the fall of
LEGEND
MEGHAN
NEW YORK TIMES BESTSELLING AUTHOR
MARCH

Visit my website at www.meghanmarch.com

ABOUT THE FALL OF LEGEND

We come from two different worlds.

I'm from the streets. She may as well live in an ivory tower.

I made my living with my fists. I doubt she could even throw a punch.

Our paths never should have crossed. We never should have met.

That doesn't change the facts.

I would sell my soul to taste those red lips.

Fight the devil himself to hear her laugh.

Burn in hell to have a single night.

Scarlett Priest shouldn't even know men like me exist, but sometimes temptation is stronger than will.

If this is how I go down, it'll be worth every second of the fall.

The Fall of Legend is the first book in the captivating and utterly addictive Legend Trilogy.

CONTENTS

THE FALL OF LEGEND

Book One of the Legend Trilogy

Meghan March

CHAPTER ONE

SCARLETT

My body hits the floor with a thump. When my eyes flick open, darkness greets me.

What the hell?

Wait. No. There's some gray mixed with the pitch black. Maybe even a glow coming from above my head?

Did I fall asleep? Roll off my bed?

I try to sit up, but I can't move. *Why can't I move?* Fear creeps down my spine because I'm 99.99% sure I didn't fall asleep. I don't take naps. I don't have time.

Plus, if I'd been taking a nap, the sound of the Proclaimers' "500 Miles" wouldn't be blasting in my earbuds.

Wait. I was running. Not napping. *So, why the hell can't I move?* I wiggle, but something that feels like carpet nap rubs against my bare arms.

What in the actual fuck is going on?

The Proclaimers go quiet for a moment before the song starts again. In that precious beat of silence, puzzle pieces snap together, and the blood chugging through my body slows like icy water in a nearly frozen river.

Oh. No. No. Just . . . no. This isn't happening. The threats weren't real. They didn't get me. Even as I try to deny it, my inner voice pops into my head, contradicting everything I want to believe.

They got me. The threats were real. They're going to kill me. I should have listened to Ryan and Christine. Why didn't I listen?

That's right, because I never take stuff like that seriously. *And now . . .* I flex my hands with my heart thundering, and my fingertips brush against what feels like . . . a rug?

My stomach plummets as reality crashes through my confusion.

I'm rolled up in a rug. Oh. My. Fucking. God. This can't be happening.

As the Proclaimers wail in my ears, vibrations shiver across my skin. *What was that? A door shutting? Are those footsteps?*

The murmur of voices comes next. I try to listen, but I can't make out the words over the music, until . . .

Something knocks into my side, and thankfully, the rug blunts the impact. *Did someone just freaking kick me?*

I'm a smart woman. Savvy. I've lived in Manhattan my whole life and survived three mugging attempts. I'm not a shrinking violet, but neither of the two women's self-defense seminars I've attended for charity covered what to do when you wake up rolled in a rug after being *kidnapped by someone who has probably made repeated death threats against you.*

The song's volume dips for some more chanting about all the things the Proclaimers would do for the woman they loved, and that's when I hear the roar.

"You did what?" a man bellows loud enough to suck the breath out of my lungs. He sounds furious—and powerful.

Fear unleashes a cold sweat over my skin.

"You said she could fix it!" Another voice, this one higher pitched, breaks through the Proclaimers' voices before the song picks up intensity again, drowning them out.

Who said I could fix something? Fix what? Where? My brain races, but it's more sluggish than normal, given the fact it's weighted down with a billion tons of dread and the urge to shrink and run.

More murmuring. More confusion rioting in my head.

Fix what? For whom? Does this mean they're not going to kill me? Because I would really like not to be killed today. Or tomorrow. Or really ever.

Then I start rolling. Literally. Like a rock thumping over on its side when kicked.

Oh my God. Oh my God. Oh my God!

Think! Think!

My body tumbles until I'm discombobulated and the earbuds fall from my ears. Bright light blinds me as I'm freed from the rug and land on my back, staring up at the ceiling.

The scents of leather and carpet cleaner hit my nostrils as I bolt to my feet, tilting to one side like I've had too much to drink. I spin around, searching for an exit, but a big hand lands on the bare skin of my shoulder.

His palm is hot, like it was just yanked from a pocket or clenched in a fist. His touch sends tingles racing down to my fingertips.

Whoa. That's never happened before.

I jerk away, stumbling forward to catch myself on the arm of a leather chair. "Please don't kill me. Whatever you need me to fix, I'll fix it."

My head bowed, I say the words to the ripped-jean-covered legs of a man standing a few feet from me, even though I have no idea when I decided trying to reason with him was a good idea. With self-preservation running the show right now, all bets are off on me behaving rationally.

I brace for a blow or some form of verbal assault, but none comes. Other than the faint sound of the Proclaimers drifting up from my earbuds on the floor, a heavy silence blankets the room.

I wait for the man in the ripped jeans to move. To come toward me. To kill me. But he doesn't.

"*Fuck.*" It comes out softly, like he's speaking under his breath and doesn't mean for me to hear it.

"Please," I whisper, finally finding the courage to look up at the rest of the body connected to the pair of massive denim-clad legs. "Please don't hurt—"

My voice goes silent as I stare into the bluest eyes I've ever seen. He could make a fortune off those eyes alone. Mostly because they're set in a ridiculously attractive face that shouldn't be attractive at all due to a slight crook in the nose and the faint white line of a scar stretching across one of his sharp cheekbones. Shaggy dark blond hair hangs in his face as his lips press into a harsh line.

This beast, albeit a gorgeous one, is going to kill me.

The voice in my head delivers the final verdict, a conclusion it reached because somehow, to the bottom of my soul, I know this man isn't afraid to cause another person pain. Raw, savage energy flows off his body in waves, and my teeth threaten to chatter at its intensity.

Beautiful and brutal. That's what I'd caption the shot I'm mentally taking right now of the last face I may ever see.

This is it. I should have listened. But I didn't. This is all my own damned fault.

I bite down on my quivering lip and straighten my shoulders as tears well in my eyes, tears I won't allow to fall.

Not yet.

First, I'm going to bargain with the grim reaper.

CHAPTER TWO

LEGEND

I'm going to kill him. After everything I've done for him, I'm going to fucking kill him.

I was already rocking on the edge of ruin, but that was nothing compared to this. There's no way out.

I always thought if I ended up in prison like they said I would, it would be for one of the crimes *I* committed. But, no. It'll be twenty-five to life because Bump kidnapped *NYC Magazine's* Most Influential Woman Under Forty—and she's only thirty-one.

Jesus fucking Christ. Fuck. My. Life.

Scarlett Priest—a blond image of untouchable class— stands in my office at Legend, my new club that's already circling the drain. She stares me down, even as she trembles with fear of what she must assume is her impending death. Because what the hell is the woman supposed to think after someone fucking kidnapped her?

Rage burns through my veins, and Bump takes a step toward the door, like he's about to run for cover. At least he's smart enough to know that he fucked up even worse than he ever has before. If Bump were anyone else, his head would be on the chopping block.

Now what the fuck do I do? *Damage control.* If that's even possible.

"Whatever you need me to fix, I'll fix it," she says again. Her voice shakes, but the words come out clear. "Please, just don't kill me."

What's going through her mind? I have no clue why she's offering to fix whatever I need her to fix . . . except she must have heard Bump.

"What did you hear?" I ask.

Her head jerks back as if the very sound of my voice is offensive to her. I can't even find it in me to be insulted. She should be screaming and threatening us with the cops, prison, the FBI, and her family's money.

Her teeth leave little marks in her lower lip as she releases it from their grip. Her throat works as she swallows, and I can't help but wonder why I'm hyperaware of her every fucking movement.

Probably because I'll be thinking about her every goddamned day as I lie in my prison bunk, wishing for freedom and the life I promised myself we'd have. A big life. The life that . . .

I shut down that line of thought as Scarlett Priest opens her mouth to speak.

"I didn't hear anything else. Just the Proclaimers singing about walking five thousand miles."

Now that she's said something, I can hear the faint cadence of the song "500 Miles" coming from the white earbuds on the marble floor.

I make a split-second decision, the kind that has saved mine and Bump's lives more than once. I only have two ways to play this, and since both involve prison time if they go wrong, I may as well try to get something out of it.

"Are you as good as they say you are?" I ask her as I reach

toward my desk and grab the copy of *NYC Magazine*, the one that started this nightmare, and hold it out to her.

Her chin dips, and she stills when she sees the glossy photo of herself on the cover. It's been photoshopped, but the real Scarlett is even better, in my opinion. Not that my opinion matters right now.

After a beat, her gray eyes lift to connect with mine once more.

"I'm better." Her voice comes out in a ragged whisper, but there's a thread of steely confidence running through it. She licks her rosy lips and adds, "Especially if it keeps me alive."

The princess from the ivory tower can think on her feet. Good to know.

"Do you know where you are or who I am?"

She breaks eye contact to look around my office, snapping her gaze back to mine when she catches sight of Bump off to her left.

"No and no. Also, for the record, I'm capable of forgetting anything you need me to forget right now. I might as well have a degree in discretion."

Her self-preservation instincts outweigh her fear. I can work with that.

"It's your lucky day, Scarlett. I'm giving you the chance to save yourself." Silently, I add, *And me.*

CHAPTER THREE

SCARLETT

Save myself?

The offer sounds seductive, especially coming from those full lips on that dangerously attractive face. But is it too good to be true? And what is that accent? It has a Southern twang, but it's almost undetectable.

I swallow another lump in my throat. *His accent doesn't matter. Getting out of here alive does.*

I lift my chin and stare him down, because that seems to be working best. And it's no hardship to stare at the man. *Jesus Christ.* I've never seen such harsh splendor in my life.

Stop thinking about that and focus on getting the hell out of here, my inner voice snaps.

"How do I know this isn't some kind of trick?"

His expression doesn't change at all. It's like his face is carved into the side of a mountain and completely devoid of emotion. Except . . . there's a nearly imperceptible flex of his jaw from side to side.

"You don't know it isn't. But you'll listen to me anyway."

The words carry so much power, I can practically feel it envelop me. I want to sink into one of the leather chairs and wrap my arms around myself protectively. No, not into a chair. I want to back away from his foreboding presence and all the chaos it has unleashed on my system and run straight for the door. Except there's the other man in the room who somehow managed to *kidnap me* while I was jogging home from a photo op. Yeah, probably not getting too far past him.

Instead, I clutch one thing no one can ever take from me —my bravado. "Then talk. I have a rather busy evening planned, and it won't take long for someone to notice I'm gone."

Mom would be proud of my haughty tone and subtle threat. She taught me that confidence is the most important accessory you can ever wear, and even if you're not truly feeling it, you have a duty to fake it.

I just wish she were still here to tell me that in person. The pang of loss shoots through me as I stare down my adversary.

His jaw flexes again, and I wonder if that means I've annoyed him. *Not smart, Scarlett.*

He rakes those piercing blue eyes over me as if he's trying to drill beneath the expertly applied makeup on my face— not by me, but my stylist—for the shoot. Well, it was expertly applied before the rug incident. But I don't really give a single shit about my appearance right now. It won't do me much good if I'm dead.

"She's got some balls on her." This comes from the guy off to my left. His accent is thicker, and that drawl is unmistakably from somewhere in the Deep South.

A big brindle dog lies on the floor at his side, and *holy Jesus. It looks like it could eat me.* Thankfully, it doesn't move.

"Shut up, Bump," the man in front of me says, his gaze spearing me.

Bump? What the hell kind of name is Bump? I can't help but wonder, but the question disappears as soon as the blue-eyed devil in front of me nods to the chair.

"Sit and listen."

I want to object to being spoken to like a dog, but I decide silence is the better part of valor right now. As soon as my butt hits the leather, he opens his mouth to tell me exactly how I can save myself.

CHAPTER FOUR

LEGEND

She stares up at me from a leather chair that Zoe, one of my employees, picked out when we were decorating the club. After my first few selections, Zoe decided I couldn't be trusted not to make the place look like a French whorehouse. She was probably right. Class and I don't exactly run in the same circles.

They say you can't buy taste, and they're fucking right. But you can learn it. One piece at a time. But the woman in front of me doesn't need to learn a damn thing about what looks good and what doesn't.

Her mother was a high-fashion model whose name even I recognized when I read the article. Hell, I think every teenage boy used to dream about her while they jacked off. She was right up there with Cindy Crawford and Christie Brinkley, back in the day. The entire country mourned when she passed away about five years ago.

Even though Scarlett is noticeably shorter than her mother and definitely not runway height, there's no mistaking the resemblance. She has the same trademark blond hair, stormy gray eyes, and curves that'll never go out of style.

She's the kind of woman I would never cross paths with before opening Legend. And now she's one of the best shots I have to save it. If I can't pump some life back into this club, I'm going to lose every goddamned thing I've worked for my entire life. Every penny I have—and a shit ton of money that's not even mine—is on the line, because I thought there was no way I could fail.

And I won't. Because she's going to fix it all.

If I believed in a benevolent God, this is where I'd start praying. But he's never been all that kind to me, so I'm used to being in the trenches and doing all the work myself. Except this time, my best isn't good enough. I need something else. Or someone else. I need Scarlett Priest, and I hate needing anyone.

So here we fucking go.

I lean back on the edge of my desk and cross my arms over my chest. "People follow you. Go where you tell them to go. Buy what you tell them to buy."

Her eyes narrow. "So?"

"This is Legend."

She blinks when I say the name of the nightclub, like it doesn't mean anything to her. *Fuck.* If that's the case, my whole goal—making sure every person in New York knows about Legend—missed the mark.

"Legend? Like . . . the new club that just opened? And . . . closed?" She tilts her head to the side as she carefully says that last part, which might as well be a sucker punch to the gut.

I guess I didn't miss my mark after all. I demolished it.

"It's not closed," I say from between clenched teeth.

Her chin lifts, and the crinkle of her brow signals unmistakable curiosity. I guess that's preferable to sheer terror, especially if it helps get her on board.

"Wasn't there some kind of shooting? Everyone assumed the place went under immediately after. That's pretty major, after all."

Bump decides to open his mouth again when he should be shutting the fuck up. "Grand opening night. Someone decided to mess things up for Gabe. But we're not closing. That's why you're here, lady. You're going to fix it and bring the people back."

I count to three and try for a deep breath, but the kid is severing the last thread of my patience.

"Bump. Outside." I snap out the order, and the closest thing I have to a little brother shoots me a shitty glance that no one else could get away with.

"But—"

When he starts to protest, I shut him up with a slicing glare.

The scrawny kid I've known most of my life creeps toward the door and slinks out before closing it silently. He'll be waiting with his ear pressed against the crack, trying to overhear everything like a six-year-old, but hopefully he'll keep his mouth shut until I get Scarlett Priest to agree to what might be the ballsiest proposal I've ever made.

When my attention goes back to the woman sitting with her hands folded neatly in her lap, I can't help but marvel at the calm she wraps over her fear. She wears self-possession like a shield.

I had no idea that could be attractive, but damn me if it's not.

She's not wasting the opportunity to study me either. Her gaze rakes over me like I'm one of the tigers behind the bars of the Bronx Zoo. Fear lingers there, even though she puts on a good front. She's not stupid. That's for sure.

While I'm choosing my next words, she opens her mouth and dives right in.

"You want me to use my influence to bring people back to your club, don't you?"

Brass fucking balls on this one.

I lift my chin. "That's what you do, isn't it?"

"By appointment only. Not kidnapping." Her jaw tilts up, like she's ready to argue the point, and *fuck me*, but I want to see her riled up.

Stop, Gabe. Fucking quit. Twenty-five to life. That's what's on the line here. Remember it and get your shit together.

"Consider this your appointment, Scarlett. Unless you can't do it. Maybe you're not as good as you think you are." I add the taunt out of instinct. I have a feeling the duchess of Manhattan doesn't like to be doubted. Her ego probably can't handle it.

As her lips purse into a pout, I block out the thought of how fucking good they'd feel on my cock. *Ha. Right. Doesn't matter.* Fifth Avenue and a New Jersey transplant from a trailer park in Mississippi don't exactly mix. Besides, I can find a willing woman any time of the day or night. That's never been a hardship. However, none of them could fix what Scarlett Priest can.

She sits up straighter in the chair. "I told you, I'm even better. I just don't normally do this particular sort of thing."

"What sort of thing?" I'm damn close to offering her anything she wants just for her word that she'll try. I'm fucking desperate, and it's a feeling I hate.

"The *get kidnapped, and in exchange for not dying, save some-one's business* thing. So, forgive me if I'm on shaky ground, because this is all new to me." The sound of her skin sliding across the leather zings through the electric air as she crosses her legs.

Stop fucking staring at her legs, man. That pussy might be gold-plated, but it's not for you.

I shift, leaning more weight against the edge of my heavy wooden desk. I have to choose my words carefully. I need her fucking help, so I go for the one thing that I think will gain her compliance.

"The alternative is what you should be worried about. This is a cakewalk job for you. Do what I need, and you never see me again. Not even in your fucking nightmares."

She bites down on her bottom lip again, and I want to tug it free.

Goddammit, she shouldn't be allowed to do that. She's a whole new level of off-limits. The kind I can't even think about touching. No matter what.

The rest of me doesn't get the memo, and my body tenses when she leans forward.

"What's a successful outcome to you then? I need to know before I can give you an honest answer about whether or not it's possible." Her hands separate, and her perfectly manicured fingers wrap around the wooden ends of the chair's arms as she explains. "If your club is on life support, waiting for someone to pull the plug, it could be beyond my help. And I'm not going to work my tail off to try to save it just to have you *off me* at the end because I couldn't do the impossible."

It's on the tip of my tongue to tell her we're not the mob, we don't *off* women, and that Bump has never kidnapped anyone before, but was just trying to help. I can't tell her that it's really not his fault his higher mental functioning isn't all there anymore. Because that's just more evidence that'll get us both locked up.

If anyone takes the blame for what happened to Bump, it's me. Which is why I keep my mouth shut and let Scarlett

Priest think the worst. I have to protect him—even when I want to fucking kill him for getting us both into this mess.

Except it's not really his mess. It's my mess, and I'm going to fix it. So I shoot straight with her.

"I need to make my payments to people who loaned me money, or they have the right to take everything I own to satisfy the debt. A successful outcome is me making those payments and them not taking my shit. You come once a week—on Saturday nights—and bring your friends, take your selfies, post that you're here. Get people in the doors so I can make some money and do what I need to do."

"Once a week?" Her voice rises as her eyes widen. "Anyone who follows me will realize that something's up. I don't ever go to the same place every week. Every other Saturday night at most, and no more than three or four times."

She uncrosses and re-crosses her fucking porcelain legs again, and it takes everything I have to fight against the blood leaving my head and going straight to my dick.

Is she really bargaining with me?

Bump was right. She's got balls on her. Then again, one thing I learned the hard way is to know your worth. Scarlett Priest clearly knows what she brings to the table, and I'm impressed, especially because she thinks she's negotiating for a hell of a lot more.

I decide to meet her in the middle.

"Two Saturdays in a row, and then every other. You keep coming until I say you're done." I hold out my hand to her. "We got a deal?"

She draws in a breath and holds it for a few beats before releasing it. It's that same controlled, Zen-type shit that I used in my previous life to keep myself from snapping before a big fight. It also tells me that I'm about to get exactly what I want.

Thank fuck.
Which means I may apologize to Bump.
Maybe.

CHAPTER FIVE

SCARLETT

The knuckles of the hand reaching out to me are scarred, like Gabriel Legend has had to fight his way through life. He's menacing, raw, and other-worldly. Every move he makes, from the way he leans on his desk to the way he offers his hand, is precise, efficient, and carries the impression of leashed power. The men who run in my circles only wish they could have that kind of presence.

Although he never introduced himself to me, I knew exactly who he was the second he said the name of the club. Gabriel Legend has made quite a name for himself over the last few years.

My hair and makeup artist, Kelsey, is always full of the hottest and most forbidden gossip about what's happening in the city. And Kelsey's brother, Jon Pak, was a big fan of the *illegal* club that Mr. Legend used to run. Jon went to Urban Legend to drink and watch the fights, both in and out of the ring, and was always telling Kelsey no when she asked to go with him. "Too dangerous," he said. "Not a place for girls like you."

And then Jon got pissed when the club closed without warning. One night while people were waiting in line, a man came out and said, "Doors aren't opening tonight or ever again. A new Legend is coming. That's where you'll want to be, if you can even get in. You won't want to miss it."

A couple of months later, rumors about the new, expensive club—and its owner—were all over town. *Legend.*

"Do we have a deal?" he asks, repeating himself.

I snap back to the present, meeting that sharp, icy gaze. "Do I have any other choice?"

"You always have a choice, Scarlett. Whether you like your options or not."

My hackles rise as I stand, because it's such a bullshit statement. Even if he's technically right.

I could tell him to go fuck himself and risk the consequences. There's a chance he won't kill me. He probably doesn't want to end up in prison for the rest of his life. Then again, they'd have to find my body and know what happened to me to put him behind bars. Do I really want to risk pissing him off, when I'm pretty sure it wouldn't even take half the strength in his rangy body to end me?

No. I don't.

I've barely begun to accomplish the things on my vision board. I'm not dying today.

In that moment, I make my choice. I'll consider saving Legend to be a challenge—and I never back down from a challenge.

I slide my palm into his calloused grip. Another shock of connection sparks through me as I squeeze and shake his hand like I do this with people who threaten me every day.

My voice sounds more confident than I feel when I say, "Fine. We have a deal."

"Good." His grasp is tight and firm, and he lets go almost as soon as I agree. Like he can't stand to touch me for a single second longer than he has to in order to seal the deal. He pulls back quickly, like I burned him.

Nice to know he doesn't want to touch me. Guess I'm safe in that respect.

I should be thrilled with the discovery, but for some reason, the voice in my head sounds like she's about to get into a snit about it. I shut her up. She's clearly confused from getting knocked out, because there's no way in hell I want Gabriel Legend to *want* to touch me. *Right?*

But, still, I jump a little in the chair when he barks, "Get back in here, Bump."

The door flies open and Bump, the man responsible for me knowing what it's like to be wrapped up in a rug, comes bounding into the office.

"I told you it would work!" He gives off the vibe of a kid hopped up on a mountain of sugar as he practically bounces on his toes.

Legend doesn't acknowledge his statement. "Where's Q?"

"Meeting. Zoe wouldn't let me interrupt."

Bump's response calls forth a scowl that deepens the lines around Mr. Legend's mouth. I don't know who Q is, but clearly, he or she is important.

"Fine. Walk her out. Put her in a cab. Don't say another fucking word until you're back in my office. Got it?"

"Got it, Gabe," Bump replies as he turns to me with a bright-eyed smile and waves me toward the door.

I grab my phone and earbuds off the floor and sneak one last look at Gabriel Legend as he seats himself behind his desk, his attention already consumed by the stack of papers and laptop in front of him. Before I walk out of his office, he makes it completely clear that he's already forgotten about my presence.

It's a foreign concept to me, and my ego doesn't like it one damned bit.

The insult of him not saying good-bye, or even *I'll kill you if you don't show up Saturday night* perches on my shoulder as Bump leads me through hallways and then into a cavernous room that reminds me of a Greek or Roman temple. It's dominated by soaring ceilings, massive columns, and translucent white silk drapery hanging from the corners that swoop across the open space.

The effect is impressive, even while empty. I can imagine the club filled with people dancing as they sip champagne or hold court on the large round daises tucked along the sides. A balcony with heavy balustrades runs all the way around the room. I imagine that's the VIP section, up above, where people like me could watch the crowd but not get crushed by it.

I point up. "How many VIP lounges are there?"

Bump stops and turns to face me, his gaze following my finger upward. His lips move from side to side, and I remember Legend told him not to speak. My money says he can't *not* reply.

"Lots. I don't go up there, though. I like to be close to the music."

While his answer isn't helpful in the least, I pause and count the separate areas I can make out from the main floor. My best guess is that there are somewhere in the neighborhood of a dozen separated VIP sitting areas, and if Legend is smart, they'd each have their own servers and security. Maybe even a separate entrance and exit, so if someone wants to avoid being seen, they can. At least, that's what I'd do if it were my club.

"Thanks, Bump," I whisper as he keeps walking. My brain is already working out a plan. "I'm going to need two of them Saturday, and then four the next time I come. After that, I'll need the whole floor."

Bump snorts a laugh. "All of them? Yeah, right. That

didn't even happen opening night before the bullets started flying."

I spin around and scan the plasterwork and the columns. "I don't see any bullet holes."

Another snort-laugh. "It's been two months. You think Gabe would let it go two fucking days without having everything fixed? Not a chance. So many guys were here after the cops left. They fixed it all like new."

I can picture Legend marshalling the troops like a general when it came to fixing his club. It had to have been the ultimate insult. I can't imagine the rage he kept banked while he put his club back to rights.

Seriously, the man should come with a blinking red light above his head and a warning sign that reads DANGER: APPROACH WITH CAUTION.

"They did a good job," I mumble as I spin back around toward the exit.

"They spun around like you," Bump says, watching my every move.

"What do you mean?" I ask, torn between wanting to get out of this building and wanting to know every single thing about Gabriel Legend and his club that I can learn. Purely to help save his club, of course.

My inner voice pipes up. *Yeah, you don't believe that either.*

"The gawkers. They're the only ones who've come since. They wanted to see carnage. But there was nothing. So they left. Then we were screwed until I got you."

Listening to this man talk about kidnapping me so casually should freak me the hell out, but it doesn't. *My system must be seriously jacked up now.*

Bump keeps rambling as we move toward the exit, like he can't handle silence, but I don't mind. Honestly, I'm glad he's not following his boss's orders, because I'm learning vital information that'll help me set the stage for Legend's comeback. After all, who doesn't love a good comeback story?

If I can pull it off.

The hint of self-doubt creeps in, but I silence it.

Not if. When *I pull it off.*

As soon as Bump opens one of the massive steel front doors, I'm blinded by the sunlight, even though it's waning. For a second, I feel as discombobulated as Cinderella running from Prince Charming before the clock finished chiming at midnight.

Except I'm not Cinderella, and Gabriel Legend is no Prince Charming. In a fairy tale, he'd be the villain.

A breeze catches the messy tendrils of my hair, sending a raft of shivers across my bare skin.

He's a villain, Scarlett. You only agreed because you had no other safe choice. But even then, I know I'm lying to myself.

I agreed because I want to see Gabriel Legend again, and I'm not ready to deal with the implications of that particular realization.

I stride to the curb, forgetting about Bump, and fling my hand into the air to summon a taxi. I have to get the hell out of here. Right now, before I make any other bad decisions.

Bump snags my wrist and yanks it down. "Gabe said I put you in a cab. I'll get it."

He releases me to put two fingers in his mouth and unleashes a shrill whistle. A yellow car signals to change lanes and approaches.

Hurry. Hurry. I chant in my head as urgency takes over. *I have to get out of here.* I scrub my hands up and down my arms, chafing the skin to bring some warmth back into it.

I'm only wearing my tank and leggings from the staged jog past one of my clients' new boutiques. Jordy was supposed to get photos of me to post on social media to help get more people into the boutique.

Oh my God. I freeze as the thought hits me. *They're going to wonder what happened to me. Shit-buckets. What am I going to tell them? What if Jordy didn't get the shot? I can't go back like this.*

The cab stops at the curb, and I dart toward it, reaching for the door handle.

"Wait a minute," Bump says, grabbing my wrist again.

I whip around to look at him. His thin face has light brown whiskers and is that of a full-grown man, but there's something very childlike about his tone and actions. I'm not sure what Bump's story is, especially with the strip of hair missing on the side of his head, but I have a feeling it's a colorful one.

"What?"

All lightness and humor drains away, leaving behind the man that kidnapped me. The chills are back, and they don't have a damn thing to do with the breeze whipping through the city.

"You don't talk about this. Not to anyone. You understand?"

"Bump—" I say his name as I tug at my wrist, but there's nothing childlike about his grip. It carries the power of a full-grown man.

"No. You listen. Gabe is my *brother.* You hurt him or hurt the club, and I hurt you. You get me, lady?"

Whatever naivete his tone carried before, it's gone. His threat is delivered with the ice of a hardened killer. At least, until his lips tilt into a lopsided smile.

"Plus, I think I could like you, and I don't really wanna hurt a girl. So don't make me. 'Kay?"

I swallow the saliva pooling in my mouth as the hair on my arms stands on end. There's something even more menacing about him when he says it with a smile.

I opt for firm and confident with my response. "We're

clear, Bump. Make sure the VIP sections are ready for me. Tell your brother I'll be in Saturday night."

He grins huge and nods three times. "See you later, Scarlett. Be safe."

I open the back door of the cab and slide inside. Only then do I release the breath I was holding. I give my address to the driver and drop my head against the seat.

Jesus Christ. What in the actual fuck have I gotten myself into this time?

I stare down at the phone in my hand.

Two new texts. One missed call. Dozens of social media notifications. And yet . . . not a single message from Jordy, the photographer who should have noticed that *I got freaking kidnapped*, or anyone wondering what happened to me.

When everyone is staring at a screen, I guess it's true that no one notices what's happening in the real world.

CHAPTER SIX

LEGEND

The magazine mocks me from the corner of my desk. I only read the first couple of pages of the article before I went off to Q, my best friend of fifteen years and second in command, about how we needed this girl—or someone like her—to come to Legend and bring all their friends with them, or else we'd be fucked within a month.

Exactly the same conversation Bump overheard that caused him to fuck up my entire world. *What the fuck was he thinking, kidnapping her?*

Fuck me. Q is never going to let me live this down. He's the one who told me recklessness couldn't fix this, and we'd have to be patient and smart.

But I'm still more comfortable with recklessness than patience, and look where that got me.

Fuck.

The T-shirt I'm wearing feels too fucking tight around the neck as I look at the clock. Fifteen minutes. That's what I figure I've got before Q's meeting is done.

Curiosity gets the best of me, and I reach for the maga-

zine again. I flip past the cover quickly, because I don't need to stare into her perfect face any longer than I have to. Scarlett Priest is shit hot, but I don't care. I *can't* care.

It's one of my tricks—blocking out all emotion. It goes right along with never getting close to anyone new. I keep my circle small for a reason, and I'm not expanding it for anyone. Especially not for a woman who would cross the street to avoid me if we were walking down the same sidewalk at night.

I don't want a steady woman in my life, anyway. I don't care if that means I'm stuck spending the rest of my days getting by with hookups and booty calls. It works for me. Caring about someone is the fucking trap of all traps, and one I'll never get sucked into again.

Flipping to the first page of the article, I skim past the part about her fashion-icon mother and the House of Scarlett brand Lourdes Priest created and sold before she passed away from cancer five years ago. That shit sucks, and I feel bad for Scarlett, which makes me move to the next section even faster.

And then I wish I hadn't. There's a picture of Scarlett and her boyfriend.

My fingers clench into a fist, crumpling the paper. I should tear the damn page out. That tool is a fucking douchebag. I don't have to read a single word about him to know I'm right. The generic smirk he wears as he wraps his arm around her says it all.

She's his cash cow. His golden fucking ticket. I wonder if she realizes—

No. No, I don't wonder. Because it's not important to me.

I sit up straighter in my chair and stare down at Chadwick LaSalle Jr.'s face. He looks like the hedge fund type, but a quick scan of the caption says he's a VP of the pharmaceutical company owned by Scarlett's father, Lawrence Priest.

Yep. She's definitely his golden ticket.

I bet they went to Yale or Harvard together and partied like entitled rich kids do.

Meanwhile, I got my GED when I was twenty-four and made my money with my fists, fighting for my fucking life, before I made enough to start my first club. I couldn't get a liquor license, but I wasn't about to let that stop me. Instead, I paid off the right people, and I was on my way.

Money talks. Something I'm sure Chadwick LaSalle Jr. is well aware of. *Fucking douche.*

I slap the magazine shut and shove it aside.

That piece of shit doesn't matter. What matters is saving my club.

Because another thing I learned is that when you're making all your money illegally, everyone wants a piece of it. I thought I'd be untouchable running my underground club, but I wasn't. I was exposed as fuck. I made a promise a long time ago to get out of that life, and I'll keep it, even if it fucking kills me. I will be totally legit, and nothing, not even a fucking shooting during my grand opening night, is going to stop me.

Except, now I have to do what I hate—depend on someone else to rescue me from the hole I've dug. And that someone is Scarlett Priest.

I saw the fear in her eyes in my office. That's not something you can hide from a junkyard dog like me.

But it doesn't matter. Fear is good. I hope she holds on to it.

A knock on the door interrupts my thoughts, and it opens before I can say *enter.* Only two people are brave enough to do that, and one of them is the man standing before me.

Marcus Quinterro, also known as Q.

In his tailored suit and slicked-back hair, the Puerto Rican looks every bit the club owner, which is good, because

I don't fit that mold. From where I sit, it's hard to believe Q was raised in a scrapyard across the river in Jersey, and narrowly avoided getting locked up for grand theft auto when he decided chopping cars was better money. I can't imagine how bad Mama and Pop Q had to have thrashed him for that. His three older sisters too.

"What'd I miss?" he asks with a questioning expression. "Because you don't look right, man."

Q knows me better than anyone, even Bump, who I've actually known longer. But given Bump's limitations, he'll never be able to read me like Q can. Which fucking sucks, but there's nothing I can do about it. Bump is what he is, and that's not changing.

Q's going to be fucking pissed, though, when he hears what went down. Might as well just tell him.

"You missed Bump trying to be a hero."

Q stops in midstride. "Jesus, fuck, what'd the kid do now?"

I pick up the magazine on my desk and fling it at him. He catches it, his brows diving together in confusion.

"Instead of bringing the rug straight back from the cleaners, he kidnapped Scarlett Priest, wrapped her up in it, drove her back here in the van, and dropped her on my office floor."

The color leaches from Q's olive-toned skin. "Please tell me that's a fucking joke, even though you don't know how to joke."

"She just left."

Q looks around the room, like he's afraid he's being punk'd. "Where are the cops then? Do we need our passports and the cash? I've got a list of places we can go. No extradition."

That's how you know someone's a true friend. They're ready to flee the country on a moment's notice. And to countries with no extradition treaties, no less. Q is the real deal.

"Hold on to the passports and cash for now. She's going to help us . . . I think."

Q jerks his head back as he strides toward my desk. "You *think?* What the fuck does that mean? Did you actually let her walk out of here with no surveillance, so we have no warning if she calls the cops? We'll be in cuffs before we can even get to the fucking airport."

I lean back in my chair and cross my arms. "I followed my gut and got her to agree to help get people in the doors of the club, starting Saturday. I don't want to go to prison any more than you do. What other choice did I really fucking have? You think I should've killed her?"

Q drops into the chair Scarlett sat in only twenty minutes ago, shaking his head in disbelief. "Fuck me. This is bad, Gabe. Really fucking bad. We have to hack her phone. Watch her calls and texts. Fuck, we need someone to tail her. I have someone I can call."

I think about the woman who marched out of here like she owned the place, pretending her pristine feathers hadn't been ruffled.

Do we need to follow her? The immediate *yes* isn't coming from my gut. It's coming from my dick. Because for some reason, it wants another reason to see her again. Soon.

Fucking idiot. She's not for you, buddy. Not a chance in hell.

"She was scared shitless. I don't think she'll talk," I say to Q, and watch as his features rearrange in an expression that I can read easily—and it's telling me I'm a fucking dumbass for taking this risk. He might be right. Only time will tell.

"Scared shitless means she'll talk," Q says, jamming a hand through his hair. "Unless you went all *Godfather* on her and pretended like we're the mob and threatened her."

My shoulders rise and fall in a quick shrug. "Something like that."

"I don't trust it, man. I'll get someone. He'll be discreet. Just for a couple days. When the hell is she coming back to allegedly save our asses, anyway?"

"Saturday," I reply, straightening in my chair and trying to keep anything out of my voice that might make me sound eager for the wrong reasons. As in, any reason that doesn't strictly have to do with Legend coming back from the brink of extinction.

Q looks down at his phone, already tapping out a message on the screen. "I'll be praying this works. Fuck, I might have Ma get her prayer circle on it. We need all the fucking help we can get. Otherwise . . ."

My head drops back against the padded leather of my chair. "I know. You don't need to spell it out for me. I know what's on the line. More than anyone."

My best friend lifts his head and shoots a glance at me. "I know you do, Gabe. That's why we're not taking any chances. I'm on damage control, and you keep tabs on Bump, so this shit never happens again."

"You know he didn't know any better," I say quietly. "He was just trying to help."

"Yeah, and he might land all our asses in prison. Think on that, and I'll catch you later. Pop's got his poker game tonight, so Zoe's taking point here. If you're done before ten, come over. Otherwise, it'll be old Puerto Rican men taking all my money."

And that's Q in a nutshell. Capable even when pissed, and a fucking good friend. When you've got someone like him at your side, even a white-trash kid like me can climb out of the gutter.

"I might see you there."

He nods, and we both know that under normal circumstances, if the club were doing what it's supposed to be, I'd be working until four. But given the minimal number of people who will likely show up tonight, there's nothing Zoe can't handle.

Q gives me a chin jerk and leaves me alone with my thoughts in my office.

Fuck. This isn't how today was supposed to go. Not one damn bit.

I lean back in my chair and grip the wooden knobs at the end of the padded arms. Zoe said the chair was perfect for conveying power and prestige. Which means right about now, I feel like I've got no claim to be sitting in it.

I had plans, big plans, and they were all leading to *this.* Every sacrifice I made. Every meal I missed to stash the cash instead. Every punch I took in the ring. Every mouthful of blood I spit out. It was all for *this.*

My dream. I huff out what is supposed to be a laugh, but I can't even fake humor under these circumstances.

Guys like me aren't supposed to have dreams. We're supposed to be living hand to mouth, scraping rock bottom, pretending we're gangsters until we catch a bullet with our name on it. That's the life I was born into. The life I nearly died with. Instead, I got free of it. Left my bad decisions and the people who'd just as soon shoot me as shake my hand behind in Mississippi after that bitch Hurricane Katrina tore my life apart.

I thought getting out of Biloxi meant I'd be someone else, and hell, I am. I left my last name there to die and became Gabriel Legend—first on the streets of Jersey, and then in the ring.

I release my punishing grip on the chair and stand. I know exactly what the hell I need tonight—to go back to the gym and remember who the fuck I am.

Because Gabriel Legend doesn't let anyone take something from him without a fight.

When I whistle, my baby girl, Roux, comes trotting into the office with her brindle coat shining under the lights. She comes over to me and rubs her massive Cane Corso head against my leg.

"Come on, sweetheart. Let's get out of here. Time to beat the shit out of something."

CHAPTER SEVEN

SCARLETT

The cab slows to a halt in front of the four-story brick building that has been one of my favorite places for most of my life. I pay the cabbie and slide out, my gaze going directly to the letters carved into the stone over the main entrance.

House of Scarlett

Every time I read it, I feel a pang of grief for my mother. Even five years after losing her, it hasn't faded much. It's duller than it used to be, but always there. Just as I feel like she's always here with me. After all, this was her favorite place too—the headquarters of one of the world's most iconic fashion houses where my mother was founder, CEO, and creative director, at least until she made the decision to sell it after receiving her cancer diagnosis. The new owner moved everything to LA, and the building came to me after she passed.

My mother spent almost a decade as a runway model before she met and married my father, something I still don't understand to this day, given their incendiary fights and legendary divorce when I was eight. My dad thought House of Scarlett was a silly little project that didn't mean anything and gave up all rights to it in the divorce settlement. Only, he would have been better off with House of Scarlett than his family's pharmaceutical company, which has been facing massive lawsuits for the last decade from selling drugs the company knew were tainted . . . but didn't recall or warn the public about them.

I choose to believe I get my business sense from my mother and not my father.

A feeling of being watched shivers down my spine, and I spin around to scan the street behind me.

Nothing but people who look completely normal, going about their business. But, then again, maybe I'm not the best judge of what completely normal looks like, because I didn't notice the guy who *kidnapped me* only hours ago.

Is he following me? I back toward the door as I continue my assessment of the potential threats on my block.

The woman with a watering can, trying to extend the life of her impatiens as the petals fall with the cooling temperature. Mrs. Wanstein, I think? And then there are the three girls in plaid uniform skirts and white blouses, who must have already started school. A man walking a greyhound. Someone trying to parallel park poorly.

All normal. Right?

I turn back around and jam my key into the first lock, noticing the large flower pots bursting with rusty red and orange mums out of the corner of my eye. Amy must have switched them out today, so we'd be ready for tomorrow's appointments.

Two more locks and I'm inside. Even the familiar fresh citrus scent of my sacred space doesn't dispel my disquiet—at least, not until the door is bolted shut behind me. I lean against the wooden panel and drop my head back against it with a thump.

Home. Safe.

Also better known as Curated. My baby.

Critics have called my social media staging store brilliant, simply elegant, and forward-thinking. Then there are the others who've called it shallow, vain, and adding to the problem of millennial vapidity. That last one stung.

But I don't care what the critics say. I don't do this for them. I do it for me. Because it makes me feel good to help level the social media playing field. Not everyone instinctively understands how to curate their surroundings to help create a great feed, and I can help. So I do.

Critics can shove it. It's a lot harder than they realize to grow up in the limelight, with paparazzi shadowing your every move because of who your mother is, and then still have the courage left to take risks. Nearly everything I do, whether business or personal, is watched, judged, and often criticized. But my detractors don't get it. My only other option is to do nothing—which means not *living*, and that is something I refuse to do.

My purpose isn't to give everyone a picture-perfect life, but to give people the tools to showcase their life in whatever way makes them happy, which I think is pretty damn cool.

And luckily, so does a lot of Manhattan and the rest of the country.

Business is going ridiculously well, and demand is always outpacing supply. We actually had to change three of our open days, Tuesday, Wednesday, and Thursday, to be by-appointment-only because of the crush of people in the store. On Fridays, when we're open to the public, a line extends from the front door all the way down the sidewalk, and we have to cut off allowing people to join it at five o'clock.

I personally stay until every single client has what they need, which usually means staying open until nine or later. On Saturdays, we start the cycle over again—restocking with one-of-a-kind pieces, moving inventory from the exclusive third floor down to the first two floors, and I occasionally still get to go on the buying trips, meet vendors, and go treasure hunting in their warehouses. Although most of the time, I have to delegate to Amy or one of the other members of the team because I get wrapped up with other things. It's a ton of hard work, and I absolutely adore it. Because it's totally and completely mine.

And right now, it's silent and utterly peaceful, exactly as it should be.

I walk through the living room, touching china and books and knickknacks as I make my way to the wide wooden staircase, with a gorgeous carved newel post and bannister, that leads upstairs. The second floor has three uniquely themed bedrooms that change weekly as we redecorate and turn over the store, along with a library, three bathrooms, a study, and a tea room. The third floor contains an entire house layout, but it's for our clients who prefer to shop without an audience and prize exclusivity. All the newest and most exciting pieces are staged on the third floor first. Anything not purchased that week is moved downstairs to the other rooms for our Friday shoppers.

I keep climbing until I hit the fourth floor. *My domain.*

Half of the square footage is taken up by office space for my team, and the other half is my sanctuary—the space that was my mother's design studio, which I now call home after I sold her penthouse overlooking Central Park. This suits me better anyway.

I miss you, Mom. I think you'd really love what I've done with the place.

After unlocking my private front door, I step inside, finally feeling the remaining tension drain out of me. *No one can get me here. This is where I'm safe.*

I don't just mean kidnappers can't get me either. *No one* also includes the press and photographers and everyone who wants something from me. It's an amazing life that I'm truly grateful for, but my privacy is more valuable to me than gold, diamonds, or vintage Chanel.

"And I think a drink is in order after this afternoon," I say out loud to the empty space.

But before I reach the antique sideboard and cut-crystal decanters, my phone buzzes in the pocket of my leggings. I yank it out, wondering if it's Jordy finally texting to find out what the hell happened to me. Or Patricia, whose shop I was running by to plug on social media.

It's neither of them. No. It's my boyfriend.

CHADWICK: Come over tonight. I'll be home by 10:30. Want to see you.

It doesn't take a genius to realize the message is a booty call. Which . . . I should be excited about, but after the day I've had, I think it's fair to say that sex is the last thing on my mind.

My first instinct is to tap the screen to call him and tell him everything that happened, but something stops me. Probably the threats that Bump made . . . but also, a pair of ridiculously blue eyes, set in a dangerously arresting face, appear in my mind.

Gabriel Legend.

I tap out a text to Chadwick, who would never deign to go by something so pedestrian as *Chad*, letting him know I'm tired. We don't even live together, but we already have our code for *sorry, you're not getting laid tonight*. I'm not sure if that's a good thing or a bad thing, but I have my theories.

SCARLETT: Sorry, working late on numbers tonight, just like every Tuesday.

Sure, it's a little passive-aggressive, but he should know that Monday and Tuesday nights are when I do the majority of the number crunching and catch up on administrative stuff that I couldn't get to over the weekend.

As I wait for his undoubtedly annoyed response, I can't help but feel resentment build in me. Somehow, it's okay for Chadwick to work late multiple nights a week, and people think he's a stud. But when he talks about how much I work, people give him looks of pity, like I'm less of a woman because of it.

Yes, I miss birthdays, holidays, and sporting events. No, I don't have many hobbies that aren't related to my business. Or much free time. And I rarely go out with my friends to any event that I'm not attending specifically for the purpose of being seen for business reasons or to help someone else.

But those sacrifices are worth it, because without them, I wouldn't have Curated.

Chadwick doesn't get it, though. Maybe because he works for my father and not for himself. Or because he's just there to climb the corporate ladder and collect the fat checks that pay for the life he lives.

Regardless of all that, I'm just not a booty-call girl. I'm an *in bed by ten and wearing my blue-light-blocking glasses and watching* Charlie's Angels *reruns* kind of girl. Sometimes I even mix it up with *Bewitched*. And if I'm feeling really salty, *Daria*. I love that cranky girl.

Not that Chadwick knows or cares, as is evidenced by the next text I get.

CHADWICK: *It's been a week since I've seen you.*

He means, it's been a week since he's gotten laid.

SCARLETT: *You know I would, but Aunt Flo is in town.*

I really shouldn't be smirking when I hit SEND, but I am.

His reply is almost instantaneous.

CHADWICK: *Good luck with your numbers. See you at dinner tomorrow.*

"Predictable as hell," I tell my living room. Because in Chadwick's world, women don't have bodily functions, let alone talk about them. And yet he keeps trying to get me to move in to his condo, and says that living above my store is negatively affecting my image.

Whatever, Chadwick. I like my store. And my image.

The reminder about dinner is welcome, though. I forgot I'm meeting Chadwick and my father tomorrow night, and I'm actually looking forward to it.

Somehow, some way, when Chadwick is around my father, our relationship makes sense. No, Chadwick isn't the perfect boyfriend, but my father becomes a different person than he is when we're alone together. Lawrence Priest never really knew what to do with a daughter, but when Chadwick joins the mix, my father comes alive in a way that makes me wish I could have that version of him all the time. *At least there's one major positive to my relationship with Chadwick.*

After pouring three fingers of Seven Sinners, my favorite whiskey, I take the glass over to the Ames chair that my mom loved for relaxing and sketching. The same chair Chadwick told me I should toss—one of the few times he came to my place. He couldn't stand the eclectic style and said "the chaos of it all" gave him a headache.

Despite being offended to the core, I smiled, as expected, and showed him to the door and promised him we'd meet up at his place from then on.

Ugh. I don't want to think about Chadwick anymore. I sip the whiskey and savor the heat and the earthy flavor as it slides down my throat, letting my mind wander.

And dammit, it goes right back to those blue eyes.

I snatch my laptop off the coffee table and type in his name. My curiosity isn't going to be tamed with anything less than a full-on, stalker-level search of Gabriel Legend. It doesn't take much, because in a fraction of a second, I'm sitting on thousands of results.

It's the videos that draw me in first. I hit PLAY on the first one, and—*holy crap*—there he is. Shirtless and in all his sweaty glory.

Oh. My. Word.

I jerk back, almost spilling my whiskey as his opponent

throws a fist and Legend dodges out of the way before firing back at him. The sound of gloved knuckles connecting with skin is primal at best and brutal at worst. I duck and shift as the guy goes after him again, forcing Legend to bob and weave. At least, I think that's what it's called. I've never been into boxing or whatever kind of fighting this is.

Legend takes a shot to the chin, and blood flies out of his mouth. But instead of hitting the floor of the ring, he launches himself at the other man and takes him to the mat. My jaw drops as they wrestle.

The way he subdues the man and uses his body to create enough leverage to nearly rip his opponent's arm from the socket is like watching cruel poetry in motion. The man slaps his hand on Legend's abs, as if begging for mercy, and then the fight is all over.

Holy. Shit. I wasn't prepared for this.

My heart is pounding. My palms are sweaty. And heat— the kind that was disturbingly absent when my boyfriend texted me about a booty call—thrums between my legs.

There's something wrong with me.

Could I have Stockholm Syndrome already? Is that even possible? Because I shouldn't think this is appealing. I should be repelled. Repulsed. Terrified to go back to Legend on Saturday night and fulfill my part of our bargain.

But I'm not. I'm practically drooling over the image of the man frozen on my screen, with sweat glistening on his skin. Sweat that makes me think *very* naughty thoughts. Like I should make my way to the bedroom and finish myself off with a vibrator.

Shit. This isn't good.

I toss back the rest of the whiskey, which is a crime, considering it should be savored, but I don't care. I put the laptop on the table and stride across to the sideboard. But instead of pouring another glass, I rearrange all the barware and decanters.

One by one, I pick up each glass and wipe it down with a bar towel and restack them, artfully. Then I dust each decanter and shift it left a half inch to compensate for the new space taken up by the crystal. It only takes me five minutes, but the mindless task calms me down and helps me put what I just watched out of my mind.

Don't think about him. Think about the club and how you're going to fix it.

Not trusting myself to halt the Google searching, I grab my phone and make a call to one of my most trusted confidants who also happens to know damn near everything about almost everyone—Kelsey Pak, my beloved hair and makeup artist.

She answers on the third ring. "Hey, babe. What's up? You need me? I can be over in a half hour if you do."

Despite the fact that I pay her very well for her services, I know Kelsey wouldn't make the offer to her other clients. I get special treatment because she's not just a service provider, she's one of my best friends.

"I'm staying in tonight, so don't worry about that . . . but I was wondering if you could help me with some information."

I can practically see the trademark smirk cross her face. "Oh . . . now you've piqued my interest. What do you need to know and about whom?"

Kelsey has made a name for herself in this city as not only being excellent at what she does, but also as a trusted source of legitimately true gossip. Of course, she'd never talk about one of her clients, though.

"Gabriel Legend. I need to know everything you—"

"Whoa. Whoa. Back up," Kelsey says, interrupting. "I didn't hear you right. Did I? Because I thought you said Gabriel Legend."

"I did." I look around the room, suddenly feeling like I shouldn't be saying his name out loud. Like if I say it three times, he might appear.

But would that be so bad? Oh my God. What is wrong with me? *Stop it, Scarlett.*

"Why? How? A sweet little thing like you shouldn't even know that man exists, let alone want to know more about him. Wait. Wait. Did you . . . hook up with him? Oh shit. Oh my God." Kelsey's tone is half *bouncing out of her chair with excitement* and half *I'm scared for your life*. It's a little disconcerting, but thrilling all the same.

"I didn't hook up with him," I say quickly, not letting her very active and vivid imagination run away with her.

"Then why?"

As much as I want to tell her the truth, Bump's warning hangs in the back of my mind. So I go with the closest thing I can say instead. "I heard about his club and the shooting, and wondered if there's a chance it can make a comeback."

Kelsey snorts. "That place is dead in the water. Not even you could resuscitate it. That grand opening party was *off the chain*. Like ridiculously insane."

"That's a good sign, though."

"Yeah, until someone came in wearing a mask and shot up the place. You know better than anyone that the who's who of Manhattan does *not* deal with gunshots and chaos. You all are way too protected to handle that level of gangster shit. No one will go back there now, no matter how hot and sexy the reclusive Gabriel Legend is. They're terrified, thinking they'll get shot at again."

I search my brain for details, and want to kick myself for not clicking on the articles about the shooting before I got sucked into the raw display of male power that was the fighting video.

"But no one got hurt, right?"

"Yeah, but that doesn't mean anything. People are afraid, and there's no way they'll chance it again. Why do you care? You aren't really a party girl if you can avoid it."

Considering she's been part of my life since I was twenty-five, trying to find my own personal style, and let me cry on her shoulder when my mom passed, Kelsey knows me better than almost anyone.

Or really, better than anyone except Ryan and Christine, my brother-sister business and financial advisor team. I inherited them from my mother, who worked with their father. The three of us were all raised together, and Ryan and Christine are the closest thing I have left to a family, other than my father. Well, except for Flynn, my former stepsister. But after Dad's ugly split with her mom last year, we don't see each other much anymore.

"Scar?"

Kelsey's prompt makes me realize I've been silent too long. One thing is for sure—if I try to bullshit her too much about Legend, she'll see right through me. I have to go with something as close to the truth as possible.

"Someone kind of dared me that I couldn't help bring the club back to life . . ."

"Oh shit." Kelsey sighs. "You have no chill when it comes to being dared. Dammit, Scarlett. This is a terrible idea. You don't want to walk into Gabriel Legend's world. I don't care how hot he is; he's dangerous in a way you aren't equipped to handle."

Kelsey has absolutely no idea how right she is about that, and I'm not talking about my reaction to his video.

"You don't think I can do it," I say, trying not to sound defeated.

"I didn't say that. You know I believe in you. You've got this drive that makes me feel like a slouch every time I see you. I know you're capable of amazing things . . . but some

45

things don't deserve your fire, girl. This might just be one of those."

"What if . . . what if I kinda already shook on it?" My question comes out hesitant, because I don't really want to tell her that, and I also don't want to remember the unsettling spark of feeling that shot up my arm when I touched Gabriel Legend's hand. Yet, I can't deny either one.

"Dammit. If you gave your word, then I guess there's nothing we can do but honor it."

I smile hearing her say *we*.

"You should've called me first. This is going to be damn near impossible. Like, you're going to need a serious miracle to have a shot. It's been—what—two months since the shooting? And from what I'm told, the only people who go are wannabe bangers and people who'd never be able to get in if the velvet rope had any kind of line. It may have been a high-class club for part of one night, but it's not anymore."

"Then challenge accepted. Tell me everything."

"There's not a lot else to tell other than gossip and hearsay, which, while entertaining, probably isn't going to cut it for this purpose. Give me a day, and I'll dig around and see what I can come up with."

"You're the best, Kels."

"Yeah . . . yeah. I know. I'll talk to you tomorrow, girl. Get your beauty sleep so I don't have to spackle concealer all over dark circles under your eyes."

"I will. Promise." She can't see that I'm crossing my fingers as I lie to her, but she knows me too well.

"Liar." She makes a kissing noise and hangs up.

I lower my phone and then take it and my laptop and head for my bedroom. It's an over-the-top feminine space, with pale yellow walls that soothe me when I'm stressed out, a cream, pale blue, and dove-gray bedroom set and coordinating drapes, mixed with antique furniture and fluffy pillows that are delicate enough to send any man running.

I suppose I can see why Chadwick isn't a fan, but that doesn't mean I'm changing a thing. I like my space. I love coming in here after a long day to unwind with a drink and whatever work I didn't finish. Which is exactly what I'm going to do tonight—review financials on my laptop, with *Charlie's Angels* on the TV for background noise, and as an incentive, a little bit of social media time to catch up on my favorite accounts.

But, first, I head to the bathroom. The color scheme extends in here, with cream subway tile, light gray paint, and cheery yellow and blue towels. After showering and applying my skin care regime—something my mother taught me from a very young age—I tug the belt tighter on my thick cotton robe and pop on my blue-light-blocking glasses and fix the messy bun about to tumble down my face.

Now I'm ready for bed, or rather, to work in bed. Welcome to the glamorous life of being an entrepreneur. Always more to do, and never enough hours in the day to get it all done.

After moving the decorative pillows, I burrow under the duvet and cue up an episode. I should dive right into numbers, but first things first . . .

I pick up my phone and tap the app of my favorite social media platform, the one I like to consider my window into everyone else's worlds. I think I love it the most because I'm a visual person, courtesy of my mother. I also love the ability to search hashtags to get me to exactly the content I want to see. And tonight, like almost every other night, I type in my favorite: *#LifeIsMessy*.

I have to scroll down the feed a little way before I start to see what I'm looking for. Three toddlers covered in flour, one with her hands in a bowl, one proudly holding up a ball of dough, and the other staring at the wall.

Oh my God. They're getting so big.

Yes, I know I sound like a stalker, but the account is public, and I absolutely love the Winston triplets. Their mom, a thirty-something woman named Tina who lives in North Carolina, doesn't have many followers, but that's not what she's about. I click on her handle, MomOutNumbered, and smile when I see a photo of Tina with her hair in a messy bun that looks a lot like mine, except she has three toddlers using her body as a jungle gym.

The caption reads:

I don't know what day it is, what time it is, or what I'm supposed to be doing right now, but I don't care. #LifeIsMessy #MomOutNumbered #TripletLife #EnjoyEveryMoment

A shot of longing rips through my body.

Families living messy lives are my weakness. They're not my target market. They truly don't give a damn about staging the perfect photo, or algorithms and engagement, or likes and followers. They're just *real.*

In my world, that's a rarity. The people who run in my circles are obsessed with appearances and image. They only show something "real" when the post is designed to elicit shock and awe and a massive comment tally.

So, why do I do what I do? Because I love it. It keeps me trying to come up with new and original ideas. It makes me work harder and think outside the box.

Still, I have to have my daily dose of *real* to keep me grounded. Because life *is* messy, and this reminder keeps me focused on where I'm headed. Not perfection, because that doesn't exist. But my own little slice of messiness that'll fuel my soul to take on the next challenge.

I'll have what Tina Winston has someday. Well, likely not triplets, but when I'm ready to take the plunge . . . I want a messy family too. Whenever that might be. With *whoever* that might be.

I should be thinking about Chadwick and making a real go at things with him when I peep in on the account of a young couple in Brooklyn who just had their first baby.

Rona's been posting hilarious stuff with the hashtag *#WhatTheyDontTellYouAboutBabies*, and her authenticity is inspiring. I'm also slightly terrified to have a baby now because *good Lord, do they ever stop with the bodily fluids?* No wonder she loves *#LifeIsMessy* because it's appropriate. So appropriate that I can't imagine Chadwick getting spit-up on his suit and tie and being okay with it. Luckily, Rona has Ben, who is a great sport and gets up to bring her the baby for nighttime feedings. I think I'm a little in love with him just for that.

Again, the thought of Chadwick doing anything remotely like that results in a totally blank image in my brain. I just can't picture it.

Which is fine, I remind myself. *I don't have to figure it all out tonight.*

I spend a few more minutes checking other accounts for updates before I finally tear myself away from the phone.

Enough fun stuff. Now, work.

I yawn, wondering how long I'll be able to go tonight. It's my personal mission to beat my productivity from yesterday, so I push through the fatigue and stare at numbers, making notes until my eyes cross.

Eventually, I drift off, one hand curled around my laptop, dreams of a little boy with dark blond hair and bright blue eyes climbing up my leg lulling me into sleep.

CHAPTER EIGHT

LEGEND

With Roux trotting on her leash by my side, I make my way to the gym I've been meaning to hit more often, but I haven't been able to make it as regularly as I should. Probably because I'm not training like I used to.

One of the biggest reasons for taking the ultimate risk and gambling so much fucking money on this club was to get me out of the cage. I've literally been fighting for my survival since I was a kid. Only once I got to Jersey did I realize I could make money with my fists. So instead of taking shit jobs, I took every fight I could. When I started to make a name for myself, it could have been a problem, except no one knew a damn thing about the man who called himself Gabriel Legend.

That was fine by me. No one needed to know my real name in order for me to put on a show for the crowd to make the betting go crazy.

And I always bet on myself. Every fight. Even when I only had a couple of bucks to my name. Because if there's one person I believe in, one person who I always think can pull through, it's *me*. Maybe I'm not supposed to have that kind of confidence after being shown by the world that I'm not worth a damn, but I do.

Or I did.

I don't know what the fuck to believe in right now.

Fifteen years of work, sacrifice, and hope are about to disappear, along with everything I put up as collateral. I have two weeks until my first payment is due, and if I miss it . . . I'm fucked, and this will all just be a memory of the time I couldn't pull off a win.

As I approach the twenty-four-hour MMA gym, the option I keep pushing out of my mind comes back with a vengeance.

I could fight for the money.

A big fight. One with a solid purse and crazy odds. The rematch that people have been dying to see. The rematch I've always been smart enough not to take because there's a good chance I won't walk out of the cage again.

Bodhi Black. A ruthless motherfucker that I beat three years ago by the grace of God.

He slipped when he was going for a superman punch, and I took him down and got in a heel hook. He refused to tap out until he tore almost every ligament in his fucking knee. And ever since, he's been out for blood, trying to get me to fight him again.

I could make enough for months of payments, buying us some time to get the club rocking again. But I told myself I wouldn't take another fight after the doors to Legend opened. No, I *promised* myself, and those are promises I don't break. Because the one time I did . . .

I cut off that train of thought because I can't ride it tonight. It isn't going anywhere new, solving my problems, or doing anything other than making me realize I'm still the same kid from Biloxi who doesn't have his shit figured out.

When I push open the door to the gym, like everywhere in Manhattan, it seems like the damn thing is never empty. Doesn't matter the time because this city doesn't sleep.

Works for me, even if I don't plan on talking to anyone, at least not beyond the kid standing in the corner watching everyone with his mouth hanging open. He'll do for holding the heavy bag.

I settle Roux in the opposite corner, giving her some pats and a scratch behind the ears. She lays her head on her paws and prepares to nap until I'm ready to go. She's a damn good dog.

Dropping my bag beside her, I dig into it for my gear, and tape and wrap my hands and wrists before slipping on my gloves and shadow boxing for a few minutes to loosen up my muscles. It's not enough of a warm-up, but it'll have to do, because I need to hit something before my mind goes back to Scarlett Priest.

Fuck. Too late.

There she is in my head as soon as her name surfaces. A face like porcelain with expressive gray eyes, rosy red lips, and framed with shiny blond hair.

Not thinking about her.

I wave the gawking kid over and point to the heavy bag. "You know what to do?"

He nods twice, fast.

"Good. I'm going hard."

His eyes widen, and I don't bother to thank him before unleashing on the bag. No real plan or workout. Just combination after combination. Strike after strike lands, and the impact of each screams up my arms and into my shoulders.

It's been too long. I shouldn't go this hard. Shouldn't move this fast. But I don't care, because nothing—not even this punishing, relentless pace—can get rid of the face in my head.

I see the rug and Bump. I feel the terror she felt. The fear pumping through her veins. And the cold metal of handcuffs wrapping around my wrists if she decides to tell anyone what the hell happened.

Q's suggestion, to have someone follow her and tap her phone, comes back to mind, and I know I'd be fucking stupid not to do it.

I don't want to fuck up her helping us, but I have to cover our asses too. If it's not already too late.

Why didn't I think of that immediately? Demand she hand over her phone so I could watch her every move?

Maybe because I was trying to do damage control, and scaring her like that wouldn't have worked in our favor. She offered to help. It's not like I forced her.

The voice in my head, the one that belongs to the only conscience I've ever had, surfaces with a tsking reprimand. *Splitting hairs, Gabriel. You could have let her walk out with no deal.*

I did what I had to do in the moment, I tell the voice.

My shoulders are screaming now. Too much time at a desk. Too much time pacing the club, wondering how the hell we're going to get patrons through the doors. Too much time getting soft and forgetting where I came from.

Then thoughts of Bump invade. I can't believe he fucking did what he did. *What the hell was he thinking?*

Oh, that's right. He wasn't thinking normally because he fucking took a bullet to the skull that was meant for me. When we ran out of Biloxi fifteen years ago, we couldn't get him all the help he needed because if we didn't move fast, we'd both be dead. Now he's never going to grow up mentally.

It's all my fucking fault. Every single bit of it. I did this. I did this to all of us.

The frustration boils over as sweat pours down my face

and neck, and I hit the bag, a 1–2 combination, with every-thing I have.

"*Umph.*" The kid lets out a grunt as his ass hits the floor.

It yanks me out of my silent tirade against myself, and I back up before moving to offer him a hand. "Shit. Sorry, kid. Didn't mean to beat you up."

"Damn, man. You hit hard," the kid says, but my eyes aren't on him after he's on his feet.

No, they're on the guy coming toward us with his eyebrows raised like he's never seen someone work out like this before. Except he's not an awestruck kid. No, he's a familiar face . . . one I've seen somewhere but can't place.

Then he holds out a fist to bump gloves. "Intense combos there. You can fucking move, man. How the hell do you do it?"

His voice kick-starts my memory, and I school my features not to show the shock at Silas Bohannon, an actor I've seen on the big screen, seeking me out in the gym.

The kid backs away, as if giving us our space, and Bohannon nods to the heavy bag. "You want to keep going?"

"Probably shouldn't. Didn't really warm up."

"I noticed. You just went to town. Working something out or working toward something?"

His question makes it sound like he truly cares, but I'm not a small-talk kind of guy.

"Something."

He huffs out a half laugh at my answer but doesn't seem affected by my lack of manners. "You've got crazy-fast hands, man. Who taught you? Not to be nosy, but damn. You're all in. No mercy."

I study the man in front of me and wonder what his angle is. *Does he recognize me, or is he going strictly off what he's seen?*

Regardless, I go with honesty. "Couldn't afford a top-notch trainer, so I worked out with buddies and offered to spar with guys who outweighed and outclassed me. Spent years getting beat up so I could learn from them."

He eyes me with curiosity. "So you're saying I should be asking to spar with you so I can take some punches and learn your ways."

This time, I choke out a laugh. "That's not exactly what I was saying—"

"My schedule's shit," he says, interrupting. "But if you're willing to beat on me, I'll find a way to make it work on your timetable."

Something about this guy doesn't put my back up, but he definitely wants what he wants and isn't used to taking no for an answer. I wonder if that's the typical MO of someone famous. I don't exactly run in those circles, not like the woman in my office this afternoon, but I'm not a complete idiot.

"Why?" I ask. His answer will determine my decision.

"Because I don't want to just be able to pretend to fight onscreen without using a body double. I don't want it to be fake. I want it to be real. I'm putting in the work either way, and I want to get skills out of the deal."

"Why me?"

Bohannon wraps an arm around the heavy bag and nods. "I saw you fight a couple years ago in person. It was harder to see your moves than on your YouTube videos, but I could feel the energy in the crowd. It was fucking electric, all because of you. That's the feeling I want to give people forking over their hard-earned money to watch my movie. I want them to have the best."

"And you want to be able to kick someone's ass for real if you need it," I add, because I'm pretty damn sure that's his other motive.

"Wouldn't you?"

I nod and undo my glove, then pull out my hand to offer him. "Gabriel Legend."

He does the same. "Silas Bohannon. You can call me Bo."

We shake hands, and I drop his wrapped fingers to hit him with the rest of the truth.

"I haven't worked out enough these last couple months. I'm not in the best shape right now."

"I'll take what I can get," Bo says.

"I can't offer more than once a week, at best—and I live in Jersey."

Bo winces, and I almost laugh at him. A lot of die-hard Manhattanites don't like going over the bridge. I'm not one of them, because I know there's a great big world outside the city.

"Fair enough. You got a phone?" he asks.

I head to my bag next to Roux and drop my gloves inside, then fish out my phone. Before Bo rattles off his number, he squats down beside my dog and pauses.

"May I?" he asks with his hand out, like he wants to pet her.

I'm glad he asked first, or I'd tell him to go fuck off about the sparring. No one should touch another man's dog without permission. Unless it's a kid, because they just don't fucking know better and can't resist not stroking the fur.

"She probably won't eat your hand. Knock yourself out."

Bo lets Roux sniff his palm and then scratches her under the chin. The man knows how to approach a dog. That's a point in his favor.

Roux licks his hand and uses her snout to lift it up to pet the top of her head. *Bossy bitch.*

"Beautiful dog."

"Her name's Roux. If she didn't like you, I wouldn't be trading numbers," I tell him.

"Fair enough," he says. "I have two of my own, and they're

too big of assholes to behave this well in public. Probably spoiled them too much."

We trade numbers, and Bo sends me a text to confirm.

"I can't promise I'll have time," I remind him. "I'm not fighting these days."

"I heard. You opened a club?"

Of course he's heard. Everyone has.

"Yeah." I stay deliberately vague because I don't want to get into the details that I know are coming next. Doesn't matter, though.

"You had some trouble there too, right?"

I nod again, keeping my mouth shut.

Bo isn't stupid and gets my drift. With one last scratch of Roux's ears, he rises, and I do the same.

"If we can connect, that'd be cool. Either way, it was good to meet you." He glances at the heavy bag. "Have a good workout, man. Looks like you needed some time with the bag. I'll let you get back to it."

He's not wrong. It's a release I need, even if I haven't been making time for it.

"I'll let you know," I say, shaking my bag to settle the gear. "See you around, Bo."

"Likewise, Legend. Looking forward to it."

I unwrap my hands and shove everything inside the bag before zipping it up and grabbing the end of Roux's leash. We're just about to the doors of the gym when I hear a familiar voice call my name. I turn around to see the big black-haired son of a bitch next to a fighter.

"Yo, Legend. Dude, it's been for-fucking-ever. How the hell are you, brother?" Rolo, my old fight promoter, says.

I walk over to him, and he holds out both arms to bring me in for a back-slapping hug. If it had been anyone else, I would have looked at him like his head was stuck up his ass. But Rolo is different. Rolo was family. At least, until I told him I was stepping out of the cage for good and broke his heart.

I slap his back with one arm and step out of the hug. Roux wags her tail happily at the sight of her old friend. Rolo used to bring cold pizza to the gym for her when I was training.

"How you been, man?" I ask.

"Been good. Damn good. Still miss watching your ass unleash pain in the cage, though. You walked away in your prime, and I know you still got rubber on those tires."

The fighter beside him stares at me with stars in his eyes, and I have to wonder if Rolo's grooming him to be the next me.

"You look like you're doing good," I reply with a nod at the guy. "What brings you to this part of town?"

"You know me, always scouting new talent, keeping my ear to the ground. Trying to put together the best fights I can to get people in the door and money in our pockets."

I force a smile that I don't feel, given my current situation. "I remember those days."

Rolo rocks back on his heels and scans me from head to toe. "Everything cool after the trouble you had with the club? Been meaning to get over there to check it out, but you know how things go . . ."

As his words hang in the air, I feel the sharp stab of my failure even more acutely, and this time, it's mixed with guilt. I purposely didn't invite Rolo to the grand opening party because I know how he gets when he's shit-faced. I also know that he'd expect me to cover his bar tab while he drank the most expensive liquor and flirted with every woman in sight while bragging about his glory days and me.

It's embarrassing as fuck, and I didn't want that in my club.

"Everything's fine. Just hit some bumps in the road. It'll sort itself out."

"If you need some quick cash, I know a guy who could get you a comeback brawl."

I shake my head. "I'm good, Rolo. Appreciate the offer, though."

Rolo shrugs, and the guy beside him continues ping-ponging his eyeballs back and forth between me and my old promoter. "It's always on the table. Everyone still asks me about you, especially when you're going to fight Bodhi Black again." Greed shimmers in Rolo's eyes. "That would be a fucking sweet payday no matter the outcome."

My molars grind together. "I'm good, man. Staying legit. Just like I planned."

The greed fades, but something that looks like it could be concern replaces it. "I know that's important to you, man, but if you ever get sick of it, you know I got you. Talk to you soon, Gabe. Don't be a stranger."

I leave the gym with Roux trotting along my side, heading back to the club to get my Bronco and get the hell out of Manhattan. As I reach the corner, a group of four girls, all dressed for the bar, cross the street and head in the same direction as opposed to walking past me.

Just like I assumed Scarlett would do.

It grates. More than it should. Especially as one of them clutches her purse tight to her side, like I'm going to fucking mug her.

I wish I could say it was the first time. Or the second. But it's not. When you walk the streets, hood hanging over your face, no woman wants to pass you on a dark street. I should congratulate them for being able to spot a danger accurately. Except it stings, because I'd never fucking hurt a woman.

Just let one think *you're going to hurt her so you can get her to save your ass?* A sweet Southern voice from my past rises, and I try to reason with her.

I didn't have a choice. It's not like I threatened her in so many words. She assumed. I played it to my advantage.

The angel on my shoulder isn't convinced. *You're better than that, Gabe, and you know it. Stop lying to yourself.*

She's right, but it doesn't change a damn thing.

After a quick check of the club and the disappointed look on Zoe's face again telling me everything I need to know about attendance, there's no reason for me to stay. Q and I normally alternate nights, but with so few bodies on the floor, we've let Zoe, the youngest of Q's three older sisters, work on her own more. She's proven to be just as capable as either of us, and if Scarlett Priest can really do what she says she can, Zoe will be proving her worth even more soon.

I'm almost afraid to hope. Hope only sets me up for more disappointment, and fuck knows I don't need any more of that. The big plans and dreams I've been trying to make happen have already been stained with blood. My revenge is still out there, waiting for me to take it. And I will, when I'm ready.

Roux hangs her head out the window of my truck as we leave the city behind, and I'm fucking ready to fall face-first in my bed and pretend today never happened. But even after I park the Bronco inside the bay of the old service station that Bump and I both have small apartments above, courtesy of Q's family, I can't shake the image of Scarlett hanging in my head.

I glance up at the darkened windows above me, which means no distraction in the form of Bump to get her off my mind. Since the lights are shining from the big white house on the other side of the scrapyard, I assume he's hanging around Q's dad and his crew, watching them insult each other while playing poker.

Which means . . . I'm all alone except for Roux.

Normally, that would suit me just fine, but I don't trust myself right now. The urge to take out my phone and search for more pictures of her face disturbs the shit out of me.

I don't give a fuck about her, I remind myself. *But . . . some recon isn't a bad idea.*

Roux and I climb the stairs, and despite the fact that the shop hasn't serviced a car in years, the scents of brake fluid, grease, and exhaust still hang in the air. After living here for fifteen years, I think it smells exactly like home, or the closest thing I've ever known to one.

Roux whines at the door as I unlock it, ready for her treats and bed. I take care of her first before mixing a protein shake for me and dropping onto the sofa in the living room. My phone sits heavy in my pocket until I can't stand it anymore.

"Fuck it," I say to the empty room as I give in.

It doesn't take me more than thirty seconds to be staring at her photo. Shit, dozens of them. Probably hundreds. Or hell, thousands. An entire gallery of the woman who has the power to make or break me.

And I can't fucking look away. I scroll down, staring at image after image of her laughing, smiling, running, hiking, buying shit at a flea market . . . it's like I'm watching her life, frame by frame.

Her perfect fucking life that Bump jacked up by kidnapping her.

I toss the phone atop the pile of old *Hot Rod* magazines on the coffee table and grab the remote to turn on the TV. Mind-numbing entertainment. That's what I need. Because I know there's no way in hell I'll be able to sleep after looking at those photos.

Halfway through a rerun of *Family Guy*, I snatch up the phone again and stare at a picture of her laughing as she dodges a water balloon on the Fourth of July, sparkler in hand.

Then I make a vow.

"After my club is in the black, I will never see your face again."

CHAPTER NINE

SCARLETT

I wake up with drool on my cheek, which is pressed against a hard surface, rather than my pillow. I'd like to pretend this is the first time I've ever woken up with the impression of the corner of my laptop on my face, but that would make me a liar.

Peeling my skin off the MacBook, I swipe the tiny pool of drool away with the edge of my sheet.

Note to self: change the bedding today. It's a mental note that I probably won't remember until I'm climbing under the covers tonight and too tired to do anything about it, but at least I'm trying.

With a yawn, I roll out of bed, my laptop clutched to my chest the way some women carry their babies.

Someday.

But not today. Today, I need to mainline coffee until I can pretend I got enough sleep to make up for the deficit I've been racking up since college. I glance at the clock and smile when I see that I only have fourteen minutes until Amy will be knocking on my door with the rundown of my schedule for the day.

Fourteen minutes is enough for *two* cups of coffee.

After washing my face, then applying my morning routine of skincare products, I make my way into the kitchen and smile at my ridiculous collection of mugs. From the kitchen setup downstairs in Curated, people might think that I only drink the nectar of the gods from dainty antique teacups, but they'd be wrong. I prefer to sprinkle as much absurdity into my morning as possible. Life is too short to take everything seriously. It's not like we're getting out alive.

As soon as the coffee is ready, I pour it into my THIS MIGHT BE WHISKEY mug, wrap my fingers around it, and inhale.

Gah. Yes.

I grab my gratitude journal off the kitchen counter and take it with me to the small table next to my open window. The sounds of the city are omnipresent, and after living here my whole life, I barely notice them anymore as I pick a pencil from my jar. Today's says BE FUCKING FABULOUS.

Duly noted.

I take my first sip and let the warmth fill my body as I consider what to write today. This is one of my most important morning rituals. I know that I was born under a pretty damn lucky star. I have a life that most people would kill for —even with a freaking kidnapping yesterday. I never want to take a single bit of it for granted . . . for however long it lasts.

I tap the eraser on the notebook until it hits me.

I am grateful for the reminder that this life is finite and every second is precious. I am grateful that I woke up this morning and have a purpose for today.

I could write more, but I don't feel moved. Some days, I write paragraphs. Others, one sentence. I don't know if I'm doing it right, but I figure as long as I write something down every single day, it keeps the spirit of gratitude flowing through me. I almost add a postscript after I take another sip, but I just think it instead.

I am grateful for coffee. Thank you to every single person whose labor and efforts brought this to my lips.

Today's brew doesn't last long as I practically inhale it. I'm just starting on my second cup when the distinctive double knock comes at the door.

Amy. Right on time.

I pop out of my seat and swerve around my antique furniture, the pieces Chadwick called *tacky* and *mismatched,* before I answer it.

Some people might expect the boss of a place like Curated to open the door looking perfectly coifed, but those people don't know me at all.

My employees have all seen me with a rat's nest of hair, no makeup, and in my pajamas. Because that's me too, and I'm not hiding my general hot-mess status every morning. It would take too much effort, and I just don't care enough to make it happen.

"Good morning, Amy," I say with a smile as I swing the door open to greet my twenty-eight-year-old executive assistant and general manager. I tried having two separate people, but things got complicated, and I decided it's easier to give all my orders to Amy, and then *Amy* has an executive assistant and staff to delegate everything to that needs to get done while she manages the store.

Unconventional, but it works for us.

"Hey, Scar. Happy hump day! You ready for me?"

"I'm always ready for you."

She laughs, because that's total bullshit. "At least you're

not using the COFFEE MAKES ME POOP mug today. That one still weirds me out."

Her comment reminds me of Chadwick and my lack of bodily functions in his brain.

"I poop. You poop. No reason to get weird about it."

"Moving on from poop. You have a call in fifteen minutes with Ryan and Christine. She specifically told me to clear your calendar from four to six Friday, and I wanted to run it by you before I go ahead and do it. Because even though I'm more scared of her than I am of you, I wanted you to know."

My financial manager is a terrifyingly capable woman who makes all my employees quake in fear. Probably because they didn't see her pee her pants climbing a tree when she was eight like I did. Still, she even frightens me with her intensity now and then, and I have to remind myself that she was a little fraidycat at one point too.

"Did she say why?"

"No, and I'm afraid to ask."

"Fair enough. Go ahead and do it. Chris wouldn't make the request if it wasn't important."

It might seem strange that I follow her instructions with blind faith, but Chris is likely the only person on this planet, other than her brother Ryan, my business adviser, who cares more about my money than I do. Chris would take it as a personal insult if I thought she was wasting my time, because that's another thing she'd never do.

"Okay. I'll do that ASAP. Kelsey will be here at ten to do your hair and makeup. I emailed you a half dozen contracts that are ready for your signature. You can check them out while she works, if you have time. Then you have appointments on the third floor from eleven thirty until three. From three to five thirty, you have time blocked to hit the two vintage shops you like. The new inventory will be there waiting for you to check out before they shelve it."

I do a little shimmy in excitement about the vintage shops. Scoping out new products is something I don't get to do as often as I like anymore, but it's the most fun part of my job.

I used to find and purchase every piece that came in the door at Curated, but our growth rate has made it so that there's no way I could keep up with supply alone. I now have an elaborate network of scouts all over the world who love to collect my finder's fee for scooping up the best and most unique goods in their area.

"And that's it? Early night?" I'm about to throw my hands up in the air and hip check her, but Amy's face falls.

"Sorry, Scar. You've got dinner at eight with Chadwick and your father."

Whoops. Chadwick just reminded me last night, and I already forgot. I shore up my happy smile.

"No, no. That's okay. It'll be good. Dad and Chadwick get along like two preppy dude-bros at a golf course. It'll be fun. After all, when else do I really get to see Dad?"

Having already lost one parent much too soon, I'm painfully aware that every minute I get to spend with my dad matters because he won't always be around. Whether he and I connect isn't the point. It's the fact that he's my father, and I'm not going to avoid him because he's still not sure what to make of me, since I don't fit into his corporate-ladder-climbing ideal.

I am, however, a CEO, which you'd think would make him happy, but not so much. But tonight . . . tonight I'm going to make him smile. Maybe he'll even say he's proud of me. That would make it all worthwhile.

With an awkward grin, Amy continues. "Do you want Kelsey to come back and touch you up beforehand? I can check with her and see if it works with her schedule."

"No, that's fine. It's a family thing. I don't have to be

perfect." As I say it, I can't help but wish I had a massive family with rowdy siblings who would put me in a headlock and mess up my hair as a matter of course. Being an only child has been tough sometimes.

"Okay, then. That's it. Is there anything you need me to add to my list for the day?"

Amy keeps a running list of every single project that's in process, and somehow manages to keep track of everything like she was born for this role.

"First, you are amazing. Second, what do you think about us designing and selling our own line of stationery products?"

Amy's eyes light up. "I was thinking the same thing. Journals, especially."

"And fun pencils!" I add with a smile. "It's like you're in my brain. I'll shoot you some notes I made yesterday morning so we can start searching for suppliers to get quotes. I also made a few terrible sketches of ideas I had to show graphic design so they could work on some mockup artwork."

"You got it, Scar. I think those would be a great addition to the gift shop area. People are seriously crazy for anything Curated. You're building an empire. Just like your mom."

My smile stretches wider, and I swallow the emotions Amy's words evoke. "It wasn't my intention, but I'll take it. I'll touch base with you after the appointments on three and before I leave to scout. Sound good?"

"Deal. I hope you have an awesome day." Amy gives me a beaming grin as she backs out of my apartment. "And don't forget to tell Christine I did what she wanted so I don't get in trouble."

"No problem."

Just before Amy shuts the door behind her beautifully curly red head, I remember the other important task I have this week. Perhaps *the* most important task. *Getting a plan and a crew together to show up at Legend on Saturday night.*

"Hey, Ames?" I call out.

"Yeah?"

"What do I have going on Saturday?"

She swipes across the screen of the phone in her hand, silent for a beat, before she looks up. "You have a dinner with Chadwick and some pharmaceutical-industry lobbyists at eight thirty."

"Shit."

Amy's shoulders shoot back, like she's ready to go to battle. "You want me to cancel it?"

I shake my head. "No, I'll take care of it. But . . . make sure nothing gets added to my calendar from seven o'clock on."

"Consider it all blocked out. Anything else?"

"No, that's it. Thanks again. Talk to you later."

She gives me another smile, but this one a bit less radiant. I get the sense that my employees aren't really fans of Chadwick, but they don't see the whole picture. Or at least that's what I tell myself. Probably because I'm not ready to take a hard look at the situation and do anything about it right now. Besides, it's not like I want to date someone else or need to be single.

As soon as the thought appears in my head, it's accompanied by blue eyes, dark blond hair, a craggy jaw, sharp cheekbones—and a body carved from granite that can perform amazing feats, like making grown men beg for mercy.

A flash of heat ignites low in my belly, and an intense need tears through me.

What in the ever-loving hell was that?

No. I am not aroused by the simple thought of Gabriel Legend. I'm not. Because that would be bad. Like, really bad. It would be the dumbest idea I've ever had in the history of ever.

No, no, and hard no.

But the word *hard* unleashes another wave of longing. I glance at the clock. The minutes are ticking down until my call with Ryan and Christine, and I have to eat breakfast, or I won't get a chance to because Kelsey will be working on me.

Food or snooping? That's the question.

After another moment of deliberation, I make my decision and stride into the kitchen with my phone in hand. *I'll multitask.*

CHAPTER TEN

LEGEND

"**G**abriel, are you there?"

I groan as I open my eyes, the bright light of morning streaking across my room telling me it's way too fucking early for someone to be at my door. But considering it's a female voice and not Bump's, I can't get too pissed. Especially because it sounds like Melanie, Q's fourteen-year-old niece who lives just down the street.

As I roll out of bed, I snag a pair of sweats and pull them on. I wish I had time to take a piss, but Melanie comes first. I've known her since she was a baby, and she doesn't bother me this early unless it's important.

I grab a bottle of water off the counter in the kitchen and chug some before opening the door.

"What's going on, Mel?" I ask the girl wearing jean shorts and a T-shirt with her hair in two thick braids. She rocks on the heels of her shoes, clutching the strap of her book bag, and won't meet my eyes. "Hey. What's up?"

When she finally looks up, she has tears in her eyes.

My first thought is, *Who the fuck do I have to kill this morn-*

ing? But because I know me being pissed won't help the situation, I duck down a little to get on her level.

"The guys at the bus stop were being dicks, so I walked away . . . and I missed the bus. Mom is gone. Dad's already working . . . and I don't really want to tell anyone else, because you know they'll get crazy and threaten to kill someone, and that'll just make it worse."

I'm even more glad I kept my initial reaction to myself. "Let me get a shirt and my keys. I'll give you a ride."

Roux shoves her way to the door as she hears Mel's voice.

"Can Roux come too? Dogs are way cooler than people."

I can't help but smile at her statement, even though I don't like her defeated tone. "You're right on that one. She can come, but only if you take her out first. I'll meet you both downstairs, and we'll go."

Happily, Melanie grabs the leash off the hook by the door and leads Roux, who comes up to the girl's elbow, out into the hallway.

Thankfully, Bump doesn't pop his head out the door as I walk by, because he'd want to go too. I shoot a quick text to Q to let him know Mel missed the bus, but I'm taking her to school so he can tell her mom and dad.

I wait until we're a half mile from my place until I start asking questions. "What did those asshole kids say to you?"

"They kept telling me that I need my V-card punched or I'll be the school prude."

My fingers grip the steering wheel almost to the point of pain. I haul in a deep breath through my nose and let it out my mouth so I don't lose it. "You're in eighth grade. Everyone's supposed to be a prude. You're way too fucking young for that shit."

Melanie drops her head against the seat. "Everyone's doing it. Like *everyone*. Even the weird girl who transferred in last year and only wears black lost her virginity. I'm like the only girl in my grade who hasn't. Everyone knows it too. It's embarrassing. Someone even shoved a bunch of note-cards with the letter *V* written on them in my locker last week, and they ended up all over the hall floor when I opened it."

As she hugs her book bag to her chest, I debate what I should do. My instinct is to walk into that school and inter-rogate every single one of those little fuckers until I find out who did it, but I can't. One, I'm not a parent, and that makes it fucking weird. Two, I'd get arrested because I'd want to beat the shit out of the kid who made her cry.

Melanie fills the silence. "Sometimes I think I should just do it so they'll stop teasing me."

I slam on my brakes at a stop sign, and Roux yelps in the back seat. I throw a hand back to pat her head as an apology as I meet Melanie's sad eyes. "Don't you fucking dare let those little pricks peer-pressure you into something you aren't ready—and shouldn't be ready—to do. Promise me right now that you won't do that shit until you're way the fuck older."

"Mom would yell at you for cursing so much," she replies matter-of-factly.

"If you're old enough to talk about sex, then you're old enough to hear me cuss."

Melanie's face turns red. "That's just it. I don't want to talk about sex. Why does everyone make such a big deal about it? Why do they care that I'm not doing it? It's my busi-ness and no one else's!"

Her voice grows louder and louder as we approach the school, and even though I'm glad about what I'm hearing her say, I don't want anyone getting the wrong idea.

"You're right, Mel. It's no one's fucking business but yours what you do, except your mom and dad. You tell those boys to fuck off because you're not into them or their dicks. And if they keep pressuring you or talking shit, tell them your uncle Gabe is going to find them when they're tooling around town and make sure they understand that you're a fucking lady and deserve to be treated with respect. We clear?"

She giggles, still blushing. "I'm going to get in so much trouble if a teacher hears me say that."

"Then don't let the teacher hear. Or better yet, tell them what the fuck the boys are saying to you."

Melanie's grin disappears as she shakes her head. "No, I'll handle this myself."

"Good. And if they give you any more trouble, you tell me, and I'll handle it. No one fucks with my people, Mel, and that includes you."

"Thanks, Gabe. You're the best."

"Now get out of here and go to school. Wait. Give Roux a pat first. She'll whine all the way home if you don't."

Melanie reaches into the back seat to give Roux a scratch behind the ears, hops out of the Bronco, and swings her book bag on her back. With a wave, she trots up the sidewalk with her head held high.

Good kid. I just hope I don't have to kill someone for her.

Then I think about Scarlett Priest and the prospect of prison if she told anyone what happened yesterday.

If I'm going down, I'll scare the living hell out of those kids first. Because that's what you do for family, even if they're not blood.

CHAPTER ELEVEN

SCARLETT

My almond-butter toast sits untouched as I stare at the screen with my mouth hanging open. Forget HGTV for a hot second, because watching sweaty men try to put their fists through each other's face is far more riveting than listening to Joanna Gaines describe all the ways you can use shiplap, and that's saying something.

It's brutal, merciless . . . and yet beautiful all the same. I don't even recognize myself right now, because I've never had thoughts like this in all my life.

My phone vibrates against the cream-and-pink china plate, and I practically jump out of my seat at the rattle. I slap my laptop closed like someone just caught me looking at porn. Which I might as well have been, because my heart is pounding, my palms are sweaty, and I can't stop shifting in the chair.

I force myself to pull it together and answer.

"H—hello?" Despite my best efforts, I sound breathless.

"You okay, Scarlett? You sound winded." This comes from

Christine, who often dispenses with normal pleasantries as a matter of course.

"Fine. Fine. Sorry, just had to run across my apartment. Left my phone in the bedroom." I cringe at my terrible delivery of the lie.

"Is this still a good time?" Ryan, Christine's twin brother, asks. "If you need a minute—"

"She just said she was fine, Ry. Now, let's get down to business. This month's numbers are looking good. We're still exceeding weekly gross-income targets, and your costs are holding steady. Don't go getting any ideas about upping your finder's fee, because I will fight you."

Christine's threat hangs in the air, and I can picture the petite brunette baring her teeth to illustrate it. Thankfully, I know how to handle her, so I agree and plant a flag in the ground, reserving my position for future arguments.

"I don't have any plans to increase the fee at present, but I'm not saying I won't in the future. You know it's only a matter of time before someone copies Curated, and then I'll be competing for product even more than I do now."

"She's got a point, Chris. Even you said the profit margin in this business is ridiculous. We have room if we need it to increase the fee," Ryan says, taking my side.

Even though he can't see it, I give him a chin jerk in solidarity. It has always taken two of us to overpower Christine, even as kids. She may be little, but she's fierce. Exactly the kind of person you want on your side in pretty much any situation.

"And until the time comes that we need to increase the fee, it stays where it is," Christine replies, putting the matter to rest with the finality of her tone. "Now, moving on—"

"I want to start a stationery line," I say, interrupting Christine as I reach for my coffee. "Something we can sell online as well. I want to increase our presence and inclusiveness, since not everyone can get here on a Friday to the store."

"I like the sound of that," Ryan says with approval in his tone. "Additional revenue streams are always good. We'd have to lease warehouse space for inventory, shipping, and receiving, though, because you're already at capacity in the current building."

Right now, we have a half dozen storage units where we stash the stuff that's waiting to go in the store, but we've outgrown those too. Ryan's right.

"I've been thinking about that. It's time. Initially, I didn't want employees at a secondary location, because I didn't want them to feel like they weren't part of the team, but I don't see a way around it. It's not like we can add more space here."

"Manhattan . . . where square-footage nightmares are made of," Christine says with a hint of biting humor. Although she was raised here, when their father retired to California, Christine moved to LA so she could be near him, just in case. Given the sharp edges of her personality, one wouldn't think she'd worry so much about her father, but she's doggedly protective of anyone she claims as her people.

Ryan jumps in, as I'd expect, since this is more his area than Christine's or mine. "I'll make some calls and find out what our options are. What's your timeline on releasing the stationery line?"

I want to say, *Considering I only said it out loud for the first time a half hour ago, I haven't really thought this through.* But I don't, because Christine will make me think about it for a year before she lets me pull the trigger.

"Thanksgiving. I want to make sure everyone has their Curated stationery supplies in time for holiday shopping."

"I like it," Christine says, shocking me.

"Really?"

"Yes, but I'm only agreeing because you're going to fight me on the next thing. I refuse to take no for an answer, so I'll say yes now and we can skip the argument."

"What?" Confusion underlies my question, but Christine doesn't elaborate.

"Just say yes. I already paid for it with your money, so technically *you* already paid for it. Resistance is futile."

"Chris, I thought we discussed that you were going to encourage her, not beat her into submission," Ryan says, trying to reason with his hardheaded sister about something that I'm completely in the dark about, and it's not a feeling I enjoy.

I sit up straighter, preparing myself for whatever is coming. "Could someone just tell me what the hell we're talking about right now? You're starting to freak me out."

"Scarlett, you know we both care about you and your safety," Ryan says, his tone calming and reasonable.

But then Christine interrupts. "You're taking real self-defense training, and I don't give a shit whether you want to or not. Ryan showed me the comments on your social media posts. You've got three trolls that creep me the fuck out, and since you flat-out refuse to increase security and you don't want to carry a gun, you have to learn to defend yourself. Unless, you know, you want to end up tied up in a hole in some crazy fucker's basement where he makes you *put the lotion on the skin.*"

My heart seizes, and I choke out a cough.

"I told you to handle this delicately, Chris. *Silence of the Lambs* isn't delicate."

Ryan and his sister trade swipes at each other while my brain shifts into overdrive.

The trolls. Oh my God. How could I forget about the trolls?

That's who I thought had taken me when I woke up in the rug. How the hell could I forget about them?

Oh, that's right. I was worried about *actually* getting kidnapped, while the trolls are still nameless, faceless ass-clowns who haven't actually done anything more than leave nasty comments on the daily to let me know all the sick and twisted things they would do to me if they could.

A shiver rips through me as I remember some of the comments they've made.

You should fucking kill yourself for being so fake.

You're a whore, and I know exactly how to treat a whore.

Your family is a fat-ass big pharma pig living off the sick. You all deserve to die like your mom.

We've screenshotted every comment, taken photos of the dummy accounts they came from, and handed them over to the NYPD, as well as notifying the FBI.

According to the authorities, there's nothing they can do about it unless or until it escalates. Christine insisted on hiring someone to look into it, and they've only come up with dead ends so far. The account disappears, and a similar comment comes another day from a different account.

It's hard to know if it's the same person every time or if I have multiple haters who wish horrible things on me. Either way, it's not a good feeling. Especially when it makes getting kidnapped by Bump and brought to Gabriel Legend appear like a best-case scenario. Things could have been so much worse. Because that is seriously *not normal.*

The memory of the bone-deep fear and desperation I felt while wrapped up in that rug comes back threefold when I think about one of those sickos waiting for me to wake up.

I never want to feel helpless like that again.

Interrupting Ryan and Christine's bickering, I blurt out, "I'll do it. I'll do it. Whatever you signed me up for, I'll do it."

They both go quiet on the line for a few beats before Ryan's voice gentles.

"Did something happen, Scar? Because these guys have never fazed you before, and now . . . Well, now you sound—"

"Scared?" I ask. "Yeah, when I think about what the hell could happen if these people are actually dangerous and not just asshole keyboard warriors, it makes me not want to leave this building ever again. But I'm not going to let them take my city or my life from me. I'll learn whatever I need to learn to make sure that doesn't happen. When do I start?"

Chris doesn't sound triumphant like I expected. More relieved. "I had Amy clear your calendar from four to six Friday. I'll text you the address. Your instructor has a bit of an . . . unorthodox reputation, but I didn't want to send you to a celebrity trainer. You need someone who knows how to maim, and he's the best I could find. If you like him and the lessons, he's agreed to see you up to twice per week for the foreseeable future. None of the other appointments will be on Friday, but that's the only time he had this week, because he doesn't normally train people who aren't fighters."

Oh Lord. My heart rate picks up at the word *fighters.* I think of the videos I've been watching of Gabriel Legend in a ring or a cage and the symphony of violence he unleashes. *Too bad he can't train me.*

Wait. What?

I push the thought from my head immediately, as if I'm afraid Christine and Ryan can read my mind. *What were we talking about again?* Oh, right. The training.

"I'll let you know if it's a good fit. If it is, I'll keep going. If not, I'll find someone else. Either way, I'm doing this." I pick up the conversation, and thankfully, neither of them notices my delayed reply.

Both the siblings cheer on the phone before we move on,

but my mind is only half on the call for the remaining ninety minutes it takes.

By the time we hang up, I need at least two more cups of coffee to keep me moving. Thankfully, I have just enough time to do that and wash my hair before Kelsey knocks.

CHAPTER TWELVE

SCARLETT

"Did you sleep at all last night? Because you look *tired.*"

"Thanks, Kels. I appreciate that," I tell her as I squeeze the water out of my hair.

"You know what I mean. You look like something's on your mind." She pauses in the middle of unloading her kit on my bathroom counter. "Or *someone.*"

Rosy heat blooms on my chest and streaks up my neck as the *someone* she's referring to comes to mind again.

How could I possibly think it was lucky *to be kidnapped by him?* Is my life really that crazy that there's a hierarchy of people I'd prefer to be kidnapped by?

The answer to that question is obvious. *Yes. Yes, it is.*

Kelsey's mouth drops open. "Oh my God. You're blushing. Like, *red.*"

I don't even bother to deny it. "Did you find out anything helpful? Because I could really use anything you've got to pull off this miracle." She shakes her head, and for a moment, disappointment creeps in. "Nothing at all?"

"I didn't say that," she says, unwinding the cord to the blow-dryer. "But I haven't decided if I want to tell you yet. Let me get you dry and then we'll talk. Because this isn't the type of stuff I want to be yelling over the dryer, if you know what I mean."

Disappointment is edged aside by apprehension, and it feels like it takes forever for my hair to dry. As soon as she turns off the dryer, I'm on her.

"You've got to give me something. I'm going crazy here."

"Legend, the club, is definitely sinking faster than a boat with a lead bottom. I asked a friend who's a promoter for all the hottest places in the city, and he said that he won't even take their money to promote it because it's a lost cause. The only people who are there lately are lurkers or women trying to get a look at Legend himself, because he almost never makes an appearance."

My mirrored reflection frowns. "Then who runs the club if he's never there?"

"Oh, he's there, all right, at least from what I'm told. But he watches from some two-way-mirrored office and doesn't come out to mix and mingle with the crowd. My promoter buddy even said he's never met him. His contacts were Marcus Quinterro and his sister Zoe."

"What do we know about them?" I ask, making a mental note of their names.

"Not much. They're Puerto Rican. Marcus Quinterro is supposed to be hot as hell, though. I wouldn't mind finding out more about him," she says, grabbing the flat iron.

"I didn't meet him, so you're on your own there," I tell her and immediately freeze. But Kelsey already caught my slip and waves the flat iron in the air.

"Hold up. Were you *at Legend*? Because by saying you didn't meet Marcus Quinterro, it sounds like you're saying you met someone else there." Her eyes go wide and her mouth drops open. "Holy fuck. You met Gabriel Legend. Didn't you?"

I press my lips together, not sure how to play this, especially when I've already said too much as it is. As much as I hate lying to her, I don't have a choice. Even if I'm not in fear for my life right now over this whole thing, I gave my word, and that matters to me.

So instead, I hedge. "Someone pointed him out to me. He was . . . impressive."

With her curiosity expanding every minute, Kelsey's shocked face morphs into an excited smile. "Oh my *God*. Do you have a crush on a very off-limits man? Is that why you want to try to save his club?"

"Kelsey . . ." I say her name, hoping she'll stop digging. It only half works.

"Look, I know what you think I'm going to say, because it's what I *should say* . . . but even though all of this is a terrible idea, I ain't mad at it. Especially if that means you're going to finally kick Chadwick-the-dick to the curb."

I meet Kelsey's dark gaze in the mirror. "Can we not dig too deeply into why I want to save his club yet? Because I'm not sure if I can even do what I said I could do."

Her face splits with a wide grin, and I'm expecting her to break into her old cheerleader moves at any moment. "Girl, we are going to make this shit happen, if for no other reason than I feel something coming from you that I can't describe, but I like it. When are we going to the club for our first appearance?"

I stare at my friend in the mirror and reach out a hand to squeeze her arm. "God, I love you, Kels."

"I know you do, and not just because I can do that thing you like with the flick on your eyeliner."

I let out a giggle of excitement, which is a hell of an improvement from the dread I was feeling earlier. "We're going Saturday night, and we're going to *slay*."

CHAPTER THIRTEEN

LEGEND

I shouldn't be here. There's no fucking earthly reason why I'm here. I already know from the guy Q has watching the place that Scarlett hasn't left, and the cops haven't been here either to raise any alarm after Bump's stunt.

And yet I'm walking down the street across from Curated with Roux beside me.

I drop my head, making my hood of my sweatshirt fall forward to obscure my face. Although in this neighborhood, I'd have been better off putting on a suit if I didn't want to be noticed. Either way, I'm assuming anyone who sees me will think I'm walking some rich person's dog. I hear they have nannies for them now, like they're kids or something. Not that I've got a problem with anyone spoiling their dogs. Bump is pretty much with Roux whenever I'm not, and it works for all of us.

With my dog blocking me, I stare at the four-story brownstone across the street with a small white sign with black typewriter-like letters reading CURATED. That's it. No description of what that means or hours or anything.

A couple of kids stand in front of it, taking pictures of the building like it's a historic landmark or something. I glance up and see HOUSE OF SCARLETT engraved into the stone above the doorway. Okay, so it is a pretty fucking historic landmark.

I googled Scarlett Priest this morning because I couldn't help it. Article after article talked about her inspired business that's helping to level the playing field on social media.

My phone hangs heavy in the pocket of my sweatshirt. I could send her a direct message on social media. Right here. Right now. Tell her I need to see her to discuss Saturday night. Or . . . I could walk right up to the fucking door and tell them I have an appointment.

Only if I'm fucking crazy.

Crouching like I'm tying my shoe, I grip the leash tighter.

I told Q I'd try to snag her phone to put an app on it to monitor all her calls, messages, and texts, just to be sure she hasn't ratted us out to the cops, but if she doesn't leave the fucking building, that's a little more of a challenge. Especially because I've learned the place isn't even open to the public until Friday. I want to trust my gut, which says if she was going to tell, she would have done it immediately.

I could let it slide. Tell Q not to worry about it. That I think we're covered.

And then he'd ask me if I'm fucking crazy enough to bet mine and Bump's freedom on the whims of a high-society snob?

My answer to that would have to be *no.*

Fuck.

But I do need to get in touch with her, if for no other reason than to make sure she's going to hold up her end of the bargain. That's a stretch. I don't *need to*, but I fucking *want to*, which is even more dangerous.

It's not like she'd see my message, though, considering her

millions of followers. *Fuck it.* I'll courier over a goddamned message that she'll actually read.

Which would be evidence if she went to the cops.

Fuck me, but I still want to do it, even though I know I shouldn't. Because if she isn't thinking about me like I am about her, I want her to be.

As I rise, I give Roux some scratches on her chest, which is her favorite spot, although it's closely tied with butt pats and ear rubs.

There's no other reason for me to be standing here, staring at the building like a dumbass without a hundred better things to do. And still, it takes a hell of a lot more effort than it should to walk away.

Why the fuck am I so drawn to her?

I have no answer to that question, but I'd better figure it out quick, because there's no room in my life for this complication.

But as I walk away, leading Roux down the cracked sidewalk, I can't help but glance over my shoulder for one last look.

CHAPTER FOURTEEN

SCARLETT

Together, Harlow Jones and Monroe Grafton are one of my private appointments today.

It works out perfectly for me, because they're easily two of the most well-connected party girls in the city —as well as my friends, despite how different we are. Harlow is married to New York's top sports agent, Jimmy Jones. Monroe's third husband, Nate, is a starting pitcher. She's hoping he doesn't get traded, which would end up in divorce number three, because Monroe will never leave Manhattan.

"I mean, can you imagine if Nate got transferred to LA or something? I don't want to live in LA. And don't even get me started on the rest of the country." Monroe re-rolls the cuffs on her white blazer, which sets off her mane of dark brown hair perfectly. And since Kelsey styles her, that mane is sleek and shiny and the envy of basically every woman who knows she exists. She's exotically beautiful, with her perfectly sculpted features and golden-brown eyes.

"Nate's not getting traded anytime soon," Harlow says as she inspects one of the cutest tea services I've ever had in the store. "Jimmy won't let it happen. He knows it would piss me off and then he wouldn't get sex for a month, and no man is about to take that risk." Leave it to Harlow to keep things in perspective as she flips her blond hair over her shoulder and holds a teacup up to the light.

Monroe studies a granite skull painted with flowers in the curio cabinet against the wall. "I know. I just . . . I really love being married to Nate. He's sweet and cute and nice, and goddammit, it would break my heart to see it end."

"Then don't let it end," I tell her, and like the true debutante she was raised to be, I only see a glimpse of emotion before she hides it away under a pearlescent smile. "You can stay married, even if he gets traded. It's not like he's home that much as it is during the season or spring training. You could treat his new city like it's a weekend adventure."

"You know I don't do well alone. My jealousy gets a little out of control when I see those cleat chasers on TV."

I know she sounds shallow, but I've never heard Monroe so worried about this kind of thing before. I won't blow her too-cool-for-school cover, but I know she really loves Nate, and she'd have to break her NYC-only rule if he got traded.

Harlow snorts from the other side of the room, where she's adding the tea set to her purchases. "You mean like that time you almost got into a legitimate fistfight with that chick outside the locker room? Yes, please. Let's not have another one of those."

"Speaking of not getting into any fistfights," I say, "what do you say about hitting up a club this weekend and seeing how much influence you have to bring more people through the doors?"

My transition may not be ideal, but neither of them will comment on it because they'll be too shocked that I'm going out and trying to get them to come with me.

"*You* want to go out this weekend?" Monroe asks, her eyes wide as she looks from me to Harlow.

"Fuck yes!" Harlow throws her arm in the air and shakes her ass with a silver teaspoon waving from her hand. "I don't know where or what or why, but I'm totally in. It's been too damn long since we've had a girls' night! We're going to dance our asses off and get *wasted*."

I don't know about wasted, but I'm not about to burst the party-planning bubble yet. Not when it's the only plan I have. "I knew I could count on you to be my wing-women."

"Wait. Wing-women?" Harlow asks, coming a step closer in this season's YSL silver-studded nude pumps. *I need a pair of those and another in black.* "Are you after a man who's not LaBoring? Because you know we are both so down for that."

Everyone in my life has a name for Chadwick, but LaBoring—a play on LaSalle—is one of my favorites, and I snicker inside.

Suddenly, it seems like everyone is telling me how they feel about Chadwick, and it's more surprising than I'd like to admit. Have I been ignoring their comments all along, or is this honesty a new development in my life?

"You don't like Chadwick?" I ask, looking from Harlow's voluminous blond waves to Monroe's sleek brown layers. "Neither of you?"

Their faces both morph into expressions of sympathy.

"You could totally do better," Monroe says. "Why do you think I'm always trying to get you to come with me to Nate's team events? I know so many players who'd love to take you out. Really hot, rich men, Scar."

"Jimmy has a lot of other clients too. You'd be a great player's wife. Can you imagine what you'd do for each other's social media?" Harlow waves a manicured hand through the air like she's reading something off a giant marquee. "Like JLo and ARod. You could be ScarPri and some other catchy nickname. And *Lord,* think of the wedding. It'd be like the event of the century."

Whoa. What am I missing here? "How long have you both felt like this?"

"We didn't like him from the very first night you introduced him to us. Jimmy hates him too," Harlow says with a perfect pink pout on her face. "We don't like the way he talks to you."

"Yeah," Monroe says. "It's like he thinks he's the *only* one who matters and that you're lucky to be with him. Um, hello? We all know it's the other way around. No one cares about Chadwick LaSalle Junior. Everyone cares about you, Scar. And if you want to know the truth, I think that drives Chad-*dick* crazy. It's like he's jealous of his own girlfriend, and that's pretty fucked up."

The pair of women may not win any Nobel Peace Prizes, but they have good hearts.

I lower myself onto an antique settee of my mother's and drop my head into my hands. "I don't know what to do. He's basically the only person who makes connecting with my father possible. I don't want to lose that. I only have one parent left."

Their heels click across the wooden floor as they come closer, and then Monroe sits beside me, sliding an arm around my shoulders for support.

"I know, honey. But that's not a reason to be with someone. I mean, you should want to climb him, at least on occasion. When's the last time you had really awesome, and I mean *killer* sex with old Chaddy boy?"

I think of the last few months. The booty calls that left me feeling less than stellar about myself. The times when he'd push me for more because it had been so long, and he was a man with needs. I can't even give them an answer out loud because of how stupid it makes me feel.

I can't remember the last time I enjoyed sex. Or even really wanted *it. I only do it because I feel obligated.*

My silence is answer enough.

"Oh, honey. I'm sorry." Monroe squeezes me tighter.

Harlow crouches between me and the coffee table, which is impressive, given her tight knee-length suede skirt. "Listen to me, Scarlett Priest. You deserve better. We're going out to have some fun and get ready for Scarlett 2.0, because next time around, you're getting what you deserve."

"Okay," I whisper, and both girls cheer. I'm excited for an update in my life, but I'll never be someone who is good at good-byes. That's probably why I've clung to Chadwick for so long.

"So, where and when are we going, anyway?" Monroe asks, and I'm grateful for the change in subject because I don't want to think about my pathetic relationship anymore.

"Legend. Saturday night. We're going to singlehandedly bring the club back to life and make it the most happening hot spot in town."

They both stare at me like I'm crazy . . . but neither of them back out. Legend's blue eyes flash through my mind, and a shiver rips down my spine.

I hope you're ready, Gabriel Legend. Because this is happening.

CHAPTER FIFTEEN

SCARLETT

I'm riding high on some awesome scores from an afternoon in my favorite vintage shops when I walk into La Familia, my father's Italian restaurant of choice. It's a far cry from the high-end, pretentious restaurants where Chadwick likes to be seen, which is fine with me. Honestly, I love the place, with its red-and-white-checked tablecloths and kitschy red candleholders. Plus, the eggplant parm is to die for.

The hostess's face lights up when she sees me. "Welcome, Ms. Priest. Your father has already arrived. Please allow me to show you to your table."

"Thanks, Lisa." I smile at her, and she gestures with her hand for me to follow her.

We wind through the tables of diners until we arrive at a table with three place settings in an intimate back corner of the dining room. No doubt my father requested it specifically.

"Enjoy," she says, returning my smile as the men rise from their seats.

"Scarlett, baby, it's good to see you. I've missed you this

week." Chadwick's light brown hair ruffles as he reaches out to grab my upper arm and pull me in for a kiss.

As soon as his dry lips slide against mine, my head jerks back, breaking the contact. His brown gaze narrows on my face while I pull myself together and try to shut down the feelings of disgust twisting in my stomach from his touch.

"Something wrong?" he murmurs in my ear as he pulls out my chair for me.

"Nothing, sorry. Thought I was going to sneeze and didn't want to surprise you." It's a lame lie, but his expression smooths out into the placid one I'm used to seeing.

"Glad you could make it, Scarlett," my father says from across the table as he reseats himself. "You're looking well."

I know he means I'm looking more like my mother every day, except for my height, which will never reach her statuesque levels. I haven't grown an inch since I was fourteen.

"Sorry to keep you both waiting," I reply, stemming the urge to check my phone and double-check the time to prove I'm not late.

"We came early for a few drinks. Long day," Chadwick says.

He reaches out to play with my fingers, and it takes everything I have not to snatch them out of his reach. I don't know why, but I really can't stand the feeling of his touch tonight.

When was the last time I actually enjoyed *his touch?* Just like the question Monroe asked earlier today, I don't have a good answer for this one either.

Now that I know all my friends think he's a douchebag, and we haven't had good sex in . . . maybe ever, the list of reasons why I should end this relationship is growing longer by the day. Except . . . there's one big, weighty reason I'm hesitant to cut it off, and he's sitting right across the table from me.

My father.

I smile across the table at my dad, wishing he were the one to stand up and wrap me in his arms in a hug and ask me how my day went. Ask how his little girl is doing. Ask if I'm happy. Ask . . . anything.

But that won't come until later, when he's had a few more vodka tonics and Chadwick's amusing comments have loosened him up, helping him remember he's my father and not just at dinner with a colleague and their significant other.

To say our father-daughter relationship is fulfilling would be a bald-faced lie.

My dad didn't want a child. He wanted an heir. A son. Someone he could groom to take over his family's business. Instead, he got me, a mama's girl with bold ideas of her own who doesn't like taking orders. Suffice it to say, he still hasn't gotten over my lack of a penis and failure at blind obedience.

Thankfully, the server comes to the table to bring the men another round of drinks and takes my order. I opt for a nice full-flavored white wine that'll go well with the eggplant parm I always get.

My father smiles in approval at my choice. "That'll accompany your usual eggplant perfectly. You're finally learning to select your pairings well. Good for you, Scarlett."

It's a crumb. A tiny taste of approval. An indication that he actually remembers what I normally order. I glom onto it like it's a five-course meal and savor the comment.

"She'll be even better after we spend next weekend in Sonoma," Chadwick says, lifting his glass to his lips.

I whip my head to the side to stare at him. "What?"

He sucks back a mouthful, and I wait for him to swallow so he can explain what the hell he just said. "Big meeting. Your father has graciously allowed us to take his place. It'll be great. You'll finally be able to get away from work and relax for a couple of days. God knows *I* need it. You're impossible to pry out of that damn store, and I'm getting pretty tired of it."

So many thoughts are firing through my head at Mach one speed that I have no idea which to address first. Before I can decide, my father chimes in like I'm not even at the table.

"That'll be a great weekend away for you two kids. You know, Chadwick, Sonoma would make an excellent place to pop the question. Time to make an honest woman of Scarlett."

What feels like every drop of blood drains out of my head. I can do nothing but gape at both of them in horror. It's like I'm watching a farce where my life is being determined, and no one thinks I need to be consulted.

Marry Chadwick? I don't even want him to touch me right now. Neither man notices my expression or shocked silence.

Chadwick tosses back the rest of his bourbon with a chuckle. "I'm going to need another drink before we talk about that, Law."

Am I in the twilight zone? Because it feels like I'm in an alternate reality right now. A glitch in the Matrix? Maybe that would explain it.

But before they can continue planning my future without my input, I force a sweet smile onto my face and interject with sympathy in my voice I don't feel. "I'm so sorry, Chadwick. I wish you would've spoken to me before you made plans. There's no way I can leave the city next weekend, let alone go all the way to Sonoma. It's just not a good time."

His sharp gaze slices through me as he turns. "Just like last night wasn't a good time? When will it be a good time, Scarlett?"

The caustic tone of his words scalds me, and heat rushes to my cheeks. *How can he possibly bring up his attempted booty call last night with my father sitting* right here?

I swallow, my smile a little shakier now. "I'll see what I

can do to clear some time next month. Weekends are really busy with restocking lately due to the heavy traffic in the store."

"That's what employees are for, my dear. What's the point of working so hard if you can't enjoy life now and again?" This comes from my dad, and I could almost cry at how fatherly he sounds.

Why can't he be this guy all the time for me? Why does he only remember my existence when Chadwick is involved?

"See, Scar? Even your dad agrees with me. Now say yes, and I'll get the flights booked so we can have a weekend alone. You never know what'll happen." He winks at me, and I want to crawl in a hole.

A weekend alone with Chadwick where he thinks he's getting laid 24/7? And might propose? The very thought puts me off my eggplant parm, and I haven't even ordered yet.

My dad smiles and waves to the server. "I think we're going to need champagne tonight. I feel like celebrating. How about the Krug?"

The server beams with faux happiness for us. "Yes, sir. I'll have the sommelier bring it right away. I'll be back for your orders momentarily if you're ready."

Chadwick leans toward me with a gleam in his eye to whisper in my ear. "I'm starving. Gonna need my energy for tonight."

Eww. Gross.

I jerk back in my chair and pretend to cough, but Chadwick doesn't even notice because he's already telling my father something about the menu. I can't find it in me to be anything but relieved that he's oblivious to how his presence is affecting me.

If my reactions to Chadwick today aren't a giant red flag that I need to break it off, I don't know what is. He's not going to take it well, and I can't have that discussion—or rather, argument—in front of my father, so it won't happen tonight. I'll just have to soldier through and talk to him alone tomorrow.

Thankfully, the men don't need me to participate in their conversation. They keep right on talking like I'm not even here.

I glance around the restaurant and get caught up staring at a family passing plates around the table so they can taste each other's dishes. They're laughing and smiling, and as much as I love seeing that, it sends a stab of envy through me.

We're not that family. We never will be that family. A corner of my heart cracks at the thought of what will never be.

The champagne comes, and then our food and another round of drinks, followed by dessert. Through it all, my mouth is as dry as sawdust, and the delicious meal is completely tasteless because of the chaos in my brain.

How is it possible that my friends see Chadwick for what he is, but my father only cares about adding a son to the family tree? What is our breakup going to do to my relationship with my father? How the hell am I supposed to handle this gracefully? Why can't there be an easy way out?

I wish I were one of those people who could just say, "I think we should end it," but I'm terrified. I know Chadwick's going to fight dirty to try to get me to stay. Or at least, I think he will. He might be a douchebag, but he's not stupid and never has been. I've always known, in the back of my mind, that if I weren't who I am, he wouldn't be with me. But, then again, I also knew that if he weren't a VP in my father's company, I wouldn't be with him either. I would have already ended things.

In a way, we're both guilty of using the other for our own reasons.

I take a long look at my father and wish we could have a normal relationship where he gave a shit about me on a regular basis, and not just when he was reminded by one of his employees that I'm alive.

Is my father just broken? Or is it me?

My mom said she'd fallen madly in love with Lawrence Priest from the very beginning, but their relationship was tumultuous. They fought and loved passionately in equal measure, until in the end, it burned them both out.

"Don't look for the raging inferno of love, Scar," my mother once told me. "Look for the steady heat of a banked flame. It'll last much longer and won't leave so many scars on your heart."

I thought I was following my mother's advice with Chadwick. There was never a raging inferno, only a low simmer of interest and mutual respect, but that seems to have disappeared.

There's no doubt in my mind that we've reached the end of the line. I just have no idea how to cut things off without a big blowup.

"You remember that, don't you, Scarlett?"

My father's question pulls me out of my thoughts.

"Sorry, what?"

"That family vacation we took to the Alps where you learned to ski. I was saying it'd make a great getaway for a family Christmas for all of us."

And there my father goes, throwing out the lure of something I'd kill for—a family Christmas. My heart practically aches at the thought, because it won't happen.

For the past few years, he's been out of the country for Christmas with his most recent wife and occasionally some of her children. I wasn't invited because she said I looked too much like my mother and she couldn't handle it.

But after they divorced this spring . . . Dad's a free agent who apparently has time for his daughter again.

"I love to ski, so you know I'm down for it. We could do New Year's there too. Make a week of it," Chadwick says.

For a moment, I contemplate if I could stomach being with him a few more months in order to have that one week with my father. *Think of the memories, Scarlett.*

I picture myself in the middle of a snow globe, laughing with my parents and tossing snowballs like we did in the Alps. My mom's golden-blond hair shone in the sun as she dodged out of the way in her black spandex ski pants and puffy pink jacket. It's a memory I've savored for years. There isn't much I wouldn't give to have another one just like it. I could wrap it up in my heart and hold on to it long after my father forgets I exist again.

"That sounds great, Dad." It breaks my heart to think the trip won't even get booked if I break up with Chadwick. My father will find some reason not to go if it's just the two of us. Like he's uncomfortable being around his only daughter alone. The disappointment shreds me.

What do I do?

Thankfully, the bill is paid and we're filing out of the restaurant a few minutes later. On the sidewalk, my father throws an arm around my shoulders and brings me in for a side hug. I swear I feel his lips briefly press against my hair with a kiss.

"Don't work too hard, Scarlett. Your mother would tell you the same thing."

The gruffly whispered words wrap around my heart, and it squeezes until it might burst.

This is why I put up with Chadwick. *This* is what I'm always hoping to get from my father.

And you're fucking pathetic, my inner voice says. *Who stays* with a guy just to get attention from her own father? That's fucked up.

Immediately, I fire back. *He's not getting any younger. What if this is all I get with him? I only have one parent left. Is it so wrong to want to see him and have his approval? Even if it's based on something that I don't like?*

Smiling through the contradictory thoughts, I press a kiss to his lined cheek. I open my mouth to tell my dad I love him, but he's already walking away to slap Chadwick on the back.

My entire body deflates like an untied balloon. I must make a noise, because both Chadwick and my father look at me.

"Something wrong, Scarlett?" Dad asks.

Honesty is out of the running, for obvious reasons, so I paste that fake smile on my face once more. "Just tired. I stayed up too late doing numbers. I should get home and make it an early night."

Chadwick shakes his head. "You work too hard, like your dad said. Come over, and I'll spoil you. You'll sleep great." He holds out his hand with a phony smile as my father watches us. I have no choice but to go to Chadwick.

Wrong. I always have a choice, I remind myself, but it doesn't change the outcome.

"I'll see you tomorrow, Chadwick. Make sure our girl gets home safe."

"'Bye, Dad," I say, hating the punishing grip Chadwick has on my fingers.

"See you tomorrow, Lawrence."

With that, my father slides into the back of a black town car, leaving Chadwick and me alone.

"You're fucking tired again? Really?" His polite smile is gone, and in its place is a sneer.

"Sorry. It's been a long week. Why don't we plan to meet up—"

Before I can finish, he drops my fingers and cuts me off. "I'm getting tired of this shit, Scarlett. I have needs too, you know. And you're my fucking girlfriend who I don't see often enough to have those needs met, and that's before we consider all your damn excuses. I'd like to get laid on a regular basis, but you might as well be a fucking block of ice."

The attack comes so quickly, I have no time to armor up before his words slice through me.

"Chadwick—" I try to get a word in, but he yanks something out of his pocket. It's a business card.

"I made you an appointment with someone Friday morning. Nine a.m. If you want a chance in hell of going on that Christmas ski trip with your dad, you'll be there. Got it?"

I want to protest. Friday is the only day we're open to the public, and I already have self-defense class taking up a chunk of the afternoon. Plus, I don't think there's any way I can stand to be around Chadwick for the months between now and Christmas.

But I don't put up a fight. I'm not the kind of woman who has arguments and breakups on a public sidewalk. Too much exposure, and the chance of a photographer catching it is far too high.

"Do you understand what I'm saying, Scarlett?"

"You're giving me an ultimatum," I reply, my voice devoid of emotion.

"Smart girl. We'll talk tomorrow. Don't forget dinner Saturday. Amy put it on your calendar. At least that's one way I can get some time with you. Maybe I should start having her add in the nights I need some ass too."

My skin feels blistered from his acerbic tone, and I remind myself that I'm not doing this in public.

"I'll talk to you tomorrow, Chadwick. Have a nice night." I turn and take a step down the sidewalk, intent on finding a cab since I told my driver I wouldn't need him, but Chadwick grabs my arm.

"Your dad said to see you home safe, so that's what I'm doing. Come on."

It's the longest, most uncomfortably silent ride home in the history of rides through Manhattan. When I finally shut the door of Curated behind me, I slide down the wooden panel into a crumpled heap on the floor. Tears spill down my face.

How the hell did I fuck up a perfect life so badly?

CHAPTER SIXTEEN

LEGEND

My phone buzzes with a text.

Q: She just got home from dinner. Boyfriend dropped her off but didn't go inside. Still no sign of cops. Wish you'd let me have one of the girls steal her fucking phone at dinner, so we'd know for sure.

All I care about is one part of that message, and it's the part that shouldn't matter to me at all.

Boyfriend dropped her off but didn't go inside.

The magazine on my desk is still open to the picture of the two of them. Why, I don't fucking know.

Probably because I'm waiting for an answer to the couriered message I sent over, and her leaving for dinner fucked that all up. I should have sent it earlier so she'd have to respond to *me* instead of spending time with Captain Dickwad.

Tomorrow. I'll hear from her tomorrow.

And if I don't, she'll find out Gabriel Legend is not a man to be ignored.

CHAPTER SEVENTEEN

SCARLETT

After wiping away my tears and taking off what's left of my makeup, I put tonight out of my mind. I don't know why I'm going to go to the appointment Chadwick booked for me on Friday, but I will.

To distract myself from whatever I'm getting into then, I should scroll my usual social media feeds or check to see if there's a new *#LifeIsMessy* photo of the Winston triplets, but instead, I do something stupid. Something really, really stupid.

I open my laptop and click over to YouTube and pick a video to watch. In this one, Gabriel Legend is shirtless and wearing tight-fitting black shorts that highlight every muscle in his thick quads, along with the bulge of his cup.

"You might as well be a fucking block of ice."

Chadwick's words come back to me, and I grit my teeth because he's *wrong* and I can prove it. *No, no more Chadwick tonight.*

I put him out of my mind as I watch Legend trade punches with the other man. I wince at every hit that connects, and I wait for the moment when he shoots out and takes the man to the mat, sweat turning his rippling back muscles into a work of art deserving of a place of honor in the Louvre.

My nipples peak, and heat builds between my legs. *I am not a block of ice.*

The bottom of my fuzzy robe slides open, and I trail my fingers up my thigh. My inner muscles clench at the sensation, and my hand keeps moving. I go higher and higher as he wrestles with the man, changing positions and taking control.

In my mind, though, the picture changes, and I see him on top of me, pinning me to my bed or any nearby flat surface. Those blue eyes stare down at me, burning with desire.

He wants me.

My fingers hit a slick of wetness, and I can't contain my moan.

I shove the computer off my lap, drop my head on the pillow, and give in fully to my fantasy. Arching my back, I stroke my center, teasing myself by not touching my clit because it just makes me even hotter.

A deep, gruff voice fills my head. *"You're mine, and I decide when you come. Until then, you're going to have to beg."*

Soft whimpers spill from between my lips as I rock my hips against my hand, wanting more. Wanting to be taken. Owned. Dominated. By a man who knows what he's doing. A man who knows what I need.

I fling out my hand and yank open my nightstand drawer. Inside is a toy I've been testing—for research purposes—and a bottle of lube.

It takes no time at all before the vibrator buzzes deliciously against me, teasing my clit and giving me just the tip. Over and over, I bring myself to the edge, imagining it's a blue-eyed devil hell-bent on destroying every barrier I have to get to the core of me. To make me lose all my inhibitions until I beg for what I really want. To give me what no one has given me before.

"Please, please." I moan out the words, my vivid imagination taking things to the next level.

He hovers over me, a wicked smile tugging at the corners of his full lips. *"You beg so pretty. I want to hear you louder."*

I buzz the vibrator across my clit before plunging it inside myself. A scream breaks loose as I shatter.

"Oh. God. *Gabriel!*"

As soon as I realize the name on my lips, I freeze. The aftermath of the orgasm wraps around me, even though I can't believe what I've done.

Holy. Shit.

I've just made a terrible mistake.

CHAPTER EIGHTEEN

SCARLETT

When I wake up Friday morning, heat from the rising sun warms my face . . . and then I remember what I've been doing lately at night. My face ignites with embarrassment. I already beat myself up yesterday, and told myself I wasn't going to make it a habit . . . but apparently, I lied.

For the love of God, why can't I stop thinking about him?

The questions circling my brain go unanswered because I can't think of a single logical, rational reason for that.

I roll out of bed quicker than normal, because if I stay, I'll dissect the situation, and since there is nothing useful left to consider, I'm ahead of the game if I just don't think about what's been transpiring in my bed late at night. Ever again.

Instead of leisurely taking my time, I rush through my morning routine like I'm already late for an important appointment. That's probably why Amy's cherry-red mouth opens in shock when I fling the door open on her first knock.

"Shit, Scarlett," she exclaims and clutches her heart.

"Sorry! Didn't mean to startle you. Busy day ahead. I'm trying to get a jump on it."

She scans me from head to toe, taking in my blue-and-white-checked gingham sundress that couldn't be any more innocent looking if I tried. Yesterday, I wore an all-white ensemble to hide my guilt, but I ended up feeling like I was wearing a scarlet letter. How apropos.

Why am I trying to hide it? I don't know. Probably because I have a big guilty splotch on my conscience, requiring me to be extra proper to make up for my misdeeds.

Except it felt pretty freaking awesome, hence the replay.

This comes from the voice in my head that I've now assigned the name *Bad Scarlett,* for obvious reasons, but mostly because she has very few inhibitions. Bad Scarlett would love nothing more than to crawl back in bed and spend the morning moaning the name of someone whose name should never be moaned in this apartment, ever again.

Good Scarlett disagrees, obviously, but that girl is weak when it comes to *he who shall not be named*, and she's easily swayed.

"Are you sure you're feeling okay?" Amy carefully steps inside, like she's afraid to spook me by moving too quickly. "I swear, something's up with you this week."

"I'm fine. Ready to tackle everything on the to-do list. Hit me," I say with a bright, wide smile that feels about as strange as the look she's giving me.

"How much coffee have you had?"

"Two cups."

She tilts her head to the side. "With a side of cocaine?"

I jerk back like I'm avoiding a punch. "Excuse me? I'm not that kind of party girl."

Her face softens with an apology immediately. "Sorry. I just mean that you seem more on edge than normal, like something's wrong. Are you nervous about your self-defense class today? I know you hate being away from the store on Fridays, but I think it's for a good reason. We can hold down the fort. I'm way more concerned about your safety anyway."

Clearly, my manager requires a rational explanation for my behavior, and since I can't tell her the truth about half the stuff that has happened this week, I lie. "I am nervous. I know it's a big day, and I've never done this sort of thing before . . ." I trail off, letting her make her own conclusions to keep my lie less guilt-filled.

"Things are changing, Scar. Really fast. It's a lot for me to keep up with too, and I only share part of the burden you carry. I can't imagine how much pressure you're under." She leans against the counter and drops the stack of folders she carried in. "Seriously, if there's ever anything at all I can do to take more off your plate—maybe somehow give you more breathing room—all you have to do is ask. I promise I can handle it."

For a moment, I imagine an alternate reality in which I tell my manager that I was kidnapped earlier this week, and not only did I not tell anyone, but I didn't call the police or FBI. *And* on top of that, *I agreed to help my kidnapper save his business.*

Oh, and I got off fantasizing about him last night and the night before.

Even in that alternate universe, I sound insane. Like, there's a good chance Amy would be concerned for my mental health. Best-case scenario, she'd call Ryan and Christine to tell them I need a vacation, stat.

Because what happened this week was crazy, and my reaction to it was even more so.

Why didn't I call the cops? Because he let me go without hurting me? Because I can't say no to a challenge? Because I'm apparently way too attracted to Gabriel Legend to see him in shackles and being led out of the courtroom onto a bus bound for prison?

I am not attracted to him.

The lie sounds hollow, even in my own brain. Especially considering my newest guilty pleasure. Still, I should have called the police. Actually, I still can. There's no statute of limitations on reporting a kidnapping, is there? It was only a few days ago, anyway.

I glance up at Amy, who is waiting patiently, but with an expectant look on her face. *Shit. She said something to me, and I'm supposed to answer her.*

Fuck. Umm, what was it? Something about taking more off my plate? *Yeah. That was it.*

"You work your butt off, Amy. I see it every day. I'm already so grateful for everything you do, I won't weigh you down with more." I deliver the oblique statement, hoping it makes sense in the context of the conversation whose thread I've lost.

"I'm always ready for more of a challenge, Scarlett. I promise. Whatever you need. Just hit me." She climbs onto the bar stool she usually perches on in the morning and crosses her matte-black leather pumps and very chicly covered legs.

"I really appreciate that. If there's anything I *can* delegate, I promise you're the first name on my list. How is today's schedule looking?" I sit across from her and finish my fourth —*so what, I lied about something else*—cup of coffee.

She shuffles through her planner and then swipes a few times on her iPad. "I don't have anything for you until your self-defense class. I do have the report from your pickers— I've highlighted everything I think we should buy—but I wanted you to see it for final selection. Also, there's a designer's rep who wants to swing by and meet with you to discuss dressing you for one of your events." She leans in to whisper excitedly. "He dressed Meryl Fosse a few months ago and said he could do ten o'clock, if that works for you. I know we open at eleven, so that doesn't give you much time, but—"

"Fuck," I say on a groan.

"What?" Amy jerks her head from side to side, as if she's looking for something jumping out of the walls at us. "What's wrong?"

"I have an appointment at nine with someone. Chadwick made it for me."

"On a Friday?" The surprise in Amy's tone expresses exactly how unwelcome an appointment on this day is.

"Yeah. I know."

I go to the small table where I leave my keys and various items removed from my pockets, and find the card. There's just a woman's name, an address, and a phone number. I'm tempted to call and cancel, but a small part of me is curious who Chadwick thinks I need to talk to in order for us to have a chance at saving this relationship.

Maybe it's couples counseling? Maybe he'll be meeting me there but was embarrassed to suggest it in front of my dad? Wouldn't that actually be somewhat sweet and thoughtful?

Skepticism swats that thought away since it would also be totally outside Chadwick's normal behavior.

Hmm. With my curiosity piqued, I grab my phone, intent on googling the woman's name on the card, but Amy snags my attention again, holding out a manila envelope.

"I totally forgot to bring this to you yesterday. A bike messenger delivered it late Wednesday afternoon after you already left, and there was no name or return address. Seemed kind of shady to me, but I didn't want to call the police or anything until after you open it and see what's inside. If it's something from those trolls on social media . . ." Amy goes silent as I study the envelope in my hands.

Do I want to open it? What if it's another one like the last time? *The time I haven't told Amy about because I didn't want her to worry.* At least Christine knows about the photo from my social media account that showed up with horrible things written all over it. Hence, why she didn't care about interrupting my Friday with self-defense lessons.

I walk to my small writing desk in the corner, grab a letter opener that looks suspiciously like a dagger, and slice the envelope open. Holding only the corners, I dump the contents onto the desk.

It's a folded piece of white paper. No photo.

That's a plus.

Amy's fingers flex by her sides, as though she's dying to grab it and read what it says, but she holds herself back. I pick it up and unfold it carefully.

Words written in heavy, bold pen strokes mark the page. I wouldn't call it neat handwriting. More like, utilitarian. One thing is for certain—it's distinctive.

Finally focusing on what it says, I read.

Ms. Priest,

If you have special requests for Saturday, please let Zoe, my assistant manager, know. She can be reached via the number or email below. We're looking forward to hosting you and your friends on Saturday night. Thank you for handling this discreetly. We've been watching.

—L

Oh. My. God.

It's from *him*. Legend. And they've been watching?

Oh. My. Freaking. God.

The piece of paper almost falls from my hand, but I keep my wits together, along with my grip.

"Is everything okay?" Amy asks, concern in her tone. "It's not something creepy, is it? Can I see?"

I refold the note, tuck it under a stack of correspondence on my desk, and turn around with what I hope is a decent impression of a cheery expression. "Nothing creepy at all. Just a reminder that I committed to an event tomorrow night, and they want to know if I have any special requests."

Her brow furrows. "What event? You had me keep your Saturday open."

"A club appearance. It's time for me to get out and live a little. Kick the all-work-and-no-play persona for a night."

The apprehension on Amy's face fades and a smile takes its place. "*Amen.* You need a night out. It's about damn time."

Thankfully, her phone rings before she can ask any more questions.

"Do you need me? Because . . ." She holds up her phone.

I wave her off. "Take the call. I'm good. I'll be gone until at least ten. Back to help on the floor, and then gone again by 3:30. Talk later."

Amy nods and then answers her cell, snatching her things off the bar, and is already speaking on her way out of my apartment. It's not until the door shuts behind her that I run back to the desk, unearth the note, and read it again. And again. And again.

Then I lift it to my nose and sniff. *He wrote this. He touched this paper.*

Stunned at myself, I freeze. *And what in the fresh hell am I doing right now?*

I put it down, but my gaze stays locked on the handwriting. It's neat enough to be legible, but there's no elegance to it. No soft edges or lazy lines. It's straight to the point. Each line and slash is confidently deliberate, just like the man himself.

Okay, so when did I become a handwriting analyst?

There's one sentence on the page that keeps repeating in my head. *"We've been watching you."*

I drift to the living area window and stare out at the street and the sidewalk across from me, and wishfully look for him before I can talk some sense into myself. He's not there, and a shaft of disappointment chases me away from the glass and back to my desk to rearrange everything on my blotter as I try to pull myself together.

Of course they were watching. Why didn't I think of that?

Oh, I don't know, probably because this was my first kidnapping?

It's a damn good thing I didn't call the police, because if I had . . . whoever was watching me would have seen the cops show up at Curated.

The subtle threat in the note hangs in my mind. But instead of it freaking me out, I can't stop thinking about him standing out there in the dark of night, watching the light in my window, waiting for a glimpse of me.

What if he was out there while I was getting myself off to him?

Oh. My. Shit.

My nipples peak and moisture blooms between my legs, and the urge to go another round, ending with me moaning Gabriel Legend's name, comes on *strong*.

What in the actual fuck is wrong with me?

I drop the pens in my hand, and they bounce on the antique wood and leather. My reorganization efforts turned what was a neat workspace into a haphazard mess.

I'm going stir crazy. Although I've never felt like this before, the sudden impulse to get out of this building and into some fresh air overwhelms me. *I should walk part of the way to my appointment and burn off this pent-up energy. Maybe that'll help.*

Then I remember that one of the places I'm going today is self-defense, and maybe I should wait until I have some skills in my back pocket before I start roaming the streets while I'm being *watched*.

I grab the note off my desk for one last glance before folding it back up and hiding it as I carefully re-reorganize everything on the surface of my desk for the next fifteen minutes. Lining up pens and making sure the blotter is perfectly even helps the knot constricting my chest to loosen.

Everything is going to be fine, I tell myself as I take a deep breath.

Ten minutes later, I punch the address into my phone from the business card Chadwick shoved in my hand, and slip into my white espadrille wedges that will need to be put away after Labor Day. Then I make my way out through the kitchen to my private entrance to the building, and sneak out to the alley to avoid the line forming on the front walk.

As I hail a cab and slide into the back seat, I have a foreboding feeling.

This week is changing everything. Even me.

SCARLETT

What in the actual fuck?

The question repeats in my brain over and over as I sit on the comfortable sofa in the bright library-like office on the ground floor of a townhouse in Chelsea that has been turned into a therapy center. I stare at the woman seated in the chair across from me, who has two fingers curled around a stylus, and the other hand supporting a tablet on which she's making notes about me for our session.

The woman who just finished introducing herself *as a sex therapist.*

What in the *actual* fuck?

"Ex—excuse me? What did you say your specialty is?"

"Sex therapy. That is why you're here, correct? Because you're having some issues with desire and inhibitions?"

My mouth hangs open so wide that I would actually catch flies if they were buzzing about the room. I blink twice, trying to compose myself, but I obviously fail as her expression grows more and more concerned.

"Ms. Priest, I'm getting the impression that you are

surprised by my profession. Didn't Mr. LaSalle explain the nature of the appointment to you? Because he was very adamant that you needed to be seen as soon as possible before you lost the nerve to talk about your issues."

I inhale deeply through my nose and release the breath through my mouth, like they taught in that yoga class I got too busy to keep attending. "You might say there's been a bit of a miscommunication, Dr. Grand. I . . . I thought this was couples counseling . . ."

"I do offer couples sessions, but I insist on meeting with each individual alone first. I generally find that partners may need a safe space to express their concerns without judgment first, but if you'd prefer to have Mr. LaSalle present—"

"No." I interrupt her, throwing up a palm in a gesture that absolutely says *stop right fucking there*. "I don't want him here. As a matter of fact . . ." I try to figure out how to say what I'm thinking without insulting the silver-haired woman across from me.

"You didn't know what you were walking into. Did you?" she asks with interest, as opposed to judgment, in her tone.

"Not even a little bit."

She flips the cover of the iPad shut and slides it onto the coffee table between us. "I discourage surprising someone with this type of discussion, so that's problematic." She crosses one ankle over a knee and leans back in her chair, her eyes on me. "As I see it, you have two options—walk out of here and forget this happened, except for that part where you need to discuss it with Mr. LaSalle . . ."

"Or?" I prompt when she goes quiet.

"Stay and talk to me about the relationship you're in, and how you happened to find yourself on my couch without knowing your boyfriend thought you needed to talk to a sex therapist."

Humiliation burns through me, along with the greasy,

oily feeling of shame. Right after that is a raging inferno of anger and betrayal. I can keep it inside . . . or I can vent to someone who's already being paid to listen. My choice is easier than one might think.

"This is all confidential, right? You can't tell Chadwick anything I say?"

"Of course, Ms. Priest. Nothing said in this room will ever leave its four walls. And I promise, they won't talk."

"Good, because I don't know what the fuck is going on, and I'm so pissed right now, I don't even know what to say to him. He springs *sex therapy* on me? Who does that?"

Her lips purse to one side. "More people than you'd think, but I understand why you're upset. This is the kind of appointment it's better to be prepared for, rather than surprised by. How long have you and Mr. LaSalle been together?"

I scratch my head but do my best to avoid messing up my hair. "A year and a half."

"And this is the first time he's suggested any kind of counseling?"

I straighten on the couch, grabbing a pillow from the corner to wrap my arms around. "He's never suggested counseling. Ever. Not even Wednesday night when he handed me this card and told me I had to be here, despite the fact that Friday is my busiest day of the week. If he paid attention to a single bit of what I said, he'd know Fridays are no good for anything but work."

Dr. Grand's thumbs tap together, and I would bet money that she's wishing she had her tablet in hand to write notes, but she abstains.

"How is your relationship in general?"

As soon as she asks the question, I cringe. "Clearly not good, if he thinks I need help in the bedroom." I shake my head. "I can't believe that *asshole* thinks that *this* is what's wrong with our relationship. That we don't have enough *sex*? And instead of talking about it, he sends me walking in here blind?"

I launch myself off the couch and toss the pillow down so I can pace her office. "He is such an *asshole*! Who does this to someone? No, seriously. This is fucked up!"

I stop at the corner table and grab the disordered stack of magazines, straightening them into a neat pile before I turn to pace back toward Dr. Grand and her couch. When I finally meet her brown eyes again, there's empathy and kindness in them.

"Do you always straighten things when you're upset?" she asks with a grin.

"Yes. It's my coping mechanism. It helps me calm my thoughts, and I find it useful on multiple levels. So, respectfully, I'm not looking to work on that either, Dr. Grand."

"Fair enough. Is there anything at all I *can* help you with during the rest of our session? Or would you prefer to leave and discuss this all with Mr. LaSalle instead?" Her question is polite but to the point.

"If you're looking for an honest answer, I have absolutely no idea what to do right now."

"Why don't you have a seat, and we'll just chat for a few minutes until you've sorted through some things."

It's her eminently reasonable tone that convinces me. I reach for my shield pillow before settling back into the corner of the sofa.

Dr. Grand gives up her fight and picks up her tablet. With both of us armed, we stare at each other in silence for a few beats.

Before she can ask me a question, I blurt out, "For the record, I'm not broken. I've been masturbating to videos of a man cage fighting, and I yell his name when I come."

My cheeks burn with the embarrassment of my confession, but Dr. Grand just nods and makes some notes.

"I see."

"I met him once. He's scary . . . dangerous, but seriously attractive. It's like . . . primal. Raw and animalistic. I don't even know what to call it."

"Primal works," she says, glancing up at me from her screen. "And I agree that you're not broken. Modern research shows that even when women *think* they have sexual dysfunction, they're often incorrect. What they have more often are thoughts and beliefs that act like roadblocks to the process of sexual arousal." She taps the stylus on the screen once, and it bounces. "For instance, a lack of trust or feeling of safety in a relationship may make it difficult to think about sex, and would likely prevent you from initiating it with your partner."

I think for a moment about my relationship with Chadwick. "But I feel safe with Chadwick. Physically, I mean. I don't think he's going to hurt me or let someone else hurt me."

"But do you feel emotionally safe with him? Can you be yourself and express your deepest fears and hopes and biggest dreams without worry?"

"Oh. Whoa." I loosen my grip on the pillow. "I see where you're going with that. And no, Chadwick and I don't really . . . I mean . . . Big conversations about our hopes and dreams aren't really part of our relationship."

Dr. Grand puts the stylus down. "Then what is part of your relationship?"

Fuck. Of course she had to ask the hard question.

"Clearly not enough sex," I say with a half laugh.

But Dr. Grand doesn't laugh with me. She has this expression on her face that makes me want to cry. Like she sees something, and she's waiting for me to reach the same conclusion.

"I don't . . . I mean, Chadwick and I don't have a very deep relationship. He does his thing, and I do mine. We meet up for dinner on occasion . . ." I trail off because other than me using Chadwick to keep my father close, there is literally no other reason I'm with him anymore. I'm not even attracted to him.

"It's okay to admit when a relationship is no longer serving you, Ms. Priest. It happens to many people and is usually no one's fault."

I jerk my head up and meet her gaze. "Then . . . where does my physical attraction to a complete stranger come into this? Why am I suddenly feeling like I need *alone time* when I shouldn't be thinking of this guy at all?" I know I'm being cryptic, but she's picking up what I'm putting down.

"Maybe he represents something your brain thinks you need more of in your life. Is he intriguing to you only on a sexual level?"

A vision of Gabriel Legend sweeps into my head. Him, standing in front of his desk, torn jeans covering his thick quads, and his messy blond hair falling into his face. His mouth as it repeats threats, which don't scare me right now at all.

There is something seriously wrong with me. Maybe Chadwick's right, and I do need therapy. And he doesn't even know about Legend!

I clutch my purse, pop out of my seat on the couch, and shoot to my feet. "I'm so sorry for wasting your time, Dr. Grand. I think I need to go. Please send me a bill for a full session. I want to make sure you're compensated for your time." I rush toward the door, but Dr. Grand's voice stops me.

"Ms. Priest."

I stop, and it takes me a second to summon the courage to turn and glance over my shoulder at her. "Yes?"

"If you ever need someone to talk to, about anything, I really am good at my job. Just because my specialty is sex doesn't mean I don't spend a lot of my time discussing more mainstream issues. Including why you're in a relationship that doesn't serve you. Please feel free to call anytime."

"Thank you, Dr. Grand. I appreciate that."

I find the knob as I give her a gracious smile and let myself out of the room. I'm so focused on getting the hell out of this office, I don't even notice the brunette sitting in the waiting area.

"Scarlett? Is that you?"

As soon as I hear my name, I'm tempted to run, but the familiar voice stays my impulse. I turn slowly, keeping my face partially shielded by my hair.

"Flynn?"

My former stepsister rises and comes toward me. "I didn't know you come here. Although I'm not surprised you need therapy, considering your father. I'm so glad my mom finally divorced his ass. What a tool, am I right?"

I find my voice again and manage to put words together that make sense. "I don't go here. Total misunderstanding."

Her gaze narrows, and she tilts her head. "I just watched you come out of a therapist's office. But it's cool if you want to pretend you didn't. I get it."

I don't know if it's the fact that we have a few shared years of history or that I'm so freaking pissed about what Chadwick did to me, but my better judgment gives way and I spill.

"My boyfriend made me an appointment with a sex therapist without telling me who I was meeting with, and now I'm pretty sure I'm going to kill him and break up with him. I'm rolling the dice on which is happening first."

Owning what I'm going to do gives me a sense of power that I desperately need right now.

"You're finally going to dump Chad-the-douchebag?" Her bright green eyes light up. "Good! He's a fucking tool, and you can do way better. Did you know he hit on me at Thanksgiving last year? It was fucking gross, but I didn't want to tell you and have you blame me for egging it on like Mom would do."

I try to remember last Thanksgiving, but it's a blur in my mind, except for the part where my dad told me he'd have his chef save the wishbone for me like Mom did when I was a kid. But Chadwick wanted to leave before dessert because he had to watch football, so we left. *Asshole.*

I meet her sharp gaze. "I know we're not technically related anymore, but regardless, I would never blame something like that on you. You have to believe that."

Flynn shrugs, but I can tell what I said matters from the way her expression changes. "You never know with crazy families. Still, I'm glad you're finally breaking it off. There's a better guy for you out there. I have no doubt. Half this city would jump at the chance to even be in the same room with you. So, how are you going to do it?"

The receptionist lifts her finger to her lips, and I move us closer to a corner with two chairs and a potted palm. "Do you want to get out of here and grab some coffee instead?"

Flynn glances down at her watch, which is a really cool artsy piece that I'd love to have in Curated. "My appointment starts in less than twenty minutes, so I'd better not. But . . . I'm here at the same time every Friday if you ever find yourself in the neighborhood."

She says it casually, as though she doesn't want to get her hopes up, and I feel like I've been a shit stepsister, even if we aren't related anymore. I always liked Flynn, probably in part because she's mouthy and bold and doesn't seem to give a shit what anyone thinks about her.

"I'll make sure I'm in the neighborhood one of these Fridays soon. Take care of yourself, Flynn."

"You too, Scarlett. And make sure to tell handsy Chadwick to go fuck himself for me." With a bright smile, she winks and makes her way back to her seat, crossing one knee over the other so that she looks like the perfect prim and proper socialite.

But I know the truth. Flynn is way cooler than any boring socialite. I definitely need to get to know my former kinda little sister better . . . and soon.

Next up, a trip to Dad's building so I can see Chadwick and tell him face-to-face exactly what I think of his sex-therapy surprise.

CHAPTER TWENTY

SCARLETT

Well, that was a hell of a letdown. I hoofed it all the way uptown to Priest Pharmaceuticals, only to be met with disappointment.

"Sorry, Chadwick's out of the office in meetings all day. Can I give him a message for you?"

The receptionist was incredibly apologetic, especially because she knows exactly who I am, but it doesn't change the fact that my trip was a complete waste. As I walk out of the lobby into the glass atrium of the building, I tap the screen of my phone to pull up Chadwick's contact. I'm not waiting until tonight to tell him what I think. *Hell. No.*

Shockingly, he picks up on the second ring. "Hey, babe! How did it go with the counselor? Did you talk to her about your problem?"

My back goes poker straight and my response is clipped. If he thought I was cold before, he'd better watch out. "Exactly what problem are you talking about?"

"Your problem in our relationship."

A wave of crimson washes across my vision.

"*My* problem in our relationship? You're going to have to

be more specific, Chadwick, because I'm pretty sure there's more than one."

I hear some garbled words and then the sound of a door opening and closing. Finally, he comes back to the line.

"Sorry, I had to step out of the meeting so we could talk."

One part of me wants to apologize for the fact that I interrupted the meeting, but that's the same accommodating part of me that didn't ask questions when Chadwick set me up on a surprise date with a sex therapist. I stay quiet, letting my anger build as I wait for him to continue.

"Good, because we definitely need to talk about what the hell you just sprang on me. I came to your office to tell you in person, but obviously you're not here."

"Wait, you're saying you left the appointment and didn't talk to her? I paid three hundred bucks for that slot, and if it didn't fix you, then you're going to have to pay for the other appointments."

The anger rising in his tone makes me see red.

"Oh, I talked to her," I say, enunciating more clearly than I ever have before. "But I'm curious about exactly why you thought I needed a freaking *sex therapist*?" My voice rises at the end, and I remember that I'm in public. I scan the atrium and spot a few people watching me.

I shove through the glass doors and walk out onto the sidewalk where I can disappear into a sea of New Yorkers who don't give a damn who I am or what I'm talking about.

"Because we hardly ever have sex, and if it were up to you, I wouldn't get laid at all. Because, trust me, I'm all for it, all the time, but you're never in the mood, which means you've got a problem, Scarlett. I'm not going to put up with it anymore. Either you fix this and start getting with the program—which means putting out or at least sucking dick a lot fucking more—or we're done. I've had it."

A sense of cold calmness settles over me, like a blanket of

freshly fallen snow has just cloaked me and the city streets. It's like I'm staring out at a landscape that's pure and unspoiled and full of second chances. This is my out. Right here. And I'm taking it.

"Then we're done. Good talk, *Chad*. Glad we worked that out so civilly. I'll mail anything I have of yours to your condo."

The other end of the call goes silent for a beat until Chadwick starts sputtering. But there's one difference now. I don't have to listen to a single word of it.

I hold my phone away from my head and tap the screen to end the call.

Just. Like. That.

In the middle of the plaza, in front of the building housing my father's company, I double over—with laughter.

It was so easy. So effortless. So perfectly *final.*

I straighten and fling my arms into a triumphant *V* in the air. "I am single!"

A woman in a suit turns to me, and her fuchsia frown turns into a smile. "Get it, girl."

I spin around in a circle and dance like Elaine from *Seinfeld*, feeling utterly and completely free for the first time in years. Like I've just broken the chains holding me down, and now I can soar.

Power fills me, bubbling to the surface until I'm fairly certain I'm a 100 percent badass.

A few people pause and watch my spectacle, but I don't care. I smile at all of them before practically skipping to the curb to hail a cab.

I text Amy to reschedule the designer and let her know I'm going off the schedule today, because I'm *unstoppable and single.*

Her reply is exactly what I need to read.

· · ·

AMY: Praise Jesus!!! We'll hold down the fort. Go have some you-time. Just don't forget about self-defense at 4.

I tuck that reminder away as I give the cabbie the address of Legend. It's time to scope out the scene of the comeback I'm staging in less than thirty-six hours.

And that wave of heat I feel? I'm not going to think about that . . . yet.

CHAPTER TWENTY-ONE

LEGEND

"How much?" I ask from between gritted teeth, hating that I'm even entertaining the possibility of a fight with Bodhi Black.

And yet, my self-preservation instincts won't let me stay silent.

I've never given up without a fight, and this won't be the first time. There's no fucking way I'm going to let my investors come in here and take everything I've worked for my entire life without doing every goddamned thing I can to dig myself out of this hole.

"You know I can't give you exact numbers, man," Rolo says with a hint of greed leaching into his tone. "Depends on the crowd. The venue."

"Bullshit, Rolo. Give me a number, or I hang up."

"Jeez, man. When'd you get so fucking serious? I miss my old buddy Legend who knew how to have a good time."

"You mean the one who made us both tons of money? The same guy you've been begging to take this fight, and now you're hesitating? What the fuck is going on?"

My fingers curl around the arm of my chair as I wait for

Rolo to shoot straight with me, something he's always done. But, now, for the first time ever, he's giving me the runaround, and I think I know why.

Like any shark, he smells blood in the water.

If Rolo knows the fight is the last option to save my ass, then he's going to use that leverage to take a bigger cut of the cash that should be going into my pocket. After all, I'm the one taking all the fucking risk on this deal. He doesn't have to stand inside a cage and face a man who might as well have sledgehammers for fists. Oh, and a man who is determined to redeem himself from defeat, at the cost of my life, if necessary.

"You know how it goes. Business is business. Let me talk to Black's people and a few venues and—"

I end the call without listening to the rest of whatever garbage Rolo is about to feed me. He's not stupid. He knows I know what he's doing. I also won't let him fuck me over just because he thinks he's got the upper hand.

Not fucking happening. I lean back in my chair and scrub my hands over my face and hair. This isn't how things were supposed to be. But they never are.

I don't plan to fail. But, *fuck*, I've done a bang-up job this time. I try to focus on my spreadsheet again—the one that shows a shit ton of numbers in red that our accountant sent over earlier attached to an email that read:

Make some fucking money this weekend or close the doors Sunday. For good.

The spreadsheet and the email pushed me into calling Rolo, because I can't stand by and do nothing while this club dies a slow death, and takes me and everyone I care about down with it.

But my concentration only lasts for a few minutes before Bump comes bursting into my office, letting the door smack on the opposite wall.

"It's her. Here."

My first instinct is to reach for a gun because he's flailing his arms and shouting shit I can't understand, but then his wheezing words penetrate.

"She's here."

There's only one *she* in my brain lately, as much as I wish I could deny the fact.

"Who?" I ask carefully, shutting my laptop. It's fair to say I'm not in a good mood.

"The woman! The one you wanted! She's here. And I didn't bring her this time. I swear. I haven't gone near her. I've been good, Gabe. I swear."

Fucking Bump. I love the kid more than any other human on this planet, exactly the way he is, but I still wish he'd never gotten shot in the fucking head. And yeah, he was liking coke a little too much back in the day, but addiction I could have helped him fix. This injury is a regret I'll take to my grave, not that it'll do a damn bit of good to change things now.

But Scarlett Priest coming to the club a full day before she's scheduled . . . what the hell does that mean?

Is she here to back out? To threaten me with calling the cops for forcing her into this? Shit. What if she's here to lead the cops to where she was kidnapped? My brain goes crazy, spiraling into more and more ridiculous shit before I force it all to go quiet, and I rise.

"Where is she?"

"With Zoe, in the club. She wants to make sure we're ready for tomorrow."

Every fiber of my being wants to walk out of this office and onto the club floor so I can see the woman whose face I've been staring at altogether too fucking often on my phone. The woman whose lips I can't stop thinking about. *Fuck.* I want to taste her so goddamned bad.

Which is exactly why I shouldn't go anywhere near her. Self-preservation.

Then Bump adds, "Zoe is showing her the VIP areas so she can pick her favorites and have them set up for tomorrow."

Favorites. That means she needs more than one. So she is planning on following through. Maybe I shouldn't have doubted her, but social media queens don't exactly inspire confidence in me.

"Can we go talk to her? Should I tell her I'm sorry? I mean, I'm not, but I can pretend." Bump is practically bouncing off the walls, which is never good.

I snap my fingers and lock my gaze onto his. "No. You're not going anywhere near her. Understand me, Bump? We need to stay away from her."

His face crumples into a devastated expression, and you'd think I just told the kid he's never allowed to have ice cream again. I hate that look, but I need him to understand that neither of us have any business going near Scarlett Priest.

She's with Zoe. Zoe will put her at ease. Reassure her that she'll have everything she needs. Zoe is incredibly capable and needs no help from me—and certainly not Bump—to do her job.

"Can we at least watch them?" Bump asks, hope budding in his tone.

Fucking kid. I should say no. But I can't. I want to see her too goddamned bad. *Fuck.*

"Only if you stay quiet. Okay? If you start yelling at them, like you did when you came in here, then—"

Bump yanks his pinched fingers across his lips like he's zipping them shut and tosses away the invisible key.

I let out a sigh and bow my head. *This is a bad fucking idea, but all the best ones are.* "Okay. Fine. Come on."

Before renovations, the club was an old Masonic temple that was supposed to be torn down, but something happened and it ended up being sold. By the time I leased it for Legend, it had been rehabbed already, and we retrofitted it for a nightclub. One thing we found that we didn't expect— hidden entrances and exits, likely used by the Freemasons who built the place.

I added my own touch—an entire wall of mirrors on the second-floor VIP area where we could watch the who's who of New York without being seen. Everything else is covered by the state-of-the-art surveillance system that I spent a fortune on. A lot of good it did, though, since it didn't even catch the face of the person who shot up the place, because he was wearing a mask.

I let Bump drag me silently out of my office by the arm and down the interior corridor that runs along the two-way mirrored wall.

As soon as we turn the corner, I see her.

Jesus. Christ.

Fuck. Me. Sideways.

She's dressed like an image out of a fantasy. All innocent and sweet in this blue-and-white-checked dress that should remind me of a milkmaid, but instead makes me think of debauching her until there's not a fucking innocent thought left in either of our heads. And the neckline shows off the curves of her perfect tits.

My dick jerks in my pants. Yeah. Bad fucking idea.

I shouldn't be anywhere near this woman. It's not safe. Or healthy. Or smart.

I can picture that pink-slicked mouth leaving lipstick prints—

"Can't believe she fucking showed up." The image leaves my head, evaporated by the sound of Q's hushed voice.

"I know," Bump says, but when I glare at him, he goes silent.

Without the music and bass beats filling the club, anything we say louder than a whisper is bound to be overheard, even if it's muffled.

"And she's actually prepping with Zoe for tomorrow. Gotta be a fucking miracle," Q adds.

"What did you expect?" I whisper.

"Cops and handcuffs. Three hots and a cot for all of us."

Bump is practically coming out of his skin with the need to talk, but I shake my head and press my finger to my lips. He nods in agreement.

"I told you not to worry, man," I say to Q with newfound confidence I didn't have twenty minutes ago. "Everything is going to work out."

Before he can reply, Scarlett tilts her head and turns toward us like she can see straight through the mirrored glass.

Fuck.

CHAPTER TWENTY-TWO

SCARLETT

The hair on my arms stands up in the middle of Zoe's explanation of how the VIP lounges are run at Legend. I shift, glancing over my shoulder, searching for *him*, because I swear I can feel his eyes on me. But all I see is my reflection in the long mirrored wall that lines the back of the entire second-floor balcony area.

I return my attention to Zoe, a pretty woman about five years older than me, with straight dark brown hair, but the feeling of being watched doesn't subside. I try to shake it off, with minimal success, and make mental notes about what she's saying.

We'll have three lounges stocked and ready to rock, but they'll all be connected rather than separated, so we can mingle between all three and not feel cramped. We have a stairway down to the club floor, where we can go shake our shit in front of the DJ booth, or stay upstairs and dance.

All in all, it's a really nice club, with what appears to be top-of-the-line everything, except *patrons.* That's where I come in.

It's still a little crazy that I'm doing this, but I can't help it.

Call me stupid, but I'm intrigued by this club. And maybe it's arrogant, but I really think I can help.

Okay, so maybe I'm not just intrigued by the club. It might have everything to do with the mysterious and reclusive owner.

Zoe goes quiet, and I can tell she's waiting for me to ask something, but I haven't been paying attention to what she was saying for the last few minutes. Not since I got distracted by the thought of Gabriel Legend's eyes on me.

I blurt out a question before I realize my intent. "Will Mr. Legend be joining us Saturday night to celebrate?"

Zoe's kind brown eyes widen with shock. "Excuse me?"

Shoving down the urge to glance at the mirror again, I smile. "Yes, well, he's the owner, isn't he? I assume he'll want to join us and celebrate the new start of the club."

"Oh, Mr. Legend doesn't really come out on the floor. He's not one for crowds. My brother, however, will be here to assist in any way that you may need. His name is Marcus, but he goes by Q, for our last name, Quinterro."

"I'm looking forward to meeting him," I reply, but I'm not feeling very appeased. I'm sure Q is a perfectly nice guy, but I haven't been moaning his name in my apartment.

No, I want to see Legend, and since I'm putting myself out to help him, the least the man can do is make an appearance.

"It's good for PR, and I'd really like to see Mr. Legend tomorrow night as well. I have some things I'd like to tell him directly. Is that something you can arrange?"

Her earrings, geometric leather shapes hanging from thin chains, dangle beneath her earlobes as she tilts her head to the side, studying me. "Do you have a personal interest in Mr. Legend, Ms. Priest? You'd be surprised how many women come in here wanting to meet the man they've watched fight, and you know . . . they get a little overzealous about it."

I'm actually impressed she's calling me out, but I was raised by a woman who might as well have had a PhD in making things happen. I straighten and meet Zoe eye to eye.

"I can promise you that I'm not like those women. After all, Mr. Legend is the one who brought me to the club and enlisted my help. The least he can do is give me a few minutes of his time after I make good on my commitments. And showing his face after a scandal—or in Legend's case, a victimless shooting—will send a message that things are under control. Maybe if he showed his face at the grand opening, whoever did it would have thought twice."

Something that looks a lot like respect flickers in Zoe's dark eyes. "I'll make sure to let him know you need to speak to him. Anything else?"

"Not off the top of my head," I say with a self-satisfied smile.

But silently, I add, *Unless he's available to see me right now . . . I'd like to introduce him to Bad Scarlett. I think they'd get along just fine.*

CHAPTER TWENTY-THREE

LEGEND

"She wants to see you." This comes from Bump, and if he weren't speaking so softly that I could barely hear him from two feet away, I'd have shut him up quick.

But I don't have to. He's already rezipping his lips and tossing away the key while he bounces from one foot to the other.

Q turns to me with a raised brow and murmurs, "Why the hell does she want to see you?"

I don't have an answer for him. All I know is that I want to walk right through this glass, wrap my hands around her waist, and carry her off to somewhere we won't be interrupted for a long, long time. I would trade burning in hell for a single night with her.

Fucking shit, this is a problem. A real one.

I don't get involved with women. Sure, I fuck them on occasion, get my fix, and move on without any ties or strings. I take care of my physical needs, and that's it. Nothing more. *Ever.*

But this woman. *Goddammit.* She's something else. She'd have to be, because there's no other explanation for why the hell I'm staring through a two-way mirror at her while I think about selling my soul to make her mine.

But she *isn't.* She can't be.

I don't do connections. I don't let new people into my circle. It's too risky. Too dangerous.

After all, the last woman I loved ended up dead.

And there it is. The only reminder that could kill any fantasy spinning to life in my brain.

I turn on my heel and march down the corridor, away from Q and Bump, intent on doing paperwork until I'm blind, deaf, and dumb. Maybe then it'll be safe to come out of my office again because Scarlett Priest, and all the temptation that comes along with her, will be gone.

Except Q won't let things lie. I'm not getting off that easy, not that I ever do. His footsteps echo in the hall as he follows me, not caring that I clearly want to be alone.

"Please tell me you're not thinking about taking that fight with Black. Because I just got a call from his trainer asking if Rolo was really serious or just wasting his time again."

"*Fuck.*" I flex my fist and manage to get my shit under control before I throw it through one of the wood panels in my office wall. "Rolo and his big fucking mouth."

Q comes inside and shuts the door. "So, you *are* thinking about it." His voice is even, the tenor he takes on when I might snap at any minute.

And maybe he's right to be concerned, because I sure as fuck don't know how long I'll last before the pressure makes me crack. I've only broken down once before, and that's not something I ever want to go through again. And I sure as hell don't want Q to witness it.

I spin around and meet his almost black eyes. "I'm not going to let them take everything from us. Not if there's a way I can stop it or buy us more time."

"At what cost? Because that motherfucker wants to kill

you, and if you die in that fucking ring, what good does it do the rest of us?" He says it like I haven't already thought about it. Which I have. In detail.

"You take the money, pay off the creditors, sell the club, and take care of Bump."

Q jams his hand through his hair, messing up the perfectly slicked-back locks.

"No. No fucking way, Gabe. I'm not doing this shit without you. Don't go trying to be a fucking hero now. We don't need that. We just need you. Breathing, and not through a fucking tube." My best friend turns and reaches for the door handle. "I'm not sure it'll work either, but you haven't even given the woman a chance to work her goddamned magic, and you're already trying to come up with a plan B. Why am I even surprised?"

"What if it doesn't work?" I ask him. "What if I was wrong about her?"

"Then you're wrong, and we figure something out that doesn't include you ending up in a fucking coma or a body bag."

I stay silent, because at this point, we're running out of time and options, and Q knows it.

"Look, give it forty-eight hours. If this doesn't work, you and I will lay all our choices on the table. It's not like I don't have some skills I can put to work to make some cash quickly if we're that desperate."

My teeth clench together because I know what he's talking about, and I won't let him do it.

"Forty-eight hours. Then we work on plan B."

CHAPTER TWENTY-FOUR

SCARLETT

W hen I walk into my self-defense class at four o'clock, there's still a spring in my step that shouldn't be there. I can't help it, though. For the first time in a long time, I'm filled with a sense of purpose that's so strong and driven, I can't possibly fail.

There's something wildly different about being on a crusade to save someone else's business, compared to attempting to become successful myself without drawing the judgment and censure of my peers.

This feels *pure.* Noble. Exciting.

I'm sure Legend doesn't see me as a badass riding to the rescue, but that's too bad. That's exactly how I feel.

At least, until I see the man I presume is my self-defense instructor.

Oh. My. Giants.

The man in front of me is around six-four and a wall of muscle. He's not as bulky as a bodybuilder, but he's got muscles on top of muscles that I can't begin to name.

"You Scarlett Priest?"

I nod because words aren't coming easily in the face of this terrifying man.

"You're on time. Good. Let's get started."

Oh. Shit.

He waves me forward, and out of instinct, I hold out a hand.

"It's nice to meet you, Mr. Black. Are you sure this is a beginner-level class? I'm not sure what Christine told you, but ..."

He doesn't reach for my hand to shake it, so I let it drop to my side.

"She made it worth my while, and that's why you're here. By the time we're done, you'll be able to disable just about anyone, and maybe kill a few people. You ready?"

Hell. This should be interesting.

When I plop onto my bed at ten, I'm sore in places I'm not sure I've ever been sore, but I do now know a half dozen ways to disable people and two ways to kill them, so that's new and different.

As I scroll through my social media feed, I see a comment from a troll that my team hasn't already caught, so I tap on the profile and look at the cat picture. It's definitely a stock photo or stolen, because the owner of a fluffy Ragdoll wouldn't really say that I should put my head in an oven and turn it on. Would she? Or he?

I don't know, but I screenshot it, delete it, and send the photo to the police detective who has my file, along with a note that there's a new profile. Then I navigate away from my page to see if my favorite families have any new photos of their messy lives, because I am *not* going to YouTube yet. *Not for at least twenty more minutes.*

That's when a message pops up on the top of my screen from *RouxDoggo.* I would have ignored it, but the dog looked familiar.

Wait. Is that the dog from Gabriel Legend's office? Brindle. Big. Looks like it could eat me?

I tap on the message.

RouxDoggo: Whatever you need, it's yours. I'll see you tomorrow.

Oh. My. God. Is that . . . Could it be . . .

I tap on the profile and find an account with no followers and only one post, a photo of a dog smiling up at the camera as a big hand scratches her ears.

I may not recognize his hand by sight, but I'm willing to bet it's his. I tap out a reply.

ScarlettPriestOfficial: Zoe has it all covered, but thank you. You'll definitely see me tomorrow. The question is—will I see you?

Because the app shows you if and when someone sees your message, I wait and stare at the screen like a teenage girl, hoping my crush will reply.

He doesn't. But that doesn't change a damn thing.

I fall asleep with Legend's name on my lips and wake up with him on my mind.

Why I'm fixated on him, I can't explain. Maybe because he lives in the shadows, while I live in the limelight. Maybe because his was the first face I saw when I rolled out of that rug, and instead of terrifying me, he captivated me. Maybe because my life is all too orderly and scripted, and his seems dangerous and exotic.

Regardless, I haven't felt this alive in years, and I want more of that feeling.

Which means, I'm ready to put my war paint on and go save his damn club.

CHAPTER TWENTY-FIVE

LEGEND

I f I look at the clock even one more time, I'm going to break it.

Friday night, the club started rocking like it already had new blood pumping through its veins. When I asked Q what the hell was going on, he handed me his phone, which showed *NYCelebSightings* and a picture of the woman I can't get out of my head walking into the club that morning.

It took everything I had not to yank the phone from his grip and zoom in on her blue-and-white dress and the smile on her face. *God. I bet she's even more beautiful when she laughs.*

Stop it, asshole. You can't have her. Stop thinking about her laugh, her smile, her fucking lips, face, and everything else. My orders to myself didn't do a damn bit of good to get the thoughts out of my head, but thankfully Q couldn't read my mind.

"Just wait until she's here with her crew, Gabe. You're not getting in the ring again. This is going to work. She's going to make it work. Bump might have risked us all going to prison, but the kid might just have saved our asses too."

We made a profit Friday night. All because of Scarlett, who wasn't even here.

Maybe Q was right. Maybe it will work.

I glance at the clock one more time, before I lose patience with myself. Five thirty. Only a few more hours.

"Come on, Roux. We're going for a walk, baby girl."

As soon as I say her name, Roux's head lifts from her bed in the corner, and a thought slams into my brain.

I messaged her as Roux yesterday. Fuck. What if she responded?

I don't normally use those social media apps because I don't give a fuck about being social. Plus, I've tried to keep my face low profile because I'm not ready to be found by the person who has wanted me dead for fifteen years. *Not ready to be found* yet, I silently correct myself.

Moses Buford Gaspard's time is coming. One way or another, I won't leave this world without putting him in the ground first. For what he took from me. For what he did to Bump.

He's living on borrowed time.

Just like I am if he gets to me first.

All thoughts of Moses slip from my mind when I see the message from Scarlett.

SCARLETTPRIESTOFFICIAL: *Zoe has it all covered, but thank you. You'll definitely see me tomorrow. The question is—will I see you?*

I can practically see her in front of me right now. That's how fucking obsessed I am with this woman, even though I shouldn't be. I've got her burned into my memory like she's meant to be there.

Fuck.

I want to reply. More than anything, I want to tell her that she won't be leaving this club without me stealing her away from her friends, sneaking her through the hidden exit, and making sure she can't stop thinking about me the way I can't stop thinking about her.

But I don't.

I can't.

And I won't.

Scarlett Priest is not for me. I need to get that fact through my thick fucking head. I shove my phone in my pocket, grab Roux's leash, and walk to the door.

Maybe the six-mile loop we take around the city will be enough to get her off my mind. Probably not. That would take a walk all the way home to Biloxi and back.

The gym, it is. Because nothing but a punishing workout could take my mind off the woman who has taken up permanent residence in it. Maybe, just maybe, if I'm exhausted, my brain will give up these ridiculous fucking ideas. I'm too old to believe in fairy tales.

Scarlett Priest will come, hopefully save my club, and then she'll go home to her fucking boyfriend. That's just how it's going to be.

"Come on, Roux. Let's go beat the shit out of the heavy bag and get you some treats."

CHAPTER TWENTY-SIX

SCARLETT

"You look *amazing.*"

Monroe squeals as I walk out of the bedroom and into the living room of my apartment.

"Like, *holy shitballs,* if I were a dude, I'd be trying to bang you up against a wall in a dark corner of the club. I wouldn't care who saw, though, because I'd have my dick so deep in the hottest bitch I've ever seen."

Harlow interjects. "Actually, if you were a dude who was into banging girls in clubs, you'd probably want someone to see, because presumably, you'd get off on that kind of thing. And Scar can totally do it now that she's broken up with Chadwick-the-dick!"

His name is a jarring reminder of the strange, yet exciting and invigorating turn my life has taken in the past few days.

I'm not Good Scarlett with the perfect life and boyfriend tonight.

No, because first off, I blocked his number like any normal person would do after a breakup. Secondly, I haven't thought about him much at all, and I have zero regrets. All of which confirms I made the right choice.

Tonight, I'm just a girl who's going to go do something a little bit crazy and, hopefully, help someone who needs it. Maybe not Good Scarlett, but not exactly Bad Scarlett either. Tonight, I'm New Scarlett.

"That means my job here is done," Kelsey says, unhooking the belt around her waist that holds the pouch with all her makeup brushes. "You have passed the *Mar-Low* test."

Mar-Low is what she calls Monroe and Harlow when they're together and drunk. Which they shouldn't be already, but Kelsey and I took longer than planned. I glance at the antique gilt-edged mirror hanging above the sideboard and smile into the aged glass.

"You're always amazing, Kels. But tonight, you killed it. I look *smokin' hot.*"

"Of course you do. That's my job. Now, let's get to the club so those paps I tipped off have something to photograph. Except, wait. Hold it right there. That downlight is incredible. I need a pic for social media or it doesn't count, right?"

I hold still and look down, to the side, and then coyly at her from under my lashes while she snaps photos.

We're not even out the door when she turns around and smiles at me. "Posted. And now everyone knows that my girl is headed to Legend, soon to be the hottest club in town."

Harlow and Monroe throw their arms into the air and do a victory dance they probably learned from watching sports with their husbands. "Let's do this, girls!"

Thirty-five minutes later, we're rolling up to a club that doesn't exactly have a line out front, but there is a small group of people milling around the two dark-suited men at the doors.

Inside the black Range Rover, Kelsey smiles at me and squeezes my hand. "You ready for this? Because you're about to make the biggest statement you've made outside Curated in a long time."

I let the wrap slip off my shoulders to reveal my vintage House of Scarlett dress—in my mother's signature color, *red*.

Red isn't normally my color, but tonight, I felt the need to go bold. Even Kelsey was surprised when I laid it out on the bed and asked for a statement lip in the exact same shade.

"I'm ready."

"Then let's do this, girl." She shoots a text to Harlow and Monroe, who are in the matching Range Rover behind us— for the sole purpose of making a statement entrance—and let them know that it's go time.

I let the driver open the door like it's a red-carpet event, because that's what I've been trained to do. With a strut that would make my runway-model mother proud, I stride toward two gentlemen manning the door. The click of heels on the sidewalk behind me tells me Kelsey and the girls are coming too.

That's when the flashes from the cameras start.

"Scarlett, why Legend? Why now?" one paparazzo calls out.

I turn and give him a blinding smile. "Haven't you heard? It's the hottest scene in town."

"Aren't you afraid of a repeat of the grand opening? You wearing body armor under that dress?"

I pause and wait a beat before I throw my head back in laughter. "Are you kidding me? I couldn't be safer here if I had Gabriel Legend guarding me himself."

The woman with the camera beside him, who has been silent until now, finally speaks up.

"Is that why you're here, Scarlett? For Legend himself? Because rumor has it you stopped in yesterday for a quick chat with the man. I can't blame you; he's fine as hell."

Her question nearly takes my breath away. It's like she

knows something that I haven't yet admitted to myself. *Am I really just here for him?*

Bad Scarlett pipes up. *Duh, Scarlett. You want him to hold you down like he did that guy in the cage. Remember? It was that fight that had you screaming his name while you came. Let's go get some of that. Stat.*

Well, hell. That's an unexpected revelation. And an awkwardly timed one as well.

When I don't answer immediately, a grin breaks out over the woman's face. "Nice, Ms. Priest. Can't blame you."

"Scarlett? Let's head inside." Kelsey's fingers close around my arm, and her touch breaks me free from my thoughts. Thankfully, Harlow and Monroe are right behind us, posing for the paps and giving them even more material for *Page Six*.

Now . . . if they'll only post it quickly so all of Manhattan knows exactly where the party's at tonight. *Legend.*

As soon as we're in the door, Kelsey pauses and looks at me. "Are you okay? Because I'm pretty sure you just handed them the biggest story of the year by *letting them think that you're here to bag Gabriel Legend*. What the hell was that, Scar?"

"Ladies, welcome."

Zoe's voice comes over the music, which I didn't even notice before because I was so shocked by Kelsey's question. She also saves me from having to come up with an explanation for something I can't explain.

Did I just put it out there to the world that I want this man? It wouldn't be a lie. But that's not something I would normally do. Not the perfectly polite Scarlett Priest.

Except I just did.

"Let me show you to the VIP area so you can get comfortable," Zoe says, holding out an arm to direct us to the marble stairs that lead to the second-level balcony where we talked yesterday.

Instead of following her, I look out at the dance floor,

which isn't empty like I expected. There's actually a crowd of about thirty people. Plus, the bars on either side have a few people sitting and standing at them, waiting for drinks or knocking them back. Every single one of them is watching us.

Kelsey pulls me along behind Zoe as we head for the stairs, but I can't tear my gaze away from the corners of the room. I'm looking for him in the shadows. I can't help it.

Maybe the pap was right. Maybe that's exactly why I'm here.

To see Gabriel Legend.

As soon as we reach the lounge area with leather sofas and marble tables, our server greets us with a large bottle of Cristal.

"I hope you're ready for a wonderful night, ladies. My name is Astra, and I will take excellent care of you."

"Yes! Let's get our drink on! I'm ready to party!"

Monroe's high-pitched squeal has to be heard by every single person in this club, because from over the railing, I can see them all staring up at us. So I do something I've never done before.

I reach for a glass, and as soon as it's poured, I walk to the edge of the balcony and lean on the railing. With the champagne flute in the air, I toast everyone down below.

"Who's ready to have fun tonight?"

Cheers fill the club. The DJ spins a sick beat, and more bodies pack the floor.

The girls crowd around me, raising their glasses high, and we all clink rims.

It's. *On.*

CHAPTER TWENTY-SEVEN

LEGEND

T he woman in the red dress and red-slicked lips is a fucking goddess meant to dare men into tempting fate. I can't take my eyes off her as she sips the most expensive champagne the club has ever *not* sold and sways to the music.

She's been here for an hour, and both the club and VIP area are more crowded than they've been since the night we opened. The till is rocking as people throw down more and more money for drinks. The door counter keeps climbing as people pay their cover—$100 tonight—and they spill inside.

"I thought I'd find you here," Q says from behind me in the corridor. "You should be out there. Thanking her for making a goddamned miracle happen. Fucking kissing her ass and begging her to do it again and again."

Q doesn't know he shouldn't have said it, but a new image barrels through my brain, obliterating every other thought. Me dropping to my knees to lift the skirt of that red dress so I can do a hell of a lot more than kiss her ass.

"So?" Q gives me a curious look, and I glance at him.

"So, what?"

"Are you even listening to me, man? Because you look like you're a million fucking miles away right now."

Not a million miles away. Just a dozen or so feet, but it might as well be the other side of the planet. Some people are untouchable, no matter how close you get to them, and Scarlett Priest is one of them.

Even though she wants to see me. I haven't forgotten her message. I just didn't know how the hell to answer it.

"Nope, clearly not fucking listening."

I tear my gaze off Scarlett Priest's face. "I'm just as surprised as you are."

Q huffs. "You were the one who had the idea. When you saw her picture on that magazine cover, something in you knew that this girl could change everything for us. This shit isn't random, Gabe. This is the universe handing you a fucking gift, and you need to treat it with the respect it deserves."

He's right. She is a fucking gift, *but not for me.* For the club. For the investors. For the friends and family who believed in me enough to plunk down their hard-earned cash to get behind my dream. Except, part of me, the part I've silenced for years, pipes up. *But what if she is meant for you?*

I stare through the two-way mirrored glass and watch her as she works the room like she was born to do it. She effortlessly talks and shifts her focus, making everyone around her feel completely at ease. They're all enraptured by her, as they should be, but she doesn't even notice. Her red dress is bold, but no bolder than the confidence she wears like a second skin. She's captivating. She *belongs.*

I've never belonged anywhere. Not even in my own club, where I won't show my face if I can help it, because I don't want it plastered all over social media until I'm ready.

It's already on those fucking YouTube videos no one was supposed to be recording, and that's dangerous enough as it is.

Still, I can't help but wonder what it would be like. *Fuck, what would it be like to belong to* her?

The question stops me cold, and I shove it away.

That can't happen.

It doesn't matter that I've never felt this fucked up over a woman I've never even seen naked. It doesn't matter that I've never wanted to taste a woman more.

Fuck.

I keep my circle small so no one gets killed. I haven't lived in the shadows as much as possible for this long just to take the risk now.

Or have I? Opening the club was always going to put me and my name in the public eye.

Deep down, I'm ready to confront my past. Because it'll only be so long before it finds me. A new name won't hide my secrets forever.

Fighting was a risk. I knew that going into it. But the money was worth it, and Moses wasn't likely to follow the underground fights circuit way up north. Besides, every minute I trained put me in shape to be ready for the war that's almost certainly coming, because his name hasn't shown up in the Biloxi obits yet.

"I'm going out there, Gabe. If you want to come, come. If not, stay here and watch where no one can see you. But I have a feeling you're going to disappoint the lady in red."

Q walks away, his footsteps barely making a sound over the beat of the thundering bass.

It's now or never.

I take one more look at Scarlett, with that wide smile on her face, holding out her glass of champagne for Astra to top it off.

Fuck it.
Here we go.

CHAPTER TWENTY-EIGHT

SCARLETT

A hand lands on my shoulder and sparks streak down my spine.

He's here. He found me. I steady myself on my four-inch heels and pivot to face . . .

Chadwick?

"What the hell are you doing here, Scarlett? Jesus Christ. And that fucking dress. You look like a—" Chadwick cuts off whatever he was about to say, but from the disgust on his face, I can tell it wasn't complimentary.

"What are *you* doing here?" I ask, and my fingers tighten around my champagne flute.

Annoyed, he bounces his fingers off his forehead, gesturing for me to think about it. "You blocked my fucking number. I had to find some way to talk you out of this ridiculous snit you're in so we can tell your father we're getting married over Christmas."

I blink twice and stare at him.

What in the actual fuck is he saying? My brain recognizes the language as English, but the words coming out of his mouth don't make any sense.

"Excuse me?" My cheeks are flaming hot, either from embarrassment or rage or both.

"You're excused—for acting like a petulant child. All I wanted to do was address your problems in the bedroom so we could fix that part of our relationship, and then we could move forward with the wedding planning."

I'm so shocked and confused that my gaze drops to my left hand, and wouldn't you know it? There's no ring there. I am indeed, *not engaged*, which means Chadwick LaSalle Jr. has lost his damn mind.

I wave my bare left hand in front of his smug face. "I don't know what you're talking about, Chadwick, but you and I are—"

"Sorting out our issues before we make it official. I know. That's the plan, but now you're acting like a fucking teenager and blocking me. It's bullshit, Scarlett, and you know it. I don't want to have this conversation here, but we *are* having it."

His index finger raises before me, and he shakes it as he continues his ludicrous speech.

"And if this is all about me not wanting to come to your place? Well, it's fucking hard to get a boner when I'm surrounded by trinkets and knickknacks—it looks like a goddamned Mother Goose nursery rhyme threw up in there —but I guess we'll deal with that too."

My lungs burn as I hold my breath, praying I don't explode and make a scene. My lips are pinched tightly shut.

"Oh, don't look at me like that," he bites out. "I'll be waiting for you at your place tonight. So stop with the fucking champagne before you get another *headache*." Chadwick grabs the glass out of my hand and finishes it in one gulp before handing it back to me. "Because I'm getting laid tonight, one way or another, and no fucking headache is going to stop me."

Bile rises in my throat at his words. Is he saying . . . is he seriously thinking that we're having sex tonight? *Whether I want it or not?* My hands ball into fists as my stomach flips.

"Scarlett? Are you—" Kelsey cuts her question short when she sees who is speaking to me—or really, speaking *at* me. "What the hell is he doing here?" she whispers.

"Good to see you brought *the help.* Seriously, Scarlett? What is going on with you?"

"Do we have a problem here?"

A man's voice joins the conversation. It's deep and just loud enough that we can all hear him over the music and the crowd.

"Listen up, buddy." Chadwick spins around to face the man with black hair and deep olive-toned skin, who I automatically assume is Zoe's brother, Q, because they look so much alike. "I'm having a discussion with my fiancée—"

I hold up my left hand again and turn it back and forth, catching Q's attention. "Funny. I must have missed the part where you proposed, *because we are not engaged,* Chadwick. We *broke up* yesterday when you gave me an ultimatum, and I *thought* I communicated exactly how I felt about it. Apparently, I wasn't clear enough."

Chadwick reaches out and grabs me by the arm. "Apparently, *I* wasn't clear enough. You don't have a choice, Scarlett. This is what your father wants, and we both know you're not going to do anything but exactly that."

Like a magnet drawing my attention, my gaze lifts over Chadwick's shoulder and I see *him.* Right there. Standing in the shadows, just beyond Q.

Gabriel Legend.

But his blue eyes aren't on me. They're on Chadwick's hand where it's wrapped around my arm. Legend's nostrils flare, and he stalks forward. The crowd moves aside, clearing a path for him as if he's a dangerous beast, rather than a mortal man.

The deep timbre of his voice vibrates up my spine along with the thumping bass when he speaks.

"Take. Your. Hand. Off. Her." Each word is a sentence of its own, carrying the weight of bloody threats if Chadwick is stupid enough not to heed his warning.

Chadwick whips around, his fingers now digging into my skin as he jerks me along with him. "Who the fuck do you think you are? No one tells me what to do, you—"

Legend takes a final step forward, and the raw power of his presence should make Chadwick wet his khakis. "You're under my roof, and I will bury you here. You have one second to decide your next move. Think fast, kid."

Legend delivers the grave warning casually, which is almost more terrifying than if he were yelling. Except, I'm not scared.

No, I feel *alive*.

I shake my arm, drawing Chadwick's attention, and he sneers at me.

"You'd better fucking tell me that this isn't why you're here. Trolling for dick, so you can get laid. No. What the hell am I thinking. That's impossible." He laughs, and it's the cruelest sound I've ever heard. "Because you're a fucking prude, Scarlett."

He drops my arm like I'm diseased and shakes his head at Legend.

"Good luck with her. You'll need it. Her pussy's so fucking frigid, it'll freeze your dick right off." Chadwick glances back at me as Legend's icy blue gaze ignites. "I'm out of here. You aren't worth a fight. You never were."

Chadwick walks away, giving a wide berth to Legend, and all I can hear is the sound of my own heart pounding in time with the music. The heat of humiliation creeps up my neck, probably turning my skin the same color as my dress, but I can't look away from Legend to check the mirror.

My gaze is held captive by his.

I know he heard every word Chadwick said. About me being a prude. About my pussy being cold enough to freeze a dick off.

Instead of dissolving into tears like I wish I could, I lift my chin higher and smile. "Being officially single for the second time in two days is a reason to celebrate. Who needs another drink?"

CHAPTER TWENTY-NINE

LEGEND

I could kill him. It would be too easy. And right now, I'd be completely justified in wiping that entitled little pretty-boy prick out of existence.

My fingers flex, and my knuckles are ready to fracture his orbital and cheek bones. He wouldn't look so pretty then.

There are only two reasons I don't move as the breeze from his escape rushes past me.

One, Chadwick-the-douchebag is leaving, and hopefully the words he said guarantee he'll never have another shot at the woman he's walking away from. And two, Scarlett wants to celebrate, and I'm not going to ruin her night. Actually, that's probably the only reason that matters.

Nothing else could have stopped me from unleashing hell on that piece of shit.

It only takes me a moment to realize causing a bigger scene would draw the attention of the crowd, so negatively impacting the club should have been on that list of reasons not to kill him too, but it was an afterthought at best. I should tell myself to get my priorities straight and focus on what matters, but with this woman in front of me, rational thoughts go right out the fucking window.

Astra, our top server, sweeps in with another bottle of champagne, and tops off Scarlett's glass. Scarlett's friends crowd around her, all getting their refills too.

Now it's time for me to make an exit.

I couldn't resist the urge to come out here. To see her again. But it's also time for me to walk away and never look back.

I take one step, and Scarlett slips through the crowd to stop right in front of me.

Jesus. She smells fucking incredible. I can't even describe it because I've never experienced anything like it.

I have to get away from her.

"Thank you for taking care of . . . that," she says, a tinge of pink darkening her cheeks. "I apologize for my . . . issues following me into your club. It won't happen again."

She's apologizing to me? Seriously? When I enjoyed scaring that preppy little prick?

She continues smiling up at me with expectation, and I realize I haven't replied.

What the hell kind of spell did this woman cast on me? I try to snap out of it, but I find myself getting sucked deeper into those stormy gray eyes of hers.

A prude? How could that fucker be so blind? There's heat burning so close to the surface that wouldn't take more than a single spark to ignite.

His loss is my gain.

As soon as the thought jumps into my brain, I shake my head and pull myself back to reality.

I can't have her. Remember that.

"You don't need to apologize," I say, then clear my throat because there's a lump in it that wasn't there a minute ago.

"You're not responsible for the actions of everyone who walks through the door."

The music gets louder as the DJ spins with more intensity.

Scarlett presses closer, until there's only an inch between us, and for the first time in years, I'm afraid to move. I'm afraid to fucking breathe.

She's so damn close.

So close she's testing my self-control. Something I thought was ironclad until right now.

She leans in, and I freeze.

"No, really. I'm a professional, and when I make appearances, I don't bring drama with me. It won't happen again. Would you have a drink with us? Join the celebration?" Her lips are slicked with red, and her delicate tongue swipes across the bottom one.

Fucking hell. I can't stand this close to her. It's not fucking safe.

"I—"

"I brought you a glass, Mr. Legend. Just in case," Astra says as she hands me a champagne flute. Up here, for the VIP section, I insisted on crystal and not barware. The bubbles sparkle as they catch the light.

Absentmindedly, I reach for it, but I'm trapped in the gray pools of Scarlett's eyes. Somehow, I find myself clinking my glass against hers as a smile lights up her face and turns those eyes to quicksilver.

What in the actual fuck is happening to me right now?

I don't think shit like this. I don't feel shit like this.

And then she fucking laughs. It sounds like pure, unadulterated happiness, and I realize I'm fucking *screwed.*

Fuck. Me.

I chug the champagne, not tasting a thing as I watch her drink, but my throat is dry. The longer I watch, the bigger her smile gets and the pinker her cheeks turn.

No. She can't . . . this can't . . .

In the middle of my denial, the air shifts behind me, and my self-preservation instincts roar to life. I turn my head, even though the last thing I want to do is look away from the most intoxicating sight of my life.

Q stands just off to my side. "Mr. LaSalle is out of the building. Just thought you'd like to know."

His statement reminds me that I already fucking forgot there was a threat before it was even removed. That's not like me. And from the raised eyebrows on Q's face, he knows there's something off about this situation.

He looks from me to Scarlett. "Is there anything else we can get you, Ms. Priest? Zoe and I are happy to take care of anything you need."

Q is giving me an out. A chance to walk away, go back to my office, and let him deal with her. An out I should take.

I never spend time on the floor of my club. I've always considered it an unnecessary risk. Moses will find me eventually, and I'm not interested in helping him do it before I'm ready. So, why are my feet glued to the floor like they're encased in concrete?

Q can handle this. Her. The whole thing. Zoe too.

Yet, I speak. "I'll take care of Scarlett tonight. I'll handle whatever she needs."

Lines crease Q's forehead, telling me he thinks I've lost my damn mind. And maybe I have. That's the only explanation I have for what happens next.

CHAPTER THIRTY

SCARLETT

I barely recognize myself, and with each glass of champagne, I care less and less. The alcohol's buzz and bubbles go straight to my head—but they can't compete with Gabriel Legend's presence.

Standing this close to him is exhilarating. Like inching nearer and nearer to the edge of the Grand Canyon because the view is incredible, but it would only take a stiff breeze to push me over. Or like walking up on a jaguar in a jungle, only to have it stand and study me before walking away, leaving me with a heart-stopping memory—but also the sense that I've been given the gift of an incredible experience.

Legend isn't a normal man. I've seen what he can do. He's capable of ending a cage match in just seconds with a dominant display of brutality and skill.

And he had a part in kidnapping me.

That little detail alone should have me backing away until I'm at a safe distance, but it doesn't. Because I don't feel a single bit threatened by him. I feel . . . invigorated.

The realization hits harder with the weight of the champagne behind it, but I'm not surprised. Somehow, I knew this would happen.

I've felt drawn to him since the second I felt his presence while still wrapped up in that rug. Then it tugged harder with each video I watched. And yes, more still when I couldn't keep him off my mind and came with his name on my lips.

Then the handwritten note. *Tug.*

And the private message. *Tug.*

If I thought I was only building him up to be larger than life in my fantasies, I was wrong. Because the man I'm standing toe to toe with has his attention completely focused on me in a way that sends a charge through my body like someone plugged me into a wall socket. He *is* larger than life.

And life is messy.

Or at least, the life I *want* is messy.

Even if I only get to have that messy life for a single night, I'm taking it.

Tonight, all bets are off. Tonight, I'm going to *live.*

"What I need, Mr. Legend, is to dance. Will you dance with me?" I hold out my free hand to him, the breath trapped in my lungs at my first daring request.

The question shocks Q, whose eyes have been darting back and forth between me and his boss. "Ms. Priest—"

Q goes silent when Legend's big hand lifts to close around my outstretched fingers. His thumb brushes over my skin, and I feel it. *The spark.*

It zips through my body as chill bumps rise on my arms, across my shoulders, and down my back. It's like touching a live wire and learning you're immune to its deadly power. I don't know who Legend is to everyone else, but to me, he's a beacon, drawing me in.

"It'd be a privilege, Scarlett." He looks to Astra, who is hovering not far behind me. "Whiskey. Three fingers."

A smile stretches my lips. "You need fortification?" I ask to be playful. I haven't flirted in a long, long time.

Legend's lips twitch, but they never fully form a smile. More like a flash of joviality that he doesn't want me to see.

His head tips back and he looks down his handsomely rugged nose at me. "Maybe it's for you."

God, he's sexy, and all the oxygen in my blood feels like it's been swapped out with helium. I'm practically levitating.

"Then make it a double."

He nods at Astra, and she leaves with our shared order.

"Did someone say dancing?" Monroe slides in beside me, and Legend releases his hold on my hand. "Because I am totally here for that."

I suck in a breath, almost thankful for the interruption. Because, *my God*, he's intense. The relief doesn't last long, though, before I already want more of him. More of whatever it was that happened when he touched me.

Harlow shimmies up to my other side. "Hell yeah. Let's shake our asses, ladies!" She grabs Kelsey by the arm, and the three of them make their way toward the stairs leading down to the dance floor.

Astra returns in moments, saving me from standing frozen in the same spot for too long. "Your drinks."

I hand off the empty champagne flute and accept the whiskey. Before I can think about what I'm doing, I tap my glass to his and whisper, "To an unforgettable night. For both of us."

He doesn't reply except for a dip of his chin.

With a smile, I tip back the whiskey, embracing the heat as it slides down my throat. "Seven Sinners. My favorite."

"You know your whiskey," he says after taking a drink.

"I have so much random knowledge, it would blow your mind, Mr. Legend."

"Just Legend. Or Gabe. I'm no mister anything," he says, correcting me before taking another sip.

I roll the glass between my palms and take advantage of how close we are, committing every scar and imperfection on his gorgeous face to memory.

"Scarlett!" We both look to the stairs as Monroe calls my name and waves. "Let's do this!"

I swallow the remainder of my whiskey before handing the glass off to Astra. She takes Legend's as well, and then he holds out his arm.

"After you, Scarlett."

I love how he calls me by my first name. Everywhere I go, I'm treated like I deserve some measure of respect I haven't earned yet. At work, it's Ms. Priest this. On the street or in a store, it's Ms. Priest that. Hearing him call me Scarlett is intimate, as if he doesn't give a damn about my clout or fame. Only my friends call me Scarlett, and I love that he's chosen to do it too.

Can I just be me with him?

I don't get a chance to dive down that mental rabbit hole before I step forward and his hand settles lightly on the small of my back. It burns through the fabric of my red dress, heating me from the outside in, finishing the job of the whiskey.

Whatever happens tonight, I will never forget exactly how I feel right now.

Anticipation fizzes through me as we walk down the stairs, his hand now gripping my arm to steady me. I can't tell you if I'm floating down those stairs, not making contact with a single tread, because my head is so far in the clouds, my feet can't even reach the ground.

And I love it.

Just like it did before, the crowd parts for him, and we follow Monroe, Kelsey, and Harlow to the center of the marble dance floor where waitresses in sharp black crop tops, skirts, and thigh-high boots circle us with trays of shots. Monroe dives right in, dropping bills on one tray before passing out shots to all of us.

Legend shakes his head, but that doesn't stop the four of us girls from tipping back the sweet concoctions and finding the beat.

Harlow and Monroe bust into their signature moves, which are guaranteed to get the attention of every man with a pair of eyes. Kelsey was born with rhythm and gives a shimmy-shake before joining Harlow and Monroe in their swaying and spinning.

That's when I remember that I need a *lot* more alcohol before I'm going to be able to cut loose from the block of ice I've suddenly become. I don't want to look stupid in front of this man.

Oh my God. Chadwick was right. I am a prude. I can't even dance without overthinking it. And here I am, pretending I'm some femme fatale who can possibly tempt a man who is utterly and completely beyond my experience.

Humiliation climbs, along with my rising flush, and there's nothing I can do to stop it. I desperately want to be the kind of woman who has crazy nights at clubs with dangerous men who make them feel like they're finally living for the moment.

But that's not what prudes do. They go home and look at other people's pictures on social media and wish they could live life so fully.

It's on the tip of my tongue to say this was a mistake. I've done my job. I should go.

But I can't get the words out.

Legend moves closer and leans down to speak into my ear. "What's wrong?"

His breath brushes over me, and the scent of male devastation overtakes my senses. Fresh, but spicy and earthy. Like citrus, bergamot, and cedar.

The woman I desperately want to be would be dancing with him. Her hands would be touching his body. The heat of him would bleed into her skin.

"I . . . I just . . ." My tongue sticks to the roof of my mouth, and the words that will get me off this dance floor won't come.

Something knowing and concerned flashes across his blue gaze, but it's gone before I can read it.

His hand curls around my hip. "It's okay, Scarlett. I've got you."

That's when it happens.

CHAPTER THIRTY-ONE

LEGEND

I recognize fear and second thoughts when I see them, but there's no fucking way I'm going to get this close to holding Scarlett Priest in my arms and not do it.

The faster her friends shed their inhibitions, the faster hers come flying back.

But I can make her forget about all the bullshit rattling around in her head that was probably put there by her piece-of-shit ex-boyfriend. *And I will.*

Like it was just yesterday that I did this last instead of well over a decade ago, my body moves to the beat, finding the rhythm. I don't think about how bad of an idea this is anymore either.

I pull her against me, her hips to my thighs, my hands gripping her waist as I help her move. Instead of fighting or bolting from the dance floor, she gives herself over to the music . . . and me.

Wherever I lead, she follows.

Her friends dance around us, one of them close enough behind me that I can feel her movements. But I don't care about anything but Scarlett.

It's like she just needed the right person to wake her up and pry her out of her shell. Even if it is just a break from reality for a few minutes.

But how can I possibly be that person? I shouldn't be. Even more, I shouldn't *want* to be. But all signs point to yes. The most terrifying part? I *want* to be exactly who she needs right now.

As she relaxes, her movements become more fluid, like the music is flowing through her veins.

The girl she called Kelsey shimmies up beside her, and Scarlett matches her for a moment, but she doesn't pull away from me. No, if anything, she comes closer. Her tits press against the top of my abs, and my dick jerks in my pants.

The pulsing warning sign forces me to pull back. I'm not a teenager letting a chick grind up on my dick until I'm ready to come in my slacks.

As I set her hips away from me, Scarlett's smile dims a few watts, and I hate it.

Fuck. I'm not supposed to care this much about her smile or how bright it is. I'm also not supposed to be dancing with her, letting the cameras that are undoubtedly in the hands of other patrons snap photos or videos of us. They'll plaster both our faces all over the internet because of the woman in my arms.

Moses will find me for sure.

My thought from earlier comes back. *Maybe it's time to deal with my ugly past—once and for all. Maybe then I'll actually get my life back.*

The one good thing about Moses popping into my head? It deflates the uncomfortable stiffness in my pants.

Whether I'm tempting fate or just thinking with my dick, I go back for more, gripping her tighter against me. Pride swells in my chest when she catches her breath and smiles. I move us faster, closer, until the music rises to a peak, and the floor clears around us for a beat. I change my grip until I've got my right hand locked around her left and meet her gaze.

"Hold on."

Her eyes go wide, but she nods. Her trust in me is completely unfounded, but I'll take it anyway.

Right at the perfect moment, I use my body to spin her out my right arm and then switch hands in a split second to spin her back down my other arm.

Her friends cheer, squealing as she does a twirl at the end. I pull her close again, her back to my front, and both my arms wrap around her.

I keep her right where she is for a few more breaths before the beat changes and the DJ spins a new track. Raising my head, I catch a flash of movement at the edge of the dance floor.

Q.

It's like the spell has been broken, because based on his posture, it's clear something's up.

As much as I don't want to, I release my hold on Scarlett and turn her around to face me.

"I have to go. Save me a dance."

CHAPTER THIRTY-TWO

SCARLETT

L egend disappears from the dance floor like a ghost fading into the night. As soon as he's gone, I smile, because his scent still clings to me, and the heat I stole from his hard body hasn't cooled yet.

Kelsey, Monroe, and Harlow swarm me.

"Oh my God!" Monroe squeals.

"Did you see that?" Kelsey says, her mouth hanging open. "Because I wouldn't believe that if I hadn't just seen it."

"I got it on video!" Harlow waves her phone in front of my face. "Now we can all watch it over and over. Oh my God. I'm going to swoon. Because seriously, that was *ah-may-zing.*"

Harlow's acrylic-tipped fingers wrap around my wrist as she pulls me off the dance floor. Monroe and Kelsey are right behind us.

"You videoed it? Oh my God, I knew you were secretly a genius hiding your powers," Kelsey says, panting for breath as she swings her attention from Harlow to me. "You just danced your ass off with Gabriel Legend in his club, where he *never* comes out on the floor."

"And he looked like he *never* wanted to let her go," Monroe adds. "He is so totally into you!"

The giddiness of the moment, and my friends' excitement, has me buzzing even harder than I was after the shot we did when we came out on the dance floor. As if my thoughts summoned her, the waitress with a tray of shooters walks by us, and Harlow tosses down some bills.

"We need more to toast this shit!"

I toss back the drink and wave at Harlow. "I want to see it. I want to see it."

"Let's go back upstairs. It'll be easier," she replies.

"Yeah, and someone will have posted it to YouTube by then too," Kelsey says, leading the way to the stairs.

"YouTube?" My voice cracks as I hustle up to the second level with my friends, wishing for another drink before I lose my mind.

Kelsey pauses at the top to sling an arm around my waist. "Don't worry, you looked like a fucking rock star out there. And just remember, any publicity is good publicity."

Monroe signals to Astra, who appears with a fresh bottle.

"Would you ladies like more champagne, or can I get something else for you?"

"We've switched to shots, so let's stick with that." Monroe rattles off three names of drinks I don't recognize, but Astra promises to be right back with them.

"Show me. Please. Before I lose my shit and decide I made a terrible mistake and I should probably never go near him again, which . . . sounds like a really awful option right now."

Monroe's eyes go wide. "Oh shit. You're into this guy. Like, for real."

"Of course she is," Kelsey says, plopping down on the leather couch beside me. "Did you see the way he moved? If she doesn't go for it with him, she's going to break my fucking heart." She takes one hand in mine and squeezes.

"Honey, you're not just doing this for you. Although we know that you really, really need this, you're doing this for all womankind. It will be a tragedy if you don't grab whatever invitation he just threw at you, hold on tight, and enjoy the ride. He's not just a man. He is a *legend*."

Kelsey's grip tightens on mine until I find myself nodding. "Really? You think I should?"

Harlow slides in on my other side and hands me the phone, which is cued up with the video. "No one say a word until we watch this. Then, we discuss."

Monroe slips behind the couch to watch over our shoulders, and I tap the screen to play it.

At first it's dark, then the strobes light us up. I see myself in red, a color that I love but don't wear enough because of its boldness, and I look . . . *vibrant*.

Then there's Legend. His dark blond hair is slicked back against his head, and he's all in black—black shirt, black slacks—and completely devastating. My body moves with his, following his lead and letting him guide me through the rhythm.

It's seamless. Effortless. And then we both pause. I can hear his voice in my head.

"Hold on."

My palms go sweaty as I witness him spin me down one arm and then back the other way. Like something out of a romantic movie where the hero is pulling out all the stops to impress the heroine. But that's not what this is. It's my life. And watching it replay before me is absolutely surreal.

He pulls me back against him, and for a second, there's this expression on his face. For the first time, he appears . . . content.

He glances up and spies something outside the frame of the camera, and then the expression disappears in an instant.

It was so fleeting, that I might never have known what Gabriel Legend looks like when he's happy.

Part of me wishes I never saw that look.

Another part tells me to forget it and move on. Embrace the moment, be grateful for what it was, but don't expect ever to feel that kind of magic again.

But then there's the rest of me—the dreamer who believes all things are possible if you're willing to work for them—and she can't unsee that pleasure on his face. She can't forget what it felt like to be in Gabriel's arms.

"You guys—" I swallow, afraid of what I'm about to say next because it might change the course of the rest of my life.

"What?" Monroe asks. "Is something wrong?"

"No. But I think Kelsey is right."

Kelsey straightens beside me. "Wait. What am I right about?"

I rise with the phone still in my hand and turn to face my three friends. "Whatever happened on the dance floor down there? I want it to happen again. With him."

"What are you saying, Scar?" Monroe asks.

I lose the hesitation and lift my chin as a smile stretches my lips. "I want Gabriel Legend."

CHAPTER THIRTY-THREE

LEGEND

I should be relieved Q pulled me away from the floor, because I shouldn't have been out there in the first place. But I was. And not just with anyone. With *her*.

Jesus. I let my guard down. Let her in. How the fuck could I be so goddamn reckless?

I know my rules. I follow them for a reason. But Scarlett makes it all too easy to throw them out the goddamned window whenever she's around. *And I fucking loved every minute of it, no matter how much I'll beat myself up for it.*

I can still feel her as I follow Q's retreating form into the shadows where he can tell me why the hell he needs me. I can still smell the scent of her on my skin. I can still feel the smooth skin of her palm gripping mine as I pulled out my old standby move.

What was I thinking?

Not about the future or how important it is to get this club back into the black, and that's *all* that should be on my mind when I see Scarlett Priest. But now when I think about her, it's got nothing to do with business and everything to do with the way she smiles when she lets go of her inhibitions and loses herself in the moment.

It was the purest thing I've seen in . . . I can't even remember how long. Which means I have absolutely no business going near her. She's so far beyond my reach that I shouldn't even dare to speak to her.

Tell that to my dick.

After all, her ass was just pressing against it, making me wish I could show her that her asshole of an ex was so fucking wrong.

She's not a prude. She just picked the wrong fucking guy.

And you're the right one? Another taunt from my conscience that I know the answer to.

No, I'm not the right guy. There probably isn't a man on this planet who actually deserves a woman like her.

"What the fuck was that, man?" Q asks as I slip behind him into the silent corridor that leads to my office.

I ignore it and respond with my own question. "Did you pull me off the floor just to ask me that?"

Q knows the answer better be fucking *no*, because I don't need him to try to save me from myself. He knows that's a lost cause.

"Just got word that the boyfriend came back. He's causing trouble out front."

I tug down the cuffs of my shirt and straighten the skull cuff links holding them together. "Is that right?" I keep my voice even, but inside, anticipation for the coming confrontation rises.

I wanted a shot at that prick, and I'm about to get it.

Q shrugs. "I figured you'd want to handle it yourself."

"You were right." I give him a nod, and we head for the club's entrance.

When we step outside, I notice two things. First, there's a chill in the air that I didn't expect for late August. Second, *we have a fucking line.* The velvet ropes that have stood empty for weeks are finally full of people dying to get inside.

Fuck. Yes.

A punch of relief fires through me because this is *exactly* what we need. People waiting outside for their chance to experience Legend. And it's all happening because of Scarlett, the knockout who dumped the douchebag raging at one of our bouncers, Peter.

"My girlfriend is in there and we have unfinished business. Do you even know who I am?"

Peter stands like a gargoyle, massive and unmoving, as he stares down the nutless asshole who is trying to shame him into not doing his job.

"I'll take it from here, Peter."

As soon as LaSalle sees me, his face contorts with rage. "You motherfucker. You're trying to steal my girl?"

Q and Peter stand behind me, blocking the people in line from seeing what's happening.

Stepping closer, I reach out like I'm going to clap him on the shoulder, but instead, my hand lands just beside his collarbone. My thumb rests right at the side of his neck, and my fingers wrap around the base of his throat. All it takes is a minuscule amount of pressure before his eyes widen with fear at the pain he feels.

"Listen up, Chadwick. I'll only say this once." I keep my voice low and my tone civil. "You don't have a girl in my club. You have an ex who doesn't want to see you. Doesn't want to hear from you. Doesn't want to know that you exist anymore. Understand me?"

"You can't—" He tries to speak, but I cut him off by pressing my thumb harder against his throat.

"I *can*. I'll do whatever the fuck I damn well please. I'm not afraid of you, your money, or your privilege. You see, kid, when a woman says you're over, you leave her the fuck alone. Do you understand that?"

He jerks, trying to get away, but I'm not about to let him go yet. His shoulders hunch forward with defeat.

"Leave Scarlett Priest alone, or I swear, you'll regret it."

I release my grip and Chadwick stumbles back a few steps, his hand clutching the base of his throat where he's going to have a hell of a sore spot for days.

But, unfortunately, Chadwick isn't as smart as I thought. His face twists into a sneer as he continues backing away.

"You think she's some hot piece of ass you're going to score with? Not even close. And trust me, she and I aren't done. She'll do whatever it takes to make her dad happy, and I'm his fucking favorite. So go ahead and fuck her. You'll be sending her back to me with a fucking bow on her head, because you won't be able to get rid of her fast enough. I'll only make her pay for fucking a piece of trash like you for the first few years we're married. Hope it's worth it. Because then, I'm going to take everything else that matters from you. This club? Gone. Your friends?" He looks at Q. "Prison. And then maybe you'll learn your lesson about not touching what doesn't belong to you."

He spins around, almost losing his balance, and stalks off down the street, still holding his neck.

Q steps up beside me. "I don't like that fucker, and I'm sure as hell not going to prison."

I glance back at the line, relieved that everyone seems focused on our doorman opening the rope to let another group in. Given the crowd and their rising voices, I think it's safe to assume they didn't hear what Captain Dickwad had to say.

"Keep an eye on him," I tell Q.

"He's all talk, boss," Peter adds as LaSalle turns the corner and disappears into the night. "Rich fucks like him make threats, but they never carry through."

"I guess we'll find out. And if he makes a move, we deal with it then."

"I don't like it," Q says, snapping his lapels straight. "He should walk the fuck away. He just got dumped, publicly, and apparently twice. So, why does he keep coming back after he's burned that bridge? It doesn't make sense. There's gotta be something else going on here."

"He mentioned her dad. Do some digging and see what you can find out. Just so we know what we're dealing with," I say to Q and then turn to Peter, shaking his hand. "Thanks, man. You did the right thing. You see him again, call me or Q."

"Yes, sir. Of course."

Q and I march through the doors of the club, and by tacit agreement, we head for my office. As soon as the door is closed, he leans against it with his arms crossed over his chest.

"Please tell me you'll stay away from her." When I don't answer immediately, he pushes off the door and stalks toward me. "You can't have her, Gabriel. We both know it."

"Don't tell me what to do, *Marcus*."

My best friend stops before me, and we lock eyes. "For as long as I've known you, you've never looked at a woman like you look at her. And then I fucking saw you dancing with her. *I didn't even know you could dance, Gabe.* What the fuck is going on? You won't take a single woman on a date for fifteen years, and now you're out there making moves on the dance floor, trying to impress some socialite with more money than God? *This isn't you.*"

I don't need Q telling me any of this. I know what I did. How it would look. I just don't care. *And she's still out there.*

"Please tell me this is temporary fucking insanity, Gabe."

I round my desk and drop into the chair. "There's something about her."

"*No*. For fuck's sake. Don't say that. I thought you understood who she was. I hate to agree with that piece of shit out on the sidewalk about anything, but she's not just out of your league, man. She exists on another fucking social stratosphere. I bet she has Beyoncé's personal number. That's her crowd. The rich and famous."

He pauses to take a breath and then keeps going, like I don't understand the point he's trying to make.

"I give you mad respect for what you've done. You showed up in Jersey with nothing. You busted your ass and took a beating to make money. Then you started giving the beatings for even bigger money. Now you're trying to make good on a promise to Jorie. I know you're still trying to be the guy she knew you could be so you can have the life Jorie wanted. Like I said, I respect the fuck out of you for that, Gabe. But don't think for one second that means there's a chance in hell you belong with a woman like Scarlett Priest. We're talking about two different fucking worlds here, man."

As soon as he says Jorie's name, I've had enough. I shoot to my feet and plant my knuckles on my desk hard enough to damn near leave dents in the wood.

"You're my best friend, and other than Bump, the closest thing I've got to a brother. That is the only reason I'm not coming at you right now for the shit you said. You know me, but you are *not* me. I don't take orders from anyone, Q, and I'm not about to start."

My best friend spins, smoothing his hands over his jet-black hair. "Fuck me, you're already in too deep."

My jaw slides from side to side in the same way it would before a fight. "I'm not in *shit*, brother. I'm assessing the situation. And that was the one and only time you'll throw Jorie in my face. You got that?"

"What about Jorie?" Bump comes in the door with Roux on a leash at his side. "I miss her. She made the best peanut butter cookies. I miss those too. Can we get peanut butter cookies on the way home?"

Roux tugs the leash from Bump's grip and comes toward me as Q replies, "Sure, bud. One of us will stop at the corner store and get some cookies on the way home."

I shove my chair back and squat down to give Roux ear scratches and a few good butt pats as the image of a woman who looks only the tiniest bit like Bump forms in my mind. She's not as vivid as she used to be. It's more like an old photograph fading with every passing day. I can't see her smile anymore, only the vague outline of her features.

Jorie Billips, the prettiest girl in Biloxi, Mississippi. The woman who taught me what it was to have a dream and go after it. The woman who died because of who she was to me, and Bump took a bullet for it too.

Regret and guilt fill me in equal measure, threatening to swallow me up like they did when I wasn't sure if I could get Bump and me out of Biloxi alive.

Then something happens. Light fills me, and a new image forms. This one isn't a brunette, but a blonde. She's smiling and laughing as I spin her along my arm and then bring her in close to my body.

Scarlett Priest.

Fuck.

Q's right. I am in too deep, and now I have to figure out what the fuck to do about it.

One thing is for sure—Chadwick LaSalle won't get another shot at her.

Not a fucking chance.

CHAPTER THIRTY-FOUR

SCARLETT

"Okay, so here's the deal," Harlow says, slipping her phone back into her clutch. "We're going to drink and dance and party our asses off, and then we're going to make a plan to get Scar what she wants—when we're sober."

"We can't wait that long," Monroe says with a shake of her head. "We have to strike while the iron is hot. But I agree on the drinking and dancing and partying our asses off." She points at me. "If he sees you having fun like the gorgeous, amazing girl you are, then he won't be able to stay away. That's step one."

I look from one to the other, and even feeling as tipsy as I am, I recognize that Harlow and Monroe are the voices of authority in this situation. Together, they've got a total of around twenty or so years of marriage under their belts, and a hell of a lot more dating experience than I have.

However, I shouldn't make decisions like this while I'm tipsy, so I just nod. "Let's have fun. Do what we came here to do, and make sure this club is off the chain by the time we leave."

Kelsey laughs. "Girl, mission fucking accomplished. Do you see what's happening out there?"

She waves an arm over the balcony, and I edge closer to see the dance floor. Unlike when we arrived, it's not just a crowd of thirty or forty people. It's *packed.* Like wall to wall, body to body, and the line at the bar is insane.

A sense of pride grows as I watch for a solid minute before I turn around.

"We did it." I look from Monroe to Kelsey to Harlow. "We actually brought this club back to life . . . in just one night."

Kelsey's perfectly sculpted brows pinch together. "Why do you sound surprised? Did you doubt for a second you could pull this off? You're Scarlett Priest, honey."

The way she says my name makes me sound like I'm not a normal woman with two arms, two legs, ten fingers, ten toes, and one asshole ex-boyfriend who showed up trying to start shit. She says my name like the brand that is Scarlett Priest, not *me.* There is a difference and Kelsey knows it, but other people don't.

Does Gabriel Legend know there's a difference? I can't help but wonder. There's no answer from the mouthy part of my brain, who has gone strangely silent since we left the dance floor. Maybe the champagne and shots have clouded my thinking.

"Ms. Priest, you didn't just bring the club back to life, you brought a *man* back to life."

We all turn and see Zoe standing just behind us.

"What do you mean?"

Her lips press together, and she looks from side to side before joining our circle. "I shouldn't have said that. Forgive me. Can I get Astra to bring you another round? Or are you ready to call it a night? I can have our car service see you all home, if so."

"Hold up," Monroe says, scooting closer to Zoe. "We need

you to elaborate on the *'brought a man back to life'* piece that you shouldn't have said."

"I can't. I'm sorry. I misspoke. I don't want to lose my job."

I'm ready to apologize to her for prying, but shockingly, Kelsey leans in. "You're not going to lose your job. You're like family, aren't you? I know it when I see it, so don't try to bullshit me."

"Kelsey, it's okay. She doesn't have to spill. It's fine. I shouldn't even be thinking about him . . ." I trail off, and Zoe's attention rivets me.

"You're into Legend? For real?"

Oh God. My entire body tenses as her questions put me in the spotlight. I just declared to my friends that I want Gabriel, but to someone as close to him as family?

"You saw them, right? On the dance floor?" Monroe asks Zoe.

The dark-haired woman nods. "I'm pretty sure everyone saw them."

Monroe keeps pushing. "And Legend doesn't usually come out on the floor, we hear."

"That's right." Zoe shifts her gaze to me. "But he's . . . he's taken a personal interest in Ms. Priest."

The words *personal interest* have never filled me with this much hope before.

"Well, I've also taken a personal interest in him," I say, and it comes out sounding demurer than my bold declaration from before.

Zoe looks around to ensure none of the other employees are within earshot, and then surveys me. "Do you have any idea what type of man you're dealing with? Because Legend is one of a kind."

"Tell us everything, Zoe. My girl needs your help." This comes from Harlow, and I could hug her right now.

Zoe glances up toward the ceiling, and my gaze follows

her. Is it a camera? It has to be. Is he watching us? Watching me?

"I can't say much. Truly, I can't. But I will tell you that he's acting differently about you than he has any other woman in a very long time. Actually, for as long as I've known him. I don't want you to get the wrong idea, though, because I don't know what's going on. But he's breaking some of his rules when it comes to you."

"We'll take that." Monroe answers for me, slipping one of her business cards from her wallet. "Thank you, Zoe. If you ever want to chat or have lunch, here's my number. And if you like baseball, I can hook you up with the most badass seats imaginable. My husband never uses all the tickets we get."

Zoe stares down at the card, hesitation clear from her slow movements, but she accepts it from Monroe anyway. "Thank you, Mrs. Grafton. I've seen your husband play before. He's impressive."

"As long as he stays in New York and doesn't get traded, he's definitely impressive."

"Monroe." Harlow barks our friend's name to get her off the *if he gets traded, I'm getting divorced* subject.

"Okay, okay. Back to partying," Monroe says as Astra approaches with her tray of drinks, then points at Zoe. "And if you see your boss watching our girl, give him a nudge. She'd love to dance with him again."

My face burns with embarrassment, but I accept another shot and hope this one contains the liquid courage I need for the rest of the night.

I nearly lose hope that I'll see Gabriel again before we leave the club. It's almost two, and the DJ is still going strong, although Kelsey is starting to droop. Other than me, she's the only one who has been up since the crack of dawn, busting ass. Harlow and Monroe are still shaking their shit on the dance floor, but I grab Kelsey's hand.

"Kels, we can go," I say with a yawn. "I'm tired too."

Harlow sees me cover my mouth with my hand and snags Monroe by the wrist. "I think we're good. You good?"

She's asking if I'm ready to give up on seeing Legend again, but part of me hopes he won't let me walk out of this building without approaching me one last time. Or maybe that's the countless shots I've had talking. Either way, I'm ready to crash.

We form a chain of linked arms and make our way out of the crush on the dance floor. When we reach the lobby, Q is there.

"Ladies, can we get our car service for you?"

"I don't want to go home yet," Monroe says with a whine. "Nate's out of town and the penthouse will be so empty."

"You can come home with me, babe. Jimmy won't care," Harlow offers, covering her own yawn.

That's when I feel him behind me. I've never been so hyperaware of another person in my life. As soon as he's in my proximity, my body buzzes from head to toe.

If this is what living feels like, what have I been doing every day before this?

As if guided by invisible hands, I turn around to face him.

His black shirt hugs his broad shoulders and muscular arms before ending with a glint of silver at the cuffs. I drag my gaze back up to his face and find his blue eyes fixed on me.

"You should get a hotel. Q can get you a suite down the street. Safer. Easier. Quicker."

"Why?" I ask, taking another step toward him. It's as if I'm sucked into his magnetic pull, and I couldn't stay away from him if I tried.

"*It's just safer,*" he repeats.

I get caught on the sharp planes and angles of his face as the word repeats in my head. *Safer.* I study his scar, his lush lips that I wish I could taste, and the five o'clock shadow that's even darker than it was a couple of hours ago.

"Are you worried about us?"

For such a large man, he moves with easy grace as he closes the distance between us. "I'd be a fool not to."

Like the rest of the world has disappeared, I hear nothing of the thumping bass or the chatter of clubgoers around me. Even my friends are invisible. All I see is him.

"You're not a fool, Mr. Legend."

"Just Legend. And you're wrong, Scarlett."

I hold my breath, searching for the courage to take another step closer as his Adam's apple bobs in his throat.

He's just as unsettled by me as I am by him. I don't know why the realization comforts me, but it does. Probably because it makes him seem more human. And if he's sometimes a fool . . . well, that means he's fallible.

"When?"

His brow creases with confusion. "When what?"

"When were you a fool?"

He inhales, making his nostrils flare, and lifts a hand between us, almost as if he wants to touch me. But he doesn't. His fingers hold there, frozen. "Earlier tonight."

"When you danced with me? That wasn't foolish." I'm proud of the steadiness in my voice and nerves.

"Knowing what you feel like in my arms will haunt me for the rest of my life."

My breath catches, and I stare at him in wonderment. "You make it sound like I'll never be there again," I whisper.

The lines of his face harden. "You deserve better than that

douchebag who was in here tonight. Stay at the hotel. Have someone get your key back from him. Don't go home until you're sure it's safe." His orders are final, but he still hasn't answered my question.

God bless alcohol, because without it, I would never be bold enough to say what is on my mind.

"You want me as much as I want you, Gabriel. Now, what are you going to do about that?"

CHAPTER THIRTY-FIVE

LEGEND

T rouble.

That's exactly what she is.

I stare at her face, her cheeks pink from the dance floor or the booze, with the question hanging between us.

She thinks I want her as much as she wants me.

Fuck.

She's dead wrong about that. Because there's no way in hell the woman in front of me knows fuck-all about the depraved things I want to do to her. The feeling of her pressed against my body hasn't faded enough yet for me to forget how much I wanted to drag her off the dance floor, find a dark corner, pin her to the fucking wall, and take everything she doesn't realize she's offering.

She's the epitome of a good girl. The high-class society princess who doesn't associate with men who've even thought about the things I've done to survive. We couldn't be from two more different worlds, and as much as I want to take her and drag her into mine . . . I can't.

Scarlett deserves better. Someone whose hands aren't

scarred from fighting night after night to bank every dollar possible. Someone who isn't more comfortable in the darkness and shadows than in the light of day.

With all that on my mind, I force myself to step back. It almost kills me to watch her expression, because every single thing she feels shows on her beautiful face.

And this is really going to fucking suck, because no matter how much I want things to be different, they're still exactly as they should be.

She's untouchable, and I know better.

"Nothing, Scarlett. I'm going to do nothing. Have a good night. Thank you for coming to Legend tonight." I turn away because I can't watch the disappointment crush her. If I see it, it'll break my resolve.

As I stride in the other direction, I tell myself she dodged a bullet. Tomorrow, the thrill Scarlett got from walking on the wild side will be gone, and she'll be relieved it didn't go any further. I'm doing the only thing keeping us both from making a giant mistake.

Walking away without looking back.

SCARLETT

"*N*othing, Scarlett. I'm going to do nothing.*"

The words echo in my head with all the finality of a guilty verdict. Stabbing pain jabs me in the chest as he turns and walks away.

"Oh shit," Harlow whispers, and I'm reminded that Legend and I were not, in fact, all alone on the planet. "That stings."

I give her my best fake smile. "I'm starving. Anyone else feel like grabbing some food?"

All three of my friends wear as much sympathy on their faces as makeup, like they just witnessed something utterly humiliating.

Oh, wait. They did.

Kelsey recovers first. "Fuck yes, I want to eat. Dolly's is around the corner. They've got the *best* biscuits and gravy, and since I only eat that shit once a year, I think I'm due." She glances at Harlow and Monroe with an expression that can only be described as militant. "You girls in?"

I know firsthand that Monroe doesn't eat anything that's not organic, so there's no way she's going to eat at a greasy spoon that would be more at home in Nashville, since Dolly's Diner is named for the legendary country star.

"Count us in." Harlow answers for them both before facing Q. "We don't need a hotel. Thanks for the offer, but we can take care of ourselves. Make sure to tell your boss he's an idiot."

"Harlow!" Her name squeaks out of my mouth.

Q's smile borders on apologetic, and his dark brown eyes meet mine. "Thank you for coming, Ms. Priest. We truly appreciate everything you've done tonight."

I hear what he's said, but my mind is still on Gabriel.

Nothing.

I can't get the word out of my brain. Even though humiliation burns my cheeks, I straighten my shoulders and hold out my hand.

"It was our pleasure, Mr. Quinterro. Please let Mr. Legend know I'll be back to fulfill my side of our agreement. Good evening."

Q shakes my proffered hand and pitches his voice low so that only I can hear it. "It's better for both of you if you don't get any ideas about Legend, Ms. Priest."

"It's none of your concern, Mr. Quinterro," I reply in my haughtiest tone.

A smile ghosts over his lips. "Maybe I'm wrong. Maybe you'd be good for him. But God knows, he'll never let you get close enough to try."

He makes the statements like he's talking to himself, and not aloud. Some of my humiliation fades away as he studies my face.

"We'll see you next week, Ms. Priest. Take care."

"He looked like he was going to fuck you right on the

dance floor." Monroe, who doesn't know how to whisper, speaks loud enough to make two tables of diners spin around and stare at us. "Like pick you up and put you on his dick and bang you right there for God and everyone to see."

Harlow tosses a sugar packet at her face. "Shhh. You're making her get all red again."

I fan my face to calm the rising color as Kelsey pops a french fry into her mouth.

"No offense, but you were impressively red. I almost went after you with the powder to calm your face down," she says.

Giving up, I drop my face into my hands as my cheeks burn with embarrassment. My buzz is finally starting to fade, and I can't believe what happened tonight.

"Let's watch the video again!" Monroe grabs Harlow's phone off the table and taps in the pass code she has apparently memorized. "Because, seriously, I think I could get myself off just watching the sexual tension between you two."

I open my mouth to tell her no, but I want to see it again too. Before, it was dark and loud in the club, and Harlow's hand wasn't exactly steady as she held out her phone.

Harlow snatches her phone from Monroe's hand, comes around the table, squats down between me and Kelsey, and cues up the video. As soon as it begins, I'm transported back into that moment, into his arms.

"His body was *hard*. I didn't know a man could be hard like that."

"Oh, honey, that's called an erection. It's what happens when a guy wants to fuck you." Monroe giggles with her witty reply.

"That's not what I mean. Like his arms and his chest and his stomach. Oh my God, do you think he still has abs? I saw them on the videos of him." As soon as my little admission is out, my lips snap shut as all the women at the table stare at me.

"What do you mean, you saw them on the videos of him?" Harlow asks as she leans toward me.

"On YouTube. He . . . he was a fighter."

Kelsey is nodding. "I watched them too. But I swear it was just to do research for you. I didn't feel remotely turned on by the sight of him rolling around on the mat with another man. Actually, that's a lie. I watched two fights and then had to go to Tumblr to find some hot man-on-man action to take care of business."

As Legend spins me on the screen, I want to do the same thing. Well, *almost.* I don't need any hot man-on-man action to get me there, but I could seriously excuse myself right now to go *take care of business.*

Has that ever happened to me before?

Dumb question. Nope. Never. Ever. Not like this.

Stop, Scarlett. You heard the man. He wants nothing *to do with you.*

The reminder kills the rest of my buzz as Harlow drops her phone onto the others piled in the center of the table.

But remember what Q said? my brain argues. *"Maybe you'd be good for him. But God knows, he'd never let you get close enough to try."* Before I can dissect that statement further, Kelsey's head jerks to the side.

"Oh my God, don't look now, but isn't that Meryl Fosse? Holy shit. What is she doing here?" Harlow says, and I thank God she can actually whisper at a safe volume.

Of course, we all look.

"It's like spotting the elusive cheetah at the watering hole," Kelsey murmurs without moving her lips.

I'm holding my breath, hoping Monroe doesn't say anything, but she shockingly doesn't and reaches for her phone.

"You should say something to her, Scar. Isn't this the perfect chance to show her how wrong she was about you?"

I still remember the sting of Meryl Fosse's rejection when I invited her to come to Curated. *"The best lives aren't Curated, Ms. Priest. They're lived. What you're selling is too perfect. Too . . . fake."*

Fake. God, the word still has the ability to make me want to break out in hives.

I'm not fake. My life isn't fake. It's real, I swear it. And it's definitely not perfect, even if I can't post fun pictures of my rambunctious family using the hashtag #LifeIsMessy.

Meryl Fosse, a third-generation Fosse who still has all the money from her forebears, runs a charity for at-risk youth. Her husband and children often accompany her to events, and I have to admit I've spent way more time looking at pictures of her social media accounts than I should. She's one woman who seems like she has it all. So, of course, because we move in similar circles, I reached out to her to see if she'd like to come to Curated.

That's when she burned me with her low opinion of what I do.

"I hope you find meaning in your life, Scarlett. Because otherwise, what's the point?"

I want to write her off as a bitch, but I can't. Something about the self-possessed way she moves and her absolute certainty about what matters in her life is mesmerizing. That, and the fact that no one else has ever been bold enough to say something like that to my face. Except, she wasn't mean about it. Just . . . dismissive. And it freaking eats at me.

"I can't talk to her. Not right now." I glance down at the red dress I have on, which coincidentally matches the dress on the cowgirl-shaped salt shaker on the table, who is paired with a cowboy in jeans, boots, and a pearl-snap shirt on the pepper.

I fucking love those salt and pepper shakers. I wonder if they'd sell them to me, or maybe they have a gift shop? Dolly of the salt is clearly Dolly from the big neon sign out front.

"Hi, Meryl, fancy seeing you here," Monroe says, waving the woman and her husband over to our table.

Mortification blows through me like a blast furnace. *Why, Monroe? Why?*

Meryl and her husband, Johan, come toward us, and her lips tilt in a bemused smile. "Now, isn't this an unexpected coincidence."

Harlow takes one look at her. "Let me guess. Charity dinner and dancing. Dinner sucked and was barely edible, but you had a few too many glasses of wine and decided to live it up like you did before you had kids."

Johan laughs and claps his hands. "You must be psychic."

"Nope, Meryl still has her name tag on."

Meryl looks down at the magnetic badge attached to her dress. "Dammit. I always forget to take them off." She moves to undo it, but her husband beats her to it.

"That was my job. I shook too many hands trying to get us out of there instead. Sorry, baby."

My heart melts at his endearment. They've been married almost fifteen years, and I think it's adorable he still calls her *baby.*

I want that. I want a partner like Johan, who will shake hands to get us out of a charity event so we can go eat breakfast at three a.m. at a greasy-spoon diner and relive the old days.

Meryl glances down at me. "I'm surprised to see you here, Scarlett. This doesn't seem like it fits your image."

It isn't a taunt, but it feels like it could be.

"I'm looking for meaning." I don't know where the words come from, but as soon as they're out, Meryl's face softens.

"Good for you."

"Our table is ready, honey," Johan says before leading her away.

Meryl smiles at me before turning to follow him.

"What was that about?" Monroe asks. "Looking for meaning? You should've said looking for some dick."

"Nothing," I say, returning my attention to the plate in front of me. I only get one bite in before someone pulls up a chair and plops into it beside me.

My jaw drops. "Flynn?"

My former stepsister is wearing tight black pants, black leather boots, a tight black tank top, and black leather gloves with big star-shaped cutouts on the back of them, which is a far cry from the designer jeans and cute blouse she had on at the psychologist's office.

"Whoa, girl. What the hell are you wearing?" Harlow's gaze is locked on Flynn's gloves. "Are you a stripper at a kinky club? Because if you are, I need to hear all about this."

Flynn tosses her leather jacket on the back of the empty chair and reaches out to grab the tip of each finger to pull her gloves off. "I'm not a stripper. If I were, I'd still be at work."

"Coyote Ugly?" Monroe asks as she steals a french fry off Kelsey's plate. "I could see you getting up and singing on a bar while you do body shots."

I stare at Flynn, concern welling inside me for what kind of trouble the twenty-year-old who is technically no longer my little sister could be getting into.

"I was working."

"You have a job?"

She yanks her head back like I suggested something stupid. "No. I'm taking twenty-four credits as soon as the semester starts. I won't have time for a job."

"Then what the hell, Flynn?" A million scenarios burst to

life in my head. "If you're—" I cut myself off because I don't even want to voice the possibilities in my head.

"I'm not stripping or hooking or dancing on bars. I'm racing."

All four of us blink at her. "What?" Our voices overlap, and other patrons turn to look at us again.

I drop my voice to a whisper. "Racing? I don't understand."

She reaches into her bra to pull out two folded pieces of paper and drops them on the table between the plates.

I snatch one, and Monroe grabs the other. I unfold the paper and stare at it. It's a title to a car.

"What the hell?" I skim down to the make and model, a 1993 Toyota Supra.

"Why do you have a title for a 2014 Camaro?" Monroe asks, sounding just as confused as me as she looks up from the other piece of paper.

Flynn plucks the titles out of each of our hands and tucks them back in her bra. "The guys thought they could take me. They don't take girl drivers seriously enough. But it's cool; being underestimated makes it even sweeter when I crush them. Me and my baby were on fire tonight."

"You race cars. For money. Or rather, for other cars?"

"It's called racing for pinks. How do you think I pay for college? I can't touch my trust fund until I turn twenty-five unless I beg my mom, which I refuse to do. I also didn't want to go into debt. It's not like NYU is cheap."

"Wait a minute." Kelsey chimes in, a french fry dangling from her fingers. "You race for pink slips and sell the cars to finance your tuition so you don't have to take out student loans that you could easily pay back when you're twenty-five and can access your trust fund without your mom?"

"Exactly. Besides, I'm really good at it. And it's fun as hell. You've never had an adrenaline rush like this before."

I turn to Kelsey. "Am I still drunk?"

"Possibly, but this is real, and your sister is an illegal street racer."

Flynn steals the fry from Kelsey and pops it in her mouth. "A damn good illegal street racer who doesn't have to worry about tuition until spring semester, and then I'm graduating a whole year early with a double major. So don't judge me. I've got my shit covered."

The door chimes, and Harlow's attention shoots to the entrance. "So those cops that just walked in aren't looking for you?"

Flynn slides down in her chair as she reaches for the empty coffee mug and pretends to sip. "Probably not. There weren't any cops called. At least, none came up on the police scanner."

I stare at Flynn like I've never seen her before. "I literally saw you yesterday, and you didn't think it was important to mention any of this?"

She shoots me a smile. "I would've at coffee. Now, pretend like I've been out with you all night if they start asking questions." She reaches out to tap my chin, signaling me to close my open mouth as she blows me a kiss. "You're the best, Scar."

LEGEND

The club is still rocking when I walk out the door with Roux and Bump on my heels. I have to get the fuck out of here, and if I could have left them behind for Q to deal with, I would have. But I always handle my responsibilities, and Bump and Roux are exactly that. *Mine.*

Unlike Scarlett Priest.

She is not and never will be.

"That lady was pretty. Like, really pretty."

I whip my head sideways to stare at Bump. "Which lady?"

"The one with the girl I brought for you. She had pretty brown hair. It looked soft. I want to touch it, Gabe. Can I touch it?"

Fucking hell. Now Bump is fixated on one of Scarlett's friends, which is the last fucking thing I need to worry about, because it means that *she* is back in my head.

We walk out to my Bronco, which is parked in an alley spot behind the club. I scan the area quickly, making sure no one has fucked with it or is waiting around to jump us, and unlock it. Bump opens the back door for Roux, and she hops up inside.

Once we're rolling out of the city, Bump is still jabbering about something, but I'm not listening to a word he says.

I can't stop thinking about Scarlett. What she felt like. What she said. How fucking badly I wanted to take her up on the invitation she made.

No. I made my decision, and that's it. There's not a fucking chance in hell that I'm going to go down that road. Nothing good could possibly come of it.

My phone buzzes in the cupholder, and Bump reaches for it as I brake at the light.

"Give it to me." I hold out my hand, and Bump's eyes widen.

"Whoa. Holy shit."

I grab it from him and stare down at the screen.

UNKNOWN NUMBER: *You were hard as a rock. Don't tell me you don't want me, because I know the truth. The real question is—are you man enough to do something about it?*

Someone honks, and I jerk my head up to see that the light has turned green.

What the fuck? How did she get my number?

I shove the phone in my pocket and punch the gas, jerking Bump and Roux back against their seats.

"Sorry about that."

"Who was that?" Bump whispers like he's in church.

"Shut up, Bump. Whatever you think you just read? You didn't."

Thankfully, he goes silent in the passenger seat for a

while. It's not until we're pulling up to the garage that he finally speaks again.

"I like her. I think Jorie would like her too." When I stare at him in the dim light, he keeps going. "She could've been real mad at me before, but she still came to help. All the other people came too. We're not going to go back to Biloxi now, right? Because I like it here. I don't want to go back. Biloxi is bad."

Every word out of Bump's mouth hits me like a sucker punch.

"Why do you think we'd go back to Biloxi?"

He shrugs, reaching into the back seat to pet Roux. "If you lose all the money, we won't have anywhere to go. But they say you can always go home. I don't want to go home, though, Gabe. I would miss Zoe and Q and—"

Bump will keep going until he lists the name of every person in Q's family, so I hold up a finger to silence him.

"Listen, kid. We're not going back to Biloxi. No matter what. I promise."

Bump's face lights up. "Good! Because that's why I brought her to help us. I'm so glad it worked. All the people were so happy tonight. I just wish you were happy too. That'd be cool."

From the mouths of innocents . . .

Fucking hell.

"I'm happy, Bump." The lie comes out sounding hollow, and Bump doesn't need to be a genius to recognize that.

"No, you're not, Gabe. But you will be. Jorie won't be happy until you are."

Fuck. Me. His words aren't like punches anymore. Now they're slashes to my soul.

Partly because he has no way of knowing how much the guilt weighs on me, because he can't comprehend concepts that complex anymore. Not since Moses Buford Gaspard's crew shot him in the head, thinking he was me because he was wearing the hat he jokingly stole off me days earlier. Right before one of Moses's guys put a bullet in Jorie and tossed them both into the floodwater, never suspecting that Bump wasn't dead—or that he wasn't me.

Bump managed to make it back to solid ground, but Jorie was already long past saving. Her younger brother was barely clinging to life when he made it home.

I'll never forget the terror I felt when I realized nothing would ever be the same. We survived Katrina, riding it out in our apartment, and then I left to find us food and water because we weren't prepared.

I never should have left them. Bump and Jorie should have stayed put. I still don't know why they left our apartment in the first place. Bump has never been able to tell me why either.

I should have known that Moses wouldn't let the opportunity to settle the score without consequences pass him by. Because in the aftermath of the storm, there were no rules. It was the Wild fucking West, and he exacted his vengeance on innocents.

Guilt threatens to crush me, and I have to jerk myself out of the memory before it destroys me. "It's late, Bump. I'll walk Roux. You head on up to bed."

"Okay, Gabe. Tomorrow is our day, though. Don't forget."

"I won't forget," I tell him. "Good night."

As soon as he climbs out of the truck and heads inside, I drop my head on the steering wheel.

"I'm so fucking sorry, Jorie. You deserved better. You both did. And I'll get you justice. I'll make it right. I promise." I whisper the words to the darkness, and then I shove it all back down inside where it can't slice me open again until next time.

"Come on, Roux. Let's go, baby girl."

I hop out of the truck, open her door, and almost forget

my phone. When I reach back inside to get it, the text is still on the screen, taunting me.

You were hard as a rock. Don't tell me you don't want me because I know the truth. The real question is—are you man enough to do something about it?

I should delete it. Fire whoever gave her my number. Tell her not to come back to the club.

But I don't. I carry the phone with me while Roux does her business, and then I read it again once I'm upstairs and the door is locked behind me.

She's not for you, I remind myself. *She couldn't handle what you'd want from her. Her life is perfect. She doesn't know shit about filthy, dirty sex that leaves you both sweating and panting for breath.*

The vision of her rising above me, riding my cock with her head thrown back and my name on her lips, is too strong to stop.

Fuck, but she'd look beautiful when she comes. I imagine gripping her around the waist, helping her ride me faster and harder before I pull her off to flip her over and fuck her from behind.

"Hands on the headboard. Don't move them."

The sliver of fear on her face is doused with anticipation, and my cock hardens to the point of pain.

Fuck.

I can't jack off to this. Not to her. Then I'll be well and truly fucked.

Too fucking bad. Because I can't not do it. It's either that, or reply to her text and get myself into more trouble.

I head for the bathroom in my one-bedroom apartment

over the service station, tearing off my clothes one piece at a time. By the time the shower spray beats down on my head, washing away her scent, I already have my cock in one hand. I brace the other on the wall as I stroke myself hard and fast, the same way I want to fuck her a second or third time.

I shouldn't be doing it, but I promise myself it'll be only this one time. Then I'll leave her the fuck alone. I won't go near her again. I sure as fuck won't touch her. This is all I need to scratch the itch.

But when I explode, cum splattering the tile wall, I know I'm a fucking liar.

I have to see her again.

I finish my shower, and before I've even dried off, my phone is in my hand.

I don't know why I do it. There's absolutely no rational explanation, but my thumbs are moving and I hit SEND before I can change my mind.

I stare down at the screen and the text I just sent.

If you think you can handle what I want from you, I'll see you on Saturday night.

SCARLETT

K elsey and I crash at my place together, and it isn't until Kelsey is leaving in the morning that we realize we weren't the only people who were here last night.

"Oh my God. Chad had a key to Curated?" Kelsey's voice sounds hushed as she stares at the single key on top of the scrawled note on a piece of my stationery on my kitchen counter.

Hope your fuck boy is worth it.

Chills skitter over my skin, like invisible spiders I can't shake.

"Oh my God. He was here," I whisper in shock. "I forgot he had a key to the side door. We have to check the security feed. Make sure he didn't do anything else."

Kelsey nods so fast that I think her chin might connect with her chest.

I rush to get my laptop from my bedroom, access the security footage in the cloud, and scroll through last night. It's after two when I see Chadwick's face on the screen, unlocking the door that leads directly to the stairwell to my apartment, but it doesn't allow access to Curated without walking through my apartment. I lose him as soon as he heads for the stairs.

From beside me, Kelsey watches as I flip to the next camera feed. All the doors in the stairwell that lead into Curated use a different key, so it's no surprise that he walks past those and unlocks the back door to my apartment.

"I can't believe he was here," she says, rubbing her hands up and down her arms. "God, that's so fucking creepy."

Once he disappears into the apartment, I have nothing. *Because I don't have cameras in my apartment.* I didn't want to lose my privacy.

"So creepy, especially because I don't know what he did in here. At all." I look at her, and I can only imagine the combination of fear and disgust that must be plastered on my face.

"Shit. Shit. Shit." Kelsey spins around and scans the room. "Would you know if he'd taken something?"

A ripple of revulsion unleashes a full-body tremor that nearly makes my teeth chatter.

"I don't know. I mean, I think so? Maybe?" My movements shaky, I drift into the bedroom, looking at the bed I just made and the jewelry on top of my dresser. My nightstands' lampshades are still perfectly level.

"Why would he come here to leave me a shitty note and his key? Why not just mail it?"

Kelsey appears behind me. "Because he wanted this. To freak you out. To make you feel unsettled in your own home.

Because that's the kind of thing a douchebag does. Ugh, I fucking hate that asshole even more now than I did before."

He knew exactly what he was doing when he violated my sanctuary. That motherfucker.

"He probably expects you to call him and ask why," Kelsey says as she turns to grab my hand. "But you can't. No communication. Just let it go. Don't give him the energy and attention he wants. He'll just try to suck you back in."

I think of the nasty things he said last night, and she's right. It still blows my mind that Chadwick really expected me to fall in line with his ridiculous ultimatum and for us to get married over Christmas. Another shudder courses through my body.

"I'm done with him. I will never let him be part of my life, ever again." It's a vow leaving my lips, one that calms the concern on Kelsey's face.

"Good. Because you don't need him. Trust me. He's been riding your coattails for so long that you got used to the weight. He needed you to secure his position at your dad's company. That's why he's been so fucking persistent."

I know she means well, but Kelsey's words are another blow. Because I didn't realize that was literally the only reason why Chadwick stayed with me. I thought, just maybe, it had something to do with *me.* But, no, it was all about what I could do for him and his status. I think of all the business dinners I attended and all the hands I shook and small talk I made. His cachet grew when he had me on his arm, and that's all he cared about.

Never. Again.

Never again will I be with a man because he wants what I can do for him more than he wants me.

Of course, my mind goes instantly to Legend and the text that was on my phone when I woke up this morning.

. . .

Unknown Number: *If you think you can handle what I want from you, I'll see you on Saturday night.*

I have a feeling that whatever he wants from me, it doesn't have a damn thing to do with my name, my status, my money, or my family.

I still haven't told Kelsey about the text, because I'm not sure what she'll say. And if there's a single chance she's going to try to talk me out of going next Saturday night so I don't get involved with him, I'm not ready to hear it.

Plus, it's still so new and exciting, I want to keep it to myself for a little bit longer. I haven't even unlocked my phone yet, because I keep glancing down at the text on the screen every few minutes to assure myself that it's real.

Then, there's the little thrill I get every time I think about the fact that somehow, Legend got my number and texted me.

Which brings up the memory of what he said before I left. *"Knowing what you feel like in my arms will haunt me for the rest of my life."*

"You okay, Scar? You want to call the cops and report the Chadwick incident? Just because Chad had a key doesn't mean he had any right to use it to get in. Maybe they can shake him down and freak him out enough that he'll leave you alone."

Kelsey's concern yanks me back to the present and away from thoughts of Legend, which I much prefer over thinking about Chadwick.

I wander to the counter and my Nespresso machine to make some coffee to help clear my racing thoughts. As soon as the shot of espresso is brewing, I shake my head and reply.

"I don't think it's worth bothering the cops with. Chadwick will just say he was returning his key, and there will be literally nothing they can do about it. I can't even really argue trespassing because *I gave him the key.*"

"True. But, still." Kelsey spins around in a slow circle. "I hate the thought that he touched even one thing in your apartment. What if he was a total creeper and stole your underwear or something?"

My gag reflex kicks in as I run to the bedroom and pull open the drawers of my lingerie chest.

Everything looks perfectly in place, including the lavender bustier I bought the other day when I saw it in a shop window. Not that Chadwick ever saw any of that lingerie on me. I think I knew, deep down, that he wasn't worth the effort. He was just an easy way to get closer to my dad.

Shit. My dad.

I shut the drawers and walk back out to the kitchen-living room area where Kelsey has taken over manning the coffeemaker. She hands me a demitasse cup before stirring sugar into hers.

"What am I going to do about my dad? How am I going to tell him? Do you think Chadwick already has?"

The possibility of losing the frayed thread of connection we have totally sucks.

"Oh, honey," Kelsey says as she slides her saucer onto the table and pulls out a chair. "I'm so sorry your dad is wrapped up in the Chadwick stuff too. I know that's why you wanted it to work. But, eventually, you're just going to have to find your own common ground with him."

I take a sip of the rich, steaming brew. "I wish it was that easy."

"Me too, babe. Me too."

Together, we sit in silence for a few minutes, and I suck

down the caffeine needed to shock my system back to normal. It's been years since I've stayed out that late, drinking and dancing and generally having an amazing night.

I danced with Legend.

My mind goes right back to the text. If I open it, I have to decide how to reply. Or if I'm going to reply. Except, who am I kidding? I'm going to reply. I can't resist. His pull is too strong.

I'm barely able to hold out thirty seconds after I hug Kelsey and she leaves my apartment. I wrap a plush robe over my pajamas and drop into a teal velvet armchair before I unearth the phone from my pocket.

On the screen, I read the message again before typing in my pass code and unlocking my phone. I tap on the text bubble and . . .

What in the actual fuck?

This wasn't just an impromptu text from him.

There's one from me to him first.

You were hard as a rock. Don't tell me you don't want me, because I know the truth. The real question is—are you man enough to do something about it?

What. The. Hell.

I didn't type that. Never in a million years would I have sent that message to the man. *But someone did—using my phone.*

The time stamp says 3:04 a.m., which means that . . . we had to be at Dolly's Diner. Which means one of my friends did it. Our phones were in a pile on the table. Easy access.

There's no way in hell it was Kelsey. She'd never . . .

Which leaves Monroe or Harlow.

Goddammit.

No longer am I thinking about how I'm going to reply. Now I'm thinking about who I need to kill—*or thank?*

Jesus. What a mess.

CHAPTER THIRTY-NINE

LEGEND

I know she hasn't replied, because like a tool, I checked my phone first thing in the morning. Nothing.

She probably passed out and hasn't woken up. It doesn't mean anything. Also, why the fuck am I thinking about this?

I roll out of bed and make my way to the bathroom to take a piss and brush my teeth. It's Sunday and preseason games are on today, which means Q's entire extended family will be having a barbecue at his folks' big white house on the other side of the scrap yard, and Bump will want to hang out there all evening.

That leaves me the morning to check out the numbers from last night and see how much room it bought us. I can't count on her coming next Saturday, so I'll have to watch the numbers closely all week and see if the Scarlett Priest effect sticks around to bring people in, or whether it was a one-shot deal. My gut says people are going to keep coming, but my gut didn't foresee a shooting on opening night.

"Gabe! You up? I made pancakes."

Bump's voice comes through the door, along with the wafting smell of burning pancakes.

I grab a pair of sweats and yank them on before I run to the door. Bump is standing there with a plate of blackened breakfast, but I rush past him to his apartment. In the kitchen, a pan is on the stove, smoke billowing from it. I grab it off the burner, flip on the fan in the stove hood, and move to the fire escape to set the skillet outside.

"Hey! That's my breakfast! What are you doing?" Bump follows me outside, his face red.

"Bump, dude. You gotta watch stuff when you're cooking. Remember what we talked about after the grease fire? You don't want us to have to find a new place to live, do you?"

Bump's face screws up into a sad expression. "I don't wanna move again. I like it here. I didn't mean to."

"It's okay, buddy. Shit happens. What do you say I take you out for breakfast instead? Just you and me?"

Instantly, his expression softens into a smile. "Really?"

I know in that moment that I haven't spent enough time with the kid lately, and it cuts deep. "Yeah, really. Get dressed. We'll take care of the pan later."

He claps his hands together like I just told him we're going to a strip club. "Okay, Gabe! Give me two minutes. I'll be ready. Don't go without me."

"I'll meet you in the truck. Take your time."

With Bump's excited humming following me out of the apartment, I head back to grab a shirt, a different pair of pants . . . and my phone.

Still no text.

Maybe it was the alcohol talking last night.

Maybe Scarlett doesn't want a damn thing to do with a guy like me in the light of day.

CHAPTER FORTY

SCARLETT

After waking up Harlow and Jimmy with my phone call, I learn that she wasn't responsible for the text to Legend.

Which means it was Monroe. Instead of calling, I hoof it over to the Upper East Side and pay her a personal visit.

"Why are you here so early? You were out last night too. Don't you ever sleep?" Monroe asks with a yawn.

"Are you going to invite me in or not?" I ask her from the airy lobby outside the penthouse door.

Monroe rolls her eyes and steps back, letting one of the double doors swing open. "Fine. But I'm making a bloody mary, and I don't want to hear about how it's not good to start the morning with vodka. It's Sunday, and I don't give a fuck."

As soon as the door closes behind me, I follow her across the travertine foyer and into the massive kitchen that Monroe mostly uses to mix drinks.

"Why did you do it?" I cross my arms over my chest and wait for her to turn around and face me.

She glances over her shoulder as she pulls a bottle of vodka from the freezer. "Do what?"

"Text Legend from my phone! And how the hell did you get his number?"

Instead of looking sheepish, a cat-got-the-canary smile spreads over her face. "Did he reply?"

"Oh my God, Monroe! What the hell were you thinking? And why didn't you tell me? I thought he was coming after *me*, but then I open the text to see he was only replying to some dirty message you sent him! What am I supposed to do now?"

"Untwist your panties from the bunch they're in and thank me."

"You don't even feel bad about it, do you?" I ask her, my voice rising with my temper. "Why would you? You never feel bad about anything you do. This isn't a game, Monroe. This is my life."

She sets the organic bloody mary mix on the counter so hard that the bottle lands with a *crack* against the granite. "And you're the one who decided you had to bring his club back to life and wouldn't tell any of us why. Don't you think that makes *you* the one going after him from the beginning?"

It's on the tip of my tongue to tell her about the kidnapping and what happened next, but I can't. Because right now, I don't trust Monroe any farther than I could throw her, and considering she's all of five foot ten, that's not very far.

"You had no right to do that."

Monroe rolls her eyes at me. "Get off your fucking high horse, Scarlett. I did you a favor. You should be thanking me, not bitching at me first thing on a Sunday morning before I've even had a drink."

My head feels like it might explode, so I suck in a few deep breaths that help calm me down a degree or two.

Monroe's inability to see that what she did was *wrong* shouldn't surprise me.

"Here, have a drink." She shoves a shot of vodka across the counter to me as I glare at her.

"I don't drink at ten a.m."

"Whatever." She adds a dash of Tabasco, followed by a few sprinkles of celery salt and a grind of pepper. Monroe pops a leafy stalk of celery into her concoction to stir it before taking a swig. "God, that's good. Almost worth being woken up at the ass crack of dawn by an ungrateful friend."

Those couple degrees of calm I felt? They evaporate.

"Why would you do that? What the hell am I supposed to do now?"

"Fuck the man so you finally know what it's like to have decent sex? Then maybe you'll get the memo that you're supposed to thank me later?"

I drop onto the white sculpture-like stool on the other side of her expansive kitchen island and bury my face in my hands. "I can't believe this."

"That you're finally single and interested in a guy who can show you what it's like to be with a real man?"

"Stop. Just stop," I mumble into my cupped hands, but Monroe doesn't listen.

"I know you think you have to plan every minute of your fucking life, Scarlett. I get it. You're perfect, and the rest of us are just a hot mess."

I jerk my head up to face her. "I don't think that at all. I'm not perfect."

Monroe responds with another eye roll and a big drink.

"Plus, I've been single for less than a day, and Chadwick broke into my apartment last night to return his key and left a shitty note on my counter, so it's not like—"

The glass smacks against the countertop. "That motherfucker did what?" Monroe snaps out the question.

"He left his key. Last night."

"Did you call the cops? Report him? That's fucking stalk-ing, Scarlett."

Monroe's instant protectiveness calms my earlier annoy-ance at her more than I thought possible.

"He had a key. There's nothing they'd be able to do."

"Maybe not, but you'd have an official record of it. What if he tries to do something else? You need that record if there's a chance you may need a restraining order. Remember when I broke up with Steve? He went batshit crazy and jacked off on my bed using my underwear."

"Oh God, Monroe. I'm so sorry. I totally forgot . . ." I trail off, wondering if I'm the one being the shitty friend here.

"It's fine," she replies with a flip of her hair. "It's not like any man would be okay with losing me. Yet more than one has had to deal with that sad reality."

Even though she plays it off like it's nothing, her earlier concern makes me realize that it wasn't *no big deal* like she told all of us when it happened.

"So, should I call the cops? I kept the note. I have the security footage of him using the key."

Monroe slides a hand into the pocket of her robe to retrieve her phone. "I'll text you the number of a detective. He's discreet. He'll document it quietly, so it doesn't end up in the press."

My phone buzzes in my pocket as soon as she finishes speaking, and when I unlock it, it opens to the screen with the text from Legend.

"He did text back," I say to Monroe, almost like a peace offering. "But I don't know what to say to him now. I don't know how to do this. I—"

With more speed that I thought she was capable of in the morning, Monroe reaches across the island and nabs the phone from my hand.

"Oh. My. God," she whispers before breaking into a dance in front of the massive stainless-steel fridge. "This is *amazing*! I knew he wanted you. The way he held you when you danced . . . and the way he made sure to talk to you before we left. He's hooked. Now all you have to do is reel him in, babe."

"I don't know how, Monroe. This isn't me. This isn't what I do."

She tilts her head to the side and scoops up the bloody mary. After taking a sip, she replaces it on the counter with a smile. "Then I guess it's time for that to change."

Her fingers fly across the keyboard, and I watch in horror as she grins.

"Done. Now all you have to do is wait."

CHAPTER FORTY-ONE

LEGEND

I'm paying for breakfast when the text comes. Bump is staring at the blond cashier as she counts out change, so he doesn't notice when I glance down at my phone.

SCARLETT: You're going to have to be more specific. Because I don't want to wait until Saturday night to find out what you want from me.

My dick jerks in my pants. *Fuck.* I shove my phone back in my pocket and take my change, ignore the inviting smile of the cashier, and hustle Bump out of the diner.

"She was pretty," Bump says as soon as we're outside. "I wish I could see her titties."

Fucking kid. He has no filter, and normally it's funny, but right now, all I can think about is Scarlett's tits, which I have no business thinking about at all.

She's sober now and she's still texting you. That's the part that sends a charge straight through me.

Whatever happened last night could easily have been written off as an alcohol-fueled mistake, but this morning . . . not so much.

Still, I have to wonder. "How the hell did she get my number?"

Bump looks over at me from the other side of the truck. "How did who get your number?"

"Scarlett Priest," I say, unable to come up with a reason I shouldn't tell him the truth.

"I gave it to her friend. The one with pretty brown hair. I want to see her titties too. They were *big.*" Bump holds out two hands in front of his chest as he demonstrates just how big.

Given his physical description—brown hair, big boobs—he has to be talking about Monroe Grafton, the wife of a starting pitcher, who was at the club with Scarlett last night.

Well, hell.

"When did you do that, bud?"

"Last night. She was walking back to the stairs. I wanted to see her up close. I told her I was your little brother so she'd talk to me."

I can only imagine how well that went over.

When I don't reply, Bump's face droops. "Did I do something wrong? Shouldn't I have told her that?"

"It's okay. Don't worry about it. Nothing bad happened."

His smile comes back instantly. "Okay. I hope the pretty lady calls you. I like her. I should probably tell her I'm sorry I knocked her on the head and wrapped her up in that rug, huh?"

I unlock the truck. "Get in. Let's get home so you're ready to watch football this afternoon at the Quinterros' with Big Mike."

His face lights up at Q's dad's name, and all thoughts of

Scarlett fly out of his head, which is exactly as it should be. I'm thinking about her enough for both of us.

What do I want from you, Scarlett? Where do I even begin?

———

I wait until I'm home and Bump is back in his apartment, getting ready for football, before I decide how to reply. I don't want to scare her off before I get a chance to see her again.

Wait. I don't?

No. I fucking don't. I'm more attached to the idea of seeing Scarlett again than I should be, and I don't care how bad of an idea that is anymore. I warned her. She didn't listen.

Maybe I should walk away, but I don't see that happening. How in the hell could I?

LEGEND: *When's the last time you let go and just had fun?*

Her response comes a few minutes later.

SCARLETT: *Last night.*
LEGEND: *What about before that?*
SCARLETT: *To be honest, I can't remember. What about you? When's the last time you just let go and had fun?*

I didn't expect her to turn the question around on me. I drop onto the couch and think back to last night. What happened on the dance floor was totally out of character. I shouldn't have left my office at all, let alone gone to her and danced.

But in that moment, there was nothing I could have done to stay away, not even my sense of self-preservation, which is pretty fucking strong.

I answer her honestly.

LEGEND: *Last night for me too.*
SCARLETT: *We have something in common then. Imagine that. ;)*

I stare down at the phone screen and read her words over and over. The statement should be false. We shouldn't have a single thing in common . . . except we do, and I can't remember the last time I felt this kind of anticipation building in me.

I want to see her again. Dance with her. Watch her let go of her inhibitions and laugh and smile and . . .

I'm totally fucked.

Completely. Totally. Fucked.

Even though I know I should block her number and never see her again, I tap out a reply.

LEGEND: *Just wait. I can do even better than that.*

CHAPTER FORTY-TWO

SCARLETT

Holy. Shit.

I'm flirting with the most dangerously attractive man I've ever seen in my life.

I roll onto my back and stare up at the ceiling. The grin on my face is so wide that it hurts my cheeks. And the butterflies in my stomach have upgraded to flop-eared rabbits running roughshod at a trampoline park.

They're just texts, and not even sexy ones at that, but they feel like more. They feel . . . bigger, somehow. Like we're actually finding common ground, me and this man who I can't stop dreaming about, or—if I'm being totally honest—fantasizing about.

Men like him aren't interested in women like me. He lives hard and fast, and I'm more comfortable at sedate afternoon tea parties.

Except, what if I could be whatever I wanted? What if I could have whatever I wanted?

It's not something I've ever considered before. Despite being raised in luxury and having ample resources available, I've lived most of my life in a box. A luxury box, but a box all the same. Opening Curated pushed the edges a little, but not much. It still fell into the category of "acceptable professions and activities" for Scarlett Priest.

Just like Chadwick fell into the category of "acceptable boyfriend material" for Scarlett Priest.

Screw the boxes and categories. I'm totally over it. I don't care what anyone else thinks. I'm following my gut, and wherever she takes me, I'm sure it will be unforgettable.

Bad Scarlett is behind the wheel now.

I carry my newfound resolve with me all the way through Monday to self-defense class.

"Better. Now practice striking with the pen. It may not look like much, but you can kill someone with something as basic as an ink pen." Bodhi, my instructor who still intimidates the hell out of me, went over everything I learned last Friday and then moved on to new material.

I swing my arm down toward the big pad on the floor, pen firmly gripped in my hand as I practice stabbing someone in the eyeball. It's kind of gross, but when I remember how helpless I felt wrapped up in that rug, I realize that if it ever happened again, it's unlikely the outcome would be as positive.

Especially since the troll is relentless right now too, but this time under a new account. I had to block him or her this morning after they commented on the photo of Kelsey, Harlow, Monroe, and me, taken before we hit the club. The comment read, *"Whores need to be taught a lesson."*

I screenshotted everything, then deleted and blocked the profile, but I still haven't forgotten about it. In fact, I was considering trying to reschedule self-defense until I saw it. Now, regardless of whether or not I like this instructor's clipped, to-the-point method of teaching, I'm committed. No one will get the best of me simply because I'm not prepared.

"That's all for today," Bodhi says twenty minutes later when he drops the pad I was kicking at. He's a freak of nature. A giant who moves so fast that he seems to defy physics.

"Thank you, Mr. Black. I appreciate your time."

"Bodhi or Black. I told you, no mister."

I give him an awkward smile at being corrected and escape to the locker where my bag is stowed. As soon as I unlock it, I grab my phone, and no, I'm not ashamed to admit it.

Texting with Gabriel Legend is the most exciting part of my day. I thought maybe I wouldn't hear from him again for a couple of days, or even until Saturday, but I was wrong.

This morning, while I was writing in my gratitude journal, my phone buzzed with a text. I forced myself to finish writing, regardless of how quivery my belly was at the possibility of what it might say. It was short and simple.

LEGEND: Have a great day.

I felt those words down to the marrow of my bones because *he was thinking about me.*

My reply was just as simple, but I hoped it conveyed everything I was feeling.

SCARLETT: Thank you. I hope yours is fantastic too.

I was proud of myself for not checking my phone during my

meeting with Amy or while I was working, but my restraint for today has run its course. I'm done trying to pretend I don't care if he's texted me. I flip my phone over as fast as I can to check the screen for a new message.

And there is one.

It just isn't from Legend.

DAD: Very disappointing to hear how you treated Chadwick. He's a good man and would make an excellent husband.

I blink twice as I reread the message.

Hurt gouges me, and instantly, I throw on some armor to protect my old wounds.

Really, Dad? You're disappointed to hear how I treated Chadwick? What about how he treated me?

I must have made a noise, because Bodhi calls out from across the gym.

"Something wrong?"

I bite down on my lip, hard, as I fend off the burning sensation behind my eyes. *I'm not going to cry about this. Especially not in front of a stranger.*

I shake my head instead, not trusting my voice, but Bodhi's features turn stony.

"Something's wrong."

"Nothing. It's fine."

He stows the pads in a storage closet and walks toward the lockers. "You sure?"

"It's nothing. I need to go." I shove my phone into my purse and hold it tight to my body.

Bodhi stands between me and the door. "I don't like being lied to, but I really fucking hate men who make women cry. You need someone taught a lesson, I know a guy."

His gruff, slightly terrifying offer is completely unexpected, but I'm not equipped to respond. All I can manage is
another nod and a whispered, "Thank you."

"If you change your mind, you know where to find me,"
he says to my back as I rush out of the room and try to pull it
together before I let my dad's comment crush me.

I form reply after reply in my head. *Why can't you just be a
normal, supportive dad? Why do you like my ex-boyfriend better
than me? Why isn't a daughter enough for you?* But, as always, I
don't ask any of the questions that run through my brain.

No, I go with something else entirely instead.

SCARLETT: *Then you marry him, Dad.*

I can barely see through the unshed tears blurring my vision
as I do something I shouldn't. I tap on Legend's name and
write a message.

SCARLETT: *Are you busy? I need to let go and have fun now. I can't
wait for Saturday. I don't even care what we do.*

CHAPTER FORTY-THREE

LEGEND

y phone buzzes as Roux and I are walking up to the door of the gym near the club. I've been crunching numbers all day, seeing how bad the damage is, even after the best night we've had since opening.

It's still bad, but instead of facing a hopeless uphill battle, we've got a small victory behind us. If the weeknight crowds hold up and we have another strong weekend, we'll be able to make the investor payment. Until then, we're watching every single penny, and I won't be sleeping much at night.

A shot of adrenaline punches through my system when I see her name on the screen. I took a risk this morning, sending that text, but it felt right. Her response felt even better.

But now . . . something's off, and I don't like it.

The only thing I want to do is see her in person to make sure she's okay. Because if that asshole of a fucking ex-boyfriend of hers came back . . . well, I'm not making any promises. I warned him. I won't warn him again.

That's second to my concern about her, though.

· · ·

LEGEND: Where are you?

She replies instantly with a location that's only a few blocks away.

LEGEND: Meet me at Bang's Gym. We'll figure it out from there, okay?

I include the address of Bang's and smile when she replies.

SCARLETT: Be there in ten. Thank you.

When I walk inside, with Roux trotting after me, I drop my gym bag and scan the fighters who are training. I recognize a few of them, but no one I really know. Bohannon's probably out making movies, and thankfully, Rolo is nowhere to be seen.

I fuck with my phone for a few minutes and check the door every time the bells hanging from the door jingle.

Until I see her.

The Bang's boxing-glove logo slides sideways as she pushes open the glass door. She's dressed like she just came from the gym herself. Normally, if a woman asked me to meet up, I'd expect it was part of a plan to get some dick, and she'd usually be all made up.

But not Scarlett. Her blond hair is up in a ponytail, there's sweat dotting her forehead, and even though her leggings and tank are cute as fuck, she's in no way dressed for seduction.

It's refreshing. Like she actually wanted to see me just to hang out and have fun.

I've got no problem with that at all.

"Hey," I say to her as she walks inside. Her face lights up when she sees me, and *holy shit,* I like it.

"Hey," she replies, a smile curving her lips as she comes toward the corner where Roux and I are parked.

Fuck, maybe we shouldn't be doing this in public, because I don't know if I can keep my fucking hands off her.

Roux takes care of that for me, though, as she jumps up from where she'd settled by my feet and trots toward Scarlett, nosing around her feet and legs.

Instead of freaking out that a giant, strange dog is sniffing her, Scarlett holds out a hand and waits for Roux to lick it before looking to me.

"May I pet her?"

I nod. "Yeah. She'll like that."

Scarlett drops to one knee and scratches under Roux's throat, which my dog eats up like she's never been shown affection before. From the way her tail is thumping against the rubber gym flooring, you'd think she'd cause an earthquake.

"What a pretty girl. Her name is Roux, right?"

Considering it's my less-than-creative social media handle, it's no surprise Scarlett remembers.

"Yeah, and she's an attention whore when it comes to new targets, so don't be surprised if she decides she's your new best friend."

Scarlett rises and gives her a few more scratches behind the ears before she closes the distance between us. "I don't think I'd mind. She's sweet."

The dog in question headbutts my leg as if reminding me that I also know how to pet her. She wedges between us and I give her a pat, but my attention is on the woman in front of me.

"What's going on? Your text . . ." I pause, watching as she bites down on her lower lip. "It seemed like there might be something wrong."

Her teeth sink deeper into the flesh for a beat before she closes her eyes. "Do you ever feel like you just need to break out of your box and live?" When her gray gaze collides with mine again, there's something in it that I can't interpret. Something did happen, and I don't know what.

"You feeling a little hemmed in today?"

Her nod is instant. "My dad . . . he and I don't have a great relationship. He's . . . traditional, I guess."

"He's giving you shit about something?" I ask, not understanding what her dad has to do with her wanting to break out of her box and live.

"Yeah. Chadwick."

"Ahh . . . the asshat from the club." I shake my head. "Your dad doesn't get how he really is, does he? No father would want that for his daughter. Not the shit I saw and heard."

Red blooms on her cheeks, and I'm kicking myself for embarrassing her.

"Hey, forget I said that."

She shakes her head. "No. You're right. No father should want that for his daughter, but my dad isn't exactly all about what's best for me. He's more worried about having someone to groom to take over his company, someone to go golfing and hunting with—and spoiler, that someone isn't me. Not just because I have more work than I can handle already with my own company, but because I'm not a good ol' boy, and that's the only kind of person my father relates to. Not his wife—who divorced him when she caught him banging his secretary, how cliché—and definitely not his daughter."

"Ouch. Fuck. That sucks."

She shrugs it off like she's used to being disappointed by

her old man. "It is what it is. I just keep hoping that someday, he'll look at me and say, 'Scarlett, I'm proud of you. You've done a hell of a job. Don't be a stranger at Christmas. It's not a holiday without family.'"

Roux nudges her hand, and Scarlett doesn't miss a beat petting my baby girl.

"So you need to get your mind off shit, and you came to me?" I'm not sure why I put it that way, but I need confirmation for a reason I can't explain. Like she didn't tap the wrong contact and send a message to me by accident.

Her gray eyes get big. "Yeah, you. You were the first person on my mind."

I'm not used to bold honesty when it comes to women in my life. Most of them are lying to me and themselves too often to even know what the truth is.

But Scarlett . . . she's different, and it doesn't have a damn thing to do with privilege or money. It's just *her*.

"I don't mind."

The corners of her mouth tug upward, and I catch a flash of dimples. *Fucking hell*, when's the last time I met a woman with dimples?

"Oh. Well, good. Also, my friends call me Scar. Or you know, since I've learned like six ways to kill someone in my last two self-defense classes, you could give me a fighter name. Like *Black Widow* or something badass. I'd be cool with that too."

I must make her nervous, because she's talking fast and bouncing from subject to subject. I grasp onto the important part, though. "Self-defense classes?"

"Yeah, I started last Friday. My financial advisor pulled rank and told me I shouldn't take any more chances after the crazy trolls we have commenting on my social media. But I probably wouldn't have agreed if I hadn't been *accidentally* kidnapped recently."

Guilt rushes in, and I dip my head. "You'll never know how sorry I am that happened. Bump is . . . well, he's special. He was trying to help, and you got caught up in something that shouldn't have touched you."

Her hand darts out and slides into mine with a squeeze. I lift my gaze to hers and drown in those clear gray eyes.

"I appreciate the apology, but I think we can let it go. Besides, if he hadn't done it, I would never have met you, Gabriel. And that would be a big problem, at least from my perspective."

I was right before. *I'm so totally fucked.*

CHAPTER FORTY-FOUR

SCARLETT

"*My* friends call me Legend. Or Gabe. No one calls me Gabriel."

"Well, I'll let you call me Black Widow if I can call you Gabriel."

He squeezes my hand before reaching up with his free one. He stops short of my face, and I desperately wish he wouldn't.

"You're more ladybug than black widow, sweetheart."

"Ladybug." I pretend to think about the name, but I'm mostly hyperventilating that his fingers are inches from my skin. "Not quite as badass, but I suppose it could work."

"Now, who do we have here?"

A man's voice comes from the doorway, and Gabriel pulls his hand from mine. The other hovering near my face drops to his side as his expression turns to stone.

"Rolo. Running into you twice in a week doesn't feel like a coincidence."

The man, tall with short black hair and tanned skin lined from what looks like years of hard living, wears a depart-ment-store-quality suit rather than gym clothes, which instantly trips my curiosity. That, and the fact that Gabriel doesn't seem happy to see him.

"I stopped by the club. Bump told me where I could find you. I got a proposition for you."

"Not the time or place. I'm busy, Rolo."

The man tilts his head to the side and studies me. "You're not even going to introduce me to this pretty lady? Come on, Legend. That's just rude."

Gabriel's lips press together into a hard line. "Rolo, Scarlett Priest. Scarlett, my old fight promoter, Rolo."

"Pleasure's all mine," Rolo says as he takes my hand and shakes it. "I've heard of you. You were all over the papers Sunday after you spent the night living it up at Gabe's club. Something about you bringing it back to life?"

"My friends and I were out having fun. It just makes sense that we'd go to the hottest place in town."

Rolo huffs out a laugh. "Yeah, I'm sure that was it. I'm sure it didn't have anything to do with you trying to be the lucky girl who finally catches this guy. Did you know that he hasn't had a girlfriend in over a decade? Not in the entire time I've known him. I hope you know what you're doing, getting mixed up with this guy, Ms. Priest."

I decide then and there that I don't like Rolo. He might be an old friend of Gabriel's, but there's nothing friendly about this exchange. It's brittle, rife with sharp edges and undercurrents I don't understand.

"That's enough, Rolo."

The older man swings his attention back to Gabriel like he's forgotten I exist. "You still need money? I'm willing to bet big you do. And Bodhi Black is a solid payday—if he doesn't kill you."

The name catches my attention, especially considering where I just came from, and what feels like all the blood drains out of my face as my attention snaps to Gabriel. "You're going to fight Bodhi Black?"

His brow furrows. "You know who he is?"

"He's my self-defense instructor," I say with horror underlying my tone. "He taught me how to kill people."

Rolo's booming laugh fills the gym, and several fighters stop punching to look at him.

"Fuck, that's great. She won't know who to cheer for. Let me know when you make up your mind, Gabe. Offer won't stand forever. So check your pride at the door and let me make us both some money."

CHAPTER FORTY-FIVE

LEGEND

R olo walks away, and all I can think is *fucking hell.*

Beside me, Roux's fur stands on end, something she's never done around Rolo. I give her a pat, trying to calm her down. She must be picking up on my irritation with the man.

I turn to Scarlett. "You're taking self-defense with Bodhi Black?"

She points at her workout clothes. "I just came from there. And what did he mean about the money? And *if he doesn't kill you?* Because that sounds really, really bad, Gabriel."

Hearing her call me by a name no one has really ever used feels foreign to me, but I like the sound of it. I just hate that I'm hearing it while we're talking about her spending time with the guy who would love nothing more than to leave me broken and bleeding in the cage.

"Black and I have history. He wants a rematch. I don't. That's all there is to it."

"And Rolo wants you to take the fight so you can make money to shore up the club's finances."

"I forget you're a CEO."

"Yeah, and you've already enlisted my help in getting customers back into the club. If you think I'm going to drop the ball on that so you have to take a fight that could end up with you *dead*, then you don't know me very well. I don't quit. Not when it matters, and certainly not when people are counting on me."

I snap out of the pall Rolo dropped over us. "Come on, ladybug. Let's get out of here."

"Where are we going?"

"I don't know yet, but first comes the fun. Then we can talk business."

"You drive this. In the city." Scarlett says it for the third time as we finally get out of Manhattan and closer to our destination.

I'm still in shock at the level of trust she places in me. I decided on a place and told her we'd need to walk back to the club so I could drop Roux off and get my Bronco and drive us there, and she's along for the ride with no questions asked. Except for her shock over my truck.

"Don't get me wrong, it's a giant pain in the ass, but I'm from the South, and that means I love jacked-up 4x4s. That's not something that will ever change."

She shakes her head like it's the most mind-boggling thing she's ever heard. Just wait until we get where we're heading. I'll bet it's something she's never done before.

Actually . . . there's one question I should have asked first, but I didn't.

"Do you know how to drive?"

Scarlett's head whips toward me. "Of course I know how to drive. I mean, I took the classes and passed the tests."

I pause and consider what she's saying. "So you know how to drive in theory . . . but how long has it been since you've been behind the wheel of a car?"

The look on her face tells me everything I need to know.

"It's been a while. A few years? I swear I drove in the Hamptons . . ."

I burst out laughing because I can't help it.

A little line forms between her brows. "What?"

"You're such a typical New Yorker. It's cute. Really."

This causes her to wrinkle her nose like I've just insulted her. "Cute? I'll have you know that I am not cute. I am a strong, capable woman who can drive if needed. Just . . . maybe not if we're in tons of traffic and I have to change lanes a lot."

She's partly wrong there. She *is* fucking cute. Way too fucking cute for her own good. And that's on top of being devastatingly beautiful and everything I can't seem to stay away from, no matter how much this could cost me.

"You'll be fine. I promise." I glance over again and see her expression morph into something akin to horror.

"We're going driving? I thought you said it was going to be fun! That's stressful, Gabe. Stressful is not fun."

Gabe. People call me Gabe all the time, but coming from her, I like it more than I've ever liked it before. Huh. Who knew?

But she's waiting for me to reply, so I push away the thought. "Not real cars. Go-karts. You'll love it. You can't break anything."

"Go-karts," she whispers at first, but then confidence grows in her tone. "I've never driven one of those before, but if a little kid can do it, I can too."

"You'll be fine, ladybug. I promise. We're almost there."

A few minutes later, we pull up to the building where Bump and I go racing every couple of months. I might not trust the kid behind the wheel of my Bronco, but he's one hell of a driver on the track, and listening to him laugh and cheer is enough to make any day better.

As we head inside, Scarlett stares at everything in quiet wonder. I may have taken the girl out of the city, but I doubt it's easy to take the city out of the girl.

"You sure you want to do this?" I ask, pausing before we approach the counter.

She nods three times but doesn't speak. Her hands are balled into fists, and I can read the tension on her face. I step closer to her, cupping her right fist in the palm of my hand, and using my thumb, I unfold her fingers one at a time. Little by little, her shoulders relax.

"I might be apprehensive about trying certain new things."

I lift my free hand to her chin and tilt it up so I can see her whole face. Her gray eyes are so wide and expressive that I'm pretty damn sure I could drown in them. Every emotion plays out across her face. Fear, excitement, nervousness. I can't stop myself from stroking my thumb across her cheek. Her skin is ridiculously soft, and *fuck*, I want to kiss her more than I want to take my next breath.

Don't do it. Don't you fucking do it.

I dip my chin, inhaling the sweet scent coming from her hair. "I promise I won't let anything happen to you. You have my word."

"And if I finish last in every race and people are pointing and laughing at me?" she whispers, and I can feel her breath on my lips.

Don't fucking kiss her. Don't.

"Fuck everyone else. We're here for you to have a good time. Nothing else matters."

She blinks twice, like my statement requires extra processing, and that's when I realize that this woman *always* has to care what people think. Every moment of every day, she's being watched and judged for everything she does.

She may be the rich one, who has never had to worry about money a day in her life, but I never considered how living like that would impact someone. It's all she knows, and suddenly, I want to change that for her. I want her to get crazy and do something new and different without the fear of judgment. I want her to *live*, not just go through the safe motions.

"Nothing else matters," she repeats quietly. A smile curls her lips upward as she considers the statement. "No one here knows who we are or cares, so I don't care what they think. Let's do this."

CHAPTER FORTY-SIX

SCARLETT

Gabriel drives like he was born with a steering wheel in his hands. After watching him effortlessly maneuver his giant truck through the bustling traffic of Manhattan, I should have known he'd race like a pro.

Even so, with his superior skills, he doesn't crush me. After a few hesitant laps, I finally get the hang of it. Now we're lined up at the start again, waiting for the green flag to wave and let us go for our final race. Except this time, I'm at the front of the line and Gabriel is at the back of the pack. I know the minor handicap won't keep him from winning, but I'm going to try my damnedest to make a good showing.

That's when I realize that coming here, to this go-kart-racing track, is the most fun I've had—other than Saturday night—in *years*. I've laughed more than I thought possible. I've cheered on little kids as they battle out what appears to be a death match, while waiting for our next race.

And it's all because of *him*.

I take one more quick glance behind me and give Gabriel a thumbs-up. He nods and gives it back to me. That small gesture, a thumbs-up, sends more of a charge through me than the smoothest move Chadwick could ever have dreamed of pulling.

More than anything, today has made me realize that my body has absolutely *no problem* getting excited over a man. It just had to be the *right* man.

Before I can think more on that discovery, the flag drops and we're off.

I grip the wheel with both hands, steering around the corners, trying to stick to the center, because I know I'm not fast enough to take the inside track. I make it almost half a lap before Gabriel's kart flies by me. I catch a hint of the grin beneath the cover of his helmet, and a surge of joy rises in me. Instantly, I snapshot it in my brain and caption it HAPPY GABE.

He looks so different when he smiles, and I want to give him more of it. I want to see that expression on his face again and again.

I force myself to focus on the race, but it's nearly impossible. I'm . . . I'm . . . in serious danger of falling for this guy who I have no business even knowing he exists.

He's not for me.

We may live in the same city, but we're from different worlds.

Yet, for the first time in my entire life, I don't care about any of that. I love how he makes me feel, and I don't want it to stop.

This is what I've been missing. This is what I need in my life. Something real.

Three laps later, all but two of the other drivers and me are off the track. I don't care that one kid looks about sixteen and the other is in his early twenties, I'm not going to be last. *No, sir. I will not.*

The older kid edges me out for the inside lane, but I jam

my accelerator to the floorboard of the kart and slide in right behind him, cutting off the younger boy. I don't know anything about racing, but I once saw *Days of Thunder*, and I remember that whole scene about drafting when Tom Cruise is pushing the sugar packets up Nicole Kidman's leg. I know he said something about doing a slingshot around the guy in front of you, but I don't think I'm equipped for that level of expertise. I'll settle for not finishing last.

I see the checkered flag waving up ahead and the younger kid is attempting to pass me, right before the finish. *Not happening. I'm going for it.* I jerk my steering wheel to the right and bump into him. *Didn't the old guy in the movie say something about rubbing being part of racing?*

I don't know, but it slows the kid down long enough for me to cross the finish line on the tail of the older kid—and *I'm not last!*

As soon as I swing my kart into the lane where I'm supposed to park, I unbuckle my seat belt and remove my helmet. Before I can climb out, Gabriel is there, lifting me into the air and swinging me around.

"You beat him! I saw that bump. You killed it, ladybug. Fucking proud of you."

I'm dizzy, and it has nothing to do with him spinning me in circles. I stare down at him, and there's only one thing I can possibly do.

I lean down and press my lips to his.

In that single instant, we stop moving and his arms wrap around me tighter, pressing me against him from ribs to hips.

The kiss takes on a life of its own. His lips move and shift, coaxing my mouth open until his tongue slips inside, tasting me and unleashing a wave of heat. One of my hands slides up from his shoulder to bury in his dark blond hair as the kiss goes deeper.

"Enough of that now. Race is done. Off the track."

The voice of the guy responsible for waving the flags steals into my consciousness, and I jerk my head back. Or at least, I try. Gabriel holds me close, taking one more taste before he lowers me.

As soon as my feet hit the ground, I know that I've either made a terrible mistake, or the best decision of my entire life.

Except, I won't know which it was until he opens his mouth.

I follow as he leads me off the track, my hand gripped in his. I expect him to stop moving as soon as we're in the viewing area, but he doesn't. He tugs me along until we exit the building and are standing outside, next to the passenger door of his truck. His expression is completely unreadable.

"Gabriel—"

He moves in and pins me against the side of the truck, one hand beside my arm and the other beside my head. "I need to do this again."

Then he swoops in.

His lips take my mouth, molding and shaping it until it's the perfect match to his, and then he devastates me completely. Slow nips, tilting heads, deep draws, and soul-drugging kisses.

Kelsey told me Gabriel Legend was dangerous, but she didn't even know the half of it.

When he finally pulls away and those piercing blue eyes lance through me, I know that I'll never recover from this man.

He's the one.

CHAPTER FORTY-SEVEN

LEGEND

I shouldn't have kissed her back the first time. I shouldn't have dragged her outside and pinned her against the side of my truck either. But I couldn't stop myself. I didn't want to stop myself. For as long as I live, I'll never forget the feel of Scarlett's lips on mine.

I pull away because I know that if I don't, there's a good chance I'm going to end up fucking her in the back seat, and she deserves better than that. She deserves better than me.

But, *fuck*, that one kiss was better than anything I've felt in a hell of a long time.

Innocent. Sweet. But with a promise of fire.

It's that scorching silent vow that scares me the most. She's just waiting for the right man and the right moment to realize her full potential. When she does, it's going to be a fucking sight to see.

A sight you won't get to see, asshole, the voice in my head reminds me. *Get your fucking hands off her, take her home, and tell her the deal is off. You're not the guy for her.*

Why not? I want to yell the question at myself, but instead

I drop my hands from the side of the truck and take a step back.

"You're a natural."

"At racing or kissing you?" she replies with a teasing grin on her face.

I have to look away. She'll fucking slay me if I don't. I buy some time to reply by digging my keys out of my pocket.

She steps away so I can open the door for her.

When she doesn't hop up, I realize she's waiting for a boost from me like I gave her before, since my lifted Bronco has no running boards and can be tough to enter if you're under five-eight. *Fuck*, do I even trust myself to touch her?

No. But I do it anyway.

I should get my hands off her as quickly as possible, but I find myself pausing as I lower her into the seat.

"Both, ladybug. You're a natural at both."

"Do you want to come in?" Scarlett asks as I pull into a shockingly empty street-parking spot in front of her four-story brownstone. "Everyone else is gone for the day."

The word *no* is on the tip of my tongue, but I can't get it out. I don't want to wipe that smile off her face.

"Come on. Let me give you a tour. I promise I won't bore you to death."

She has no idea that it's not boredom that scares me. It's her. She's got me so off-balance; I don't know which way is up.

There are fifteen texts I need to answer. Some from Bump, Q, Zoe, Rolo, and a few others. But I don't want to talk to them. I want to talk to her.

You're fucked. So fucked.

I nod, and Scarlett's wide smile shines a thousand watts more brilliantly.

"Good. Come on."

She opens her door, but my brain is throwing my body into high gear. I'm out of the truck and around the side to lift her down to the ground before she can jump.

I slowly lower her along my body, breathing in her sweet scent and committing it to memory. I don't know what the hell it is, but I'll always associate it with her.

"Thank you," she whispers before threading her fingers through mine and leading me up the sidewalk to the front door.

As she reaches into her purse with her free hand to pull out her keys, I stare down at our joined hands.

When is the last time I held a woman's hand while we walked? For the life of me, I can't think of a single instance in the last fifteen years. Not since I was young and idealistic and full of dreams. Before life showed me exactly how ruthless it could be, and how easily it could take everything from you.

It's such a simple thing to hold a woman's hand, but when you haven't done it in about fifteen years, it feels a hell of a lot bigger.

The door opens, and she tugs me inside.

"Welcome to Curated," she says with pride in her voice as she releases my hand.

Part of me doesn't want to let go, but I force my fingers to relax.

"Everything in here is for sale, except for a few pieces of the furniture. We're open to the public on Fridays and by appointment Tuesday through Thursday. I used to handpick every single item we sell, since no two are alike, but the bigger we've gotten, the faster inventory moves, so I've had to enlist the help of a network of finders all over the country.

We turn over our inventory every week. People get one chance to buy it, and after that, it's gone forever."

My brain finally clicks into logical, rational mode as I listen to her describe her business model. It's fucking brilliant. "One of each and only one chance to buy before it's gone forever means that you feed off impulse buys and scarcity. Shit must fly out of here on Friday."

Scarlett nods. "Fridays are insane. We have a line out front hours before we open. We only let a certain number of people inside at once, but there's also no limit to the number of items you can buy. We've had people come in and literally take home an entire roomful of product. It blows my mind."

I take a few steps forward, scanning the bookshelf of classics, peppered with knickknacks that even I can tell are unique and cool and probably expensive as fuck.

"Where do your finders dig all this up?"

"Flea markets, garage sales, antique stores, eBay . . . everywhere, really. My only requirement is that it's something we've never sold before, and we will only stock one. Unless it's a set, then we'll sell the entire thing."

I walk toward the kitchen area, where mismatched dishes are arranged on a table that looks like it's waiting for a family to sit down to a homecooked meal. The chairs don't match either, and somehow it's still fucking perfect and makes me wish I'd had even a sliver of this kind of home life as a kid.

"Why this?" I ask, turning to face Scarlett as she moves a salt-and-pepper-shaker set three times to get them to sit at the perfect angle next to a napkin holder.

She bites down on her lip and pauses. "You want the real answer or the one I give the media?"

"Both."

"I want everyone to have the chance to have the perfectly curated home and life on their social media feeds. I don't think that should be the exclusive purview of the wealthy, creative, or those who have great taste. I think it should be accessible to all."

"That's the canned answer, right?" I ask her.

"Yeah."

"So, what's the real reason?"

Scarlett glances out the side window before looking back to me and answering. "I hate the idea of all this amazing stuff not getting a second chance to be important. I hate the idea of it sitting in a storage unit or closet or garage—or even worse, in the dump. I don't like living in a disposable world where we don't value what we have. Each piece in here has a story, and that makes it special. I want other people to appreciate that too."

The corners of my mouth tug my lips into a brief smile. "I think you're doing a hell of a job, ladybug."

"Chadwick thought it was stupid. He thought all of this was junk and that I should work for my dad."

I close the distance between us as the light in her eyes fades with the memory of that fucking loser. I should have taught him a lesson Saturday night. He deserves to bleed for how he made her feel. But that doesn't help me now.

"Chadwick clearly didn't appreciate special. Otherwise, he'd still have you." The words come out without thought, and as soon as I speak them, I know I've fucked up.

She leans against me, and I have no choice but to kiss her.

Just. One. More. Time.

CHAPTER FORTY-EIGHT

SCARLETT

I watch him walk down the sidewalk from between the lace curtains in the front room. I know firsthand how strong that muscled body of his is now. I've felt the hardness against me. I've heard him laugh. I've seen him smile. I've tasted his lips.

And I want more.

That's the only thing I'm completely certain about right now.

More Gabriel Legend is the only cure for whatever is happening to me. My skin heats when he's near, and I can't hold still. I want to touch him, strip off his shirt, run my hands over his bare skin . . .

He fires up the truck and glances toward Curated once more. I wave from the window, not caring that he can see me watching him. He lifts his chin and pulls away from the curb, leaving me staring at taillights that disappear a moment later.

I wrap my arms around myself and smile *big*.

"He calls me ladybug," I whisper to the empty room. "And I really, really love that."

I wander upstairs and unlock my apartment. I wanted to

show him this too, but . . . a tiny bit of apprehension kept me from doing it.

"What the hell am I doing? Am I really doing this?" When no one answers my question, I grab my phone and call Kelsey. Thankfully, she answers on the third ring.

"Hey, babe, I'm just walking out of my last appointment of the day. You need me to head your way? I didn't have you on my calendar for tonight."

"I kissed Gabriel Legend." I blurt it out without preamble.

"What? Hold on, let me get out of this building. My service is acting weird, because I could swear you just said—"

"I kissed Gabriel Legend. *Three* times."

"Ho-ly shit. No way! Where? When?" Kelsey's screeching nearly deafens me.

"Today. This afternoon. We hung out. We drove go-karts. And I kissed him, and then he dragged me out of the go-kart place and kissed me against his truck and then again in Curated's kitchen. Oh my God, Kels. It was . . . Jesus. The man is a kissing savant. My knees could barely handle it."

"I don't know what to say. For the first time ever, I think I'm totally speechless," she says, this time sounding dumbfounded.

"I know. I don't know how it happened, but it was amazing. No. Awesome. He's . . . he's . . . I like him, Kelsey. *Like, like* him. *A lot.* I think . . . I'm falling for him."

"Oh fuck. I'll be right over. Don't leave your place. I'll bring food. And wine. Give me forty-five minutes." Kelsey hangs up, and I stare down at my phone.

Oh fuck?

That wasn't the response I expected.

My bell rings an hour later, and I open the back door of my apartment to find Kelsey and Harlow in the doorway.

"You told her?" I shoot Kelsey some major side-eye.

"I needed reinforcements for this conversation. I'm sorry I didn't tell you first, Scar. This is serious shit." Kelsey squeezes by me with two massive bags of takeout, leaving Harlow holding two bottles of wine.

"I tried Monroe, but Nate's home, and she said she's getting dicked down tonight and can't leave."

"Why does this feel like an emergency meeting to prevent Scarlett from making a major mistake?"

Harlow leans forward to air kiss both my cheeks. "It's not an intervention, so don't get dramatic. This is a planning session. We're in uncharted Scarlett territory here, which means we need all the dirty details so we can come up with a strategy for how to move forward."

"Why?"

"Because if my girl wants her some Gabriel Legend, she's getting her some Gabriel Legend."

CHAPTER FORTY-NINE

LEGEND

I've written and deleted a half dozen texts.

~~I'm really glad Bump kidnapped you~~ . . . The fuck?

~~Your lips are a fucking gift~~ . . . Totally true.

~~Holding your hand was better than sex.~~ Well, as far as I know. We haven't gotten there. Yet.

~~I really want to see you again. Soon.~~ And for longer than a few hours.

~~Are you busy right now?~~ Lame.

God, get it together, asshole. Keep it simple. Don't fucking creep her out or sound like you've never fucking done this before.

Keep. It. Together. Act like a fucking adult.

I finally settle on something simple.

LEGEND: *It was great to see you smile today. I'm looking forward to Saturday night.*

When her reply doesn't come immediately, I force myself to

drop my phone and get the fuck out of my apartment. I don't have any destination in mind, but when I hit the hallway with Roux beside me, Bump is holding two bags of Cheetos and a six-pack of beer and heading for the stairs.

"Wanna watch Monday night football at Big Mike's?"

Q's dad is one of the biggest NFL fans on the planet. For the first Monday-night game of the season, he pulls out all the stops, which means Q's ma has probably been cooking up a storm.

My stomach growls in response.

"Sounds like you're coming, even if it's just for Ms. Joanie's food."

"Fuck it, yeah. I'll come. Let me go grab my phone." I should leave it upstairs, but if I'm going to be gone for hours, I need people to be able to reach me.

Bullshit. You just can't wait that long to see if she replies. The voice in my head is a dick to call me out.

It's also right.

I jog back up to grab the phone, glance down to see there's been no response, and shove it in my pocket.

"Where'd you go today, Gabe? Q told me I was on Roux duty and not to bother you. He gave me a ride home too, but he was in a shitty mood."

I remember the look Q gave me when he saw me bring Roux back to the club with Scarlett beside me. It was one of those *I sure as fuck hope you know what you're doing, but I'm pretty fucking sure you don't* expressions that also promised we'd be talking about it later.

I was in no hurry to have the conversation, but now I'm walking right into it. Maybe it's for the best. Maybe Q can talk some sense into me, because I sure as fuck don't know what I'm doing breaking every one of my goddamned rules.

Bump and I walk the stretch of grass, bordered on one side by a long green fence that blocks the scrapyard from the road, and head up the stairs of the big white house on the other side.

Q's granddad started the scrapyard when he first came up from Puerto Rico. He passed away a few years back, six months after his wife, but Big Mike has kept running it in his father's tradition—sometimes shady, but mostly straight, because no one wants to go to prison.

Still, Q grew up chopping cars when cash was tight and the mortgage needed to get paid to keep the bank from taking the yard. When Bump and I ran from Biloxi, we had nowhere else to go. I knew about the scrapyard from Jorie. She'd met a girl at a music camp she got a scholarship to one summer. Q's cousin, Anita. She'd told Jorie to come visit anytime she made it up to Jersey, and they traded cards at least once a year, keeping in touch until Jorie died.

I took a chance. I didn't know what else to do. I wasn't even sure Bump was going to make it. The drunk of a doctor I paid to patch him up in Mississippi told me I'd be better off letting him die, because his quality of life would never be the same.

But I couldn't let that happen.

I showed up on the Quinterros' doorstep, homeless, bloodstained, and on the run with Bump. They would have been justified in calling the cops, but instead, they took one look at us and invited us in. That's how we ended up living above the service station Big Mike used to run for his dad, and I've never had a reason to leave. The Quinterros are the closest thing Bump and I have ever had to a family. They know everything, because I wasn't going to keep secrets from the people who gave us a home. A second chance.

I knock on the door, although it's unnecessary, and Joanie yells, "Come on in! Soup's on!" Just like always.

"Is that Bump?" Big Mike hollers from his ancient La-Z-Boy.

My sidekick answers, "And Gabe and Roux."

"No shit. Come on in, boys! Game's getting ready to start, and you do not want to miss this fucking seven-layer dip. Actually, forget I said anything. I don't want to share."

Bump and Roux bound inside, and I close the door carefully behind me. When I look up, Q looms like an all-knowing gargoyle.

"Hope you knew what the fuck you were doing today, man. Because this is a dangerous road to walk." Even though he keeps his voice down, Joanie overhears him.

"You better not be doing anything dangerous, Gabriel. I'm not sure my heart can handle it."

"What's Gabriel doing?" Q's second oldest sister asks.

"Nothing," I tell her with a chin lift. "Good to see you, Carrie."

"It's not nothing if Q's worked up about it. You fighting again?" Carrie pops a carrot stick in her mouth and chews while she waits for me to answer.

Both Q and I are silent for a long moment, and I wonder if he's going to tell his whole family what's going on.

"He's not fighting. Don't worry about it, Carrie."

Joanie comes out of the kitchen holding a massive pan of dip. "Thank God. Now, come get some of this before Mike eats it all. He doesn't need two pounds of seven-layer dip, despite what he thinks."

I take a step to follow her and Carrie down the hallway to the living room, but Q blocks me.

"Seriously, man, what the fuck are you doing? You know this can't go anywhere. She's so fucking far out of your league, it isn't even worth thinking about."

Q's not telling me anything I don't already know, but I don't want to hear it.

"She's coming back to the club Saturday. If everything

goes right, we'll be making our payments to the investors with no problems."

"And then you're done with her." It's not a question.

"I haven't decided yet."

He shakes his head, and those black eyes of his drill into me. "We have a plan, and the plan doesn't include her. Unless you've decided that everything you've worked for in the last fifteen years doesn't matter anymore."

I glare at my best friend. "Don't fucking question me. You know it matters. The plan hasn't changed."

He shakes his head. "Pussy's a hell of a drug, man. That's all I'm saying. Be smart and be fucking careful."

We lock eyes, and I lie to Q's face. "I know what I'm doing, Marcus."

The skepticism on his features tells me he doesn't believe a word I'm saying.

"I sure as hell hope so, *Gabriel*, because this has disaster written all over it."

CHAPTER FIFTY

SCARLETT

"So, this is how it's going to go," Harlow says from her reclined position on the divan in my bedroom, a glass of white wine dangling from between her fingertips.

We left the remnants of the takeout in my kitchen, which we devoured while I told them everything that happened this afternoon.

"We're going to pick out something drop-dead sexy for you to wear, then we're going to invite the troops for Saturday night. When we get to the club, you're going to look so unbelievably amazing, you won't be able to help catching everyone's attention."

"Agreed. We definitely need to figure out what she's wearing," Kelsey says, setting her wineglass on a coaster on the side table before heading to my closet. "I know there are some gorgeous dresses in here that you've collected and never worn because you thought they were too risqué for your appearances."

From my position on my bed, a pillow tucked under my chin while I lie on my belly, I take another sip of wine. "There are definitely a few. There's a gold one—"

"Not gold," Harlow says quickly, interrupting. "No offense, but gold isn't going to get the job done."

"Well, she already wore red, so that's out too. And black isn't attention-grabbing enough." Kelsey sounds muffled from her position in the closet.

"Green?" Harlow tilts her head and looks at me. "It would be stunning with your coloring. Or blue . . ."

"Oh no . . . no. I have it. Right here." Kelsey's tone takes on a new level of excitement as she pokes her head through the doorway, a dress bag hidden behind her back.

"Let's see it. Don't hold out on us, ho."

With a grin on her face broader than I've seen in ages, Kelsey whips out a clear plastic garment bag and dangles it in front of her.

"Ohhh. *White. Yesss.* I love where you're going with this. Innocent. Practically virginal. But oh-so-classy and sexy." Harlow is a man-eater from way back, and it's showing.

I stare at the dress, remembering trying it on and knowing that I had absolutely nowhere to wear it, but it was too gorgeous not to buy.

"You gotta try it on, Scarlett. It looks sheer enough that I'm afraid you're going to look completely naked in it, but I know you wouldn't have bought it if that was the case."

Kelsey holds it out to me, and I carefully roll to my side to get off the bed without spilling my wine.

"I don't know," I reply, setting the glass down to take the dress bag from her. "But you're right. I love this dress . . . it just never seemed to perfectly suit an occasion."

"That's because the occasion hadn't come yet," Kelsey says with a smile.

"Go. Go." Harlow shoos me off into the bathroom, and I follow orders and strip.

A few minutes later, I'm staring at myself in the mirror

with a smile on my face. *This is* definitely *the dress I'm going to wear to seduce Gabriel Legend.*

I don't need approval from Kelsey and Harlow, because they're going to lose their minds.

The hem of the white fabric stops high on my thigh, but is just long enough I won't have to worry about whether I'm showing my ass to everyone all night. The sleeves are long, ending just beyond my wrist bones. The neckline is demure, with a slight drape, leaving the full-blown sexiness to the back, where the dress plunges in a deep *U* that just covers the top of my butt crack. Thank God for the built-in bra, or I'd never be able to pull it off.

"Do you need help? I'm dying of anticipation here, Scar," Kelsey calls out to me.

With a smile, I slip out of the bathroom to stand in my bedroom.

"Holy shit. If I had a dick, I'd definitely fuck you." This comes from Harlow, along with a slow clap. "Damn, girl. You look like a goddess in that."

"Hold on. We need shoes! I know the perfect ones!"

Kelsey disappears back into the closet, then emerges with four-inch nude heels that have a simple strap across my toe and one that goes around my ankle. Thankfully, they're also insanely comfortable and won't cripple me before we even get to the club. Where many of my other tall heels qualify as "sitting shoes," these are functional *and* beautiful.

I slide them on my feet and buckle them before turning in a slow circle so they can see the whole effect.

Kelsey is already making plans by the time I'm facing them again. "Your hair goes up. I know that's not your normal, but with that back, we don't want anything covering it. We'll keep it super simple and sexy. Like a chignon, with a few wispy pieces around your face to soften the look."

"And long earrings. Statement pieces," Harlow says, clapping her hands. "Where are the pretties? I want to pick through."

"Safe is in the closet. Let me grab a few trays. One sec."

Moments later, I reappear, and we lay the trays on the bed. Harlow and Kelsey sort through the collection I inherited from my mother, as well as the new pieces I've added here and there.

"I like these. Simple and elegant." Harlow holds up an earring made of a half dozen gold snake chains about three inches long, with diamonds dangling from the ends.

"Oh yes. Those are perfect. I can pick up the gold in the makeup. I'll smoke it out a little too with some earth tones, and you'll look *phenomenal.*" Kelsey has her phone out, making notes about the look we're going to create, and the lop-eared rabbits are back bouncing in my belly.

This is really happening. I'm actually going to do this.

A smile spreads over my face as Harlow and Kelsey debate the rest of the makeup choices and decide on a nude lip and a blinding highlight.

Gabriel Legend, you're not going to know what hit you.

CHAPTER FIFTY-ONE

SCARLETT

I find myself back at Dolly's Diner on Friday with Flynn, steaming bottomless cups of coffee in front of us.

Normally I wouldn't leave Curated on a Friday, but things are different lately because *I'm living.* And apparently, so is my former stepsister.

"When did you start street racing? How?"

Flynn's wearing a light pink cardigan over a white cami and a jean skirt. It's a far cry from the all-black-and-leather outfit from Saturday night, which makes this conversation even weirder. It's like I never knew her at all, which I suppose is the truth. We both spent most of the time we were around each other watching the shit show that was our parents' relationship.

"Senior year of boarding school."

"What? No way. That's impossible."

"Oh, stop. You know they let us get away with murder—and the parking lot is like a luxury car dealership. Every kid has the latest and greatest, even if they don't know what the hell they're driving."

"But that doesn't explain how you got into *racing them.*"

Flynn leans back in her chair and sips her coffee. "I met a guy."

"I swear, that's how these stories always start," I comment dryly.

Her dark hair falls over her shoulder as she tilts her head. "Do you want to hear the story or not?"

"Sorry, go ahead."

"I met a guy. A townie. He hit on me one night when I was out with some friends, but he was really checking out my car. I was driving a BMW M3 in those days, and he cornered me in the bar and bet me that a pretty little rich girl like me didn't know how to drive it the way it was meant to be driven."

I have so many things I want to say, but I keep my mouth shut and let Flynn continue.

"I took the bait, ditched my friends, and followed him in his little Honda CR-X out to some abandoned strip of road on the other side of the tracks—"

I almost choke. "Jesus Christ, Flynn. Really? He could've killed you."

When she glares at me, my teeth clack together and I shut up.

"We raced a quarter mile, and he kicked my BMW's ass in his two-thousand-dollar Honda."

"Did you lose the car to him?"

She shakes her head. "No, we weren't racing for pinks."

"What were you racing for then?"

Her face turns red, and I can imagine what it was. "You slept with him because he won?"

"Blow job. Turns out, I wasn't great at those either, but I learned a lot that night."

"Flynn!"

"I would've banged him either way, so it's not like it mattered. It just made the whole experience even more exciting. Anyway, we started dating, and he taught me about cars and racing, and how not to underestimate other people. A car might look like a piece of shit, but you don't know what they have under the hood or what modifications they've made. He also helped me tune up the Bimmer and taught me to drive for real. I was hooked after the first night."

She pauses to take another sip of her coffee.

"It's hard to explain the adrenaline rush you get when you're at the line, waiting for them to drop the flag. And then they do . . . and you launch the car and hold on for your damn life. It's *epic*."

From her voice, I can tell how much she loves it, and I'm happy for her, despite the fact that her favorite hobby is *illegal*. And dangerous.

"And when you came home, you kept doing it?"

"Yeah, but I'd earned enough money for my freshman year of college before I left boarding school. It got so bad that no one in the school would race me because everyone knew I would take their cars, and then they'd have to explain to Mommy and Daddy what happened. It didn't make me a lot of friends, and the guys whose egos I crushed steered clear of me." She laughs, and I can't help but love the hearty sound.

"How often do you do it?"

She shrugs. "As often as I can safely. It's hard to keep a low profile in Manhattan's street-racing community, so I race in Jersey and Pennsylvania too."

"You're living a double life!"

Flynn slants her head and meets my gaze. "Aren't you too? I mean, you and this Legend guy? That's like an alternate reality, Scar."

I press my lips together and think of the white dress I'm going to put on tomorrow night before we head to the club. The dress that I've never been able to wear in my normal life. Maybe Flynn's right.

"Does it matter if it's a double life, as long as I'm living?" The question is rhetorical, but Flynn answers anyway.

"No. Not at all. You've always been so perfect and strait-laced. When our parents first got married, I have to admit, I didn't really like you. You were the ideal I would never be *and* didn't want to be."

I reach out to cover her hand with mine on the chipped Formica table. "I'm sorry you felt that way, Flynn. I never wanted you to feel like you weren't . . ."

She shakes her head to silence me. "Don't worry about it, Scar. Our parents couldn't make that shit work, even if they'd both been trying instead of secretly looking for an exit. But, hey, we're here now, and I'm cool with that. Maybe we should just make plans to meet up at Dolly's a couple times a month. We can have our own breakfast club. The *legendary* breakfast club."

A flush rises up my face at the play on Legend's name, but I just nod. "That sounds perfect, Flynn. It's a date."

CHAPTER FIFTY-TWO

LEGEND

"Today's the day! She's coming back!" For the last forty-eight hours, Bump has been bouncing around like a kid hopped up on sugar and counting down to Christmas.

Me? Well, I'm fucking counting down too.

The text waiting on my phone this morning was enough to send me straight to the shower to take care of business.

SCARLETT: *I hope you're ready for me tonight, because I'm beyond ready for you.*

All I can picture is her laid out on my bed, telling me those words with a blush climbing her cheeks. Which is why I had to jack off before I came like a teenager in my pants.

I shouldn't be on such a hair trigger for her, but I can't help it. Scarlett is everything I never knew I could want. Hell, I didn't know women like her existed. She's . . .

So fucking out of your league, the voice in my head fills in for me.

I want to tell it to shut the hell up, but Q is right outside my office, no doubt waiting for another chance to tell me to keep my dick in my pants because Scarlett Priest isn't for me.

But Q doesn't get it. All week, Scarlett and I have been texting and getting to know each other. It hasn't even been dirty. We've talked about a ton of different shit, from my dog to her never having owned a pet, to flea markets and the best places to get dim sum in the city.

In all my years since I lost my virginity and women became a goal, I've never connected with one like this on a totally nonsexual level, while wanting to get inside her so badly that I don't think I'll make it another day without at least tasting her again.

But what about Jorie?

That fucking voice in my head that's *not* Jorie is pissing me off today, because it insists on making constant comparisons between the two women. But the truth is—there is no way to compare.

Jorie was a girl from a foster family with a voice that could have taken her all the way to the top. She and I were just fucking kids when we decided we were it for each other. I was going to build her a club where she could sing every night, and together we'd live this insane life of limos and champagne, and she'd be dripping with diamonds.

That's the kind of shit you think about when you're a kid, growing up with your stomach always growling because there's never enough food to go around. We dreamed of the shit we saw on TV and in magazines. They were all just fantasies for kids with stars in their eyes.

Reality isn't like that.

I was hustling, trying to get us enough money to get out of Biloxi so we could go to LA and Jorie could try to get a record deal. Then I fucked over the wrong guy. Moses Buford Gaspard.

And he took everything from me.

That's how shit worked in Biloxi. If you reached too high above your station, you got knocked the fuck back down so hard that you wouldn't ever try to reach again.

But after we ran, after Jorie was gone, I put all those dreams front and center in my head. I was going to build that club we talked about, and I was going to be somebody no one would ever fuck with. Then we got to New York, and I realized I wasn't the only guy in this town with big fucking dreams. At least it was a place where shit was happening and there were opportunities.

So little by little, I stashed away cash from hustling and then fighting. Until the fights got bigger and bigger and I staked a club of my own. It grew and made good money, but being illegal, it could never be good enough. I had to go legit.

And here I am, once again, reaching high as hell above my station.

What if you get Scarlett killed too? What then, big man?

I turn to Bump, where he's brushing Roux in the corner. "Where's Zoe?"

"I dunno."

"She's talking to the servers before the doors open," Q replies from the doorway. "Why? You have another extra-special request for Ms. Perfect?"

"Would you get off my dick about her, man? Jesus Christ," I snap at Q.

"Yeah, Q, what's your deal?" Bump asks as Roux thumps her tail. "She's pretty, and he likes her. Can't he just like a pretty girl?"

Q's gaze shoots to Bump and then back to me. "You know I'm on your side. Always, brother."

I incline my head, indicating he can keep going if he's got more to say. And knowing Q, he's always got more to say.

"This girl is different, man. She doesn't live in the same world as the rest of us. She doesn't play by the same rules. If she wants something, she barely has to think about it. It just shows up in front of her like the tooth fairy brought it."

Then it hits me. "This isn't about Scarlett, is it, Q? This is about *you*."

His expression darkens. "I'm only warning you because I know what it's like when a spoiled little rich girl sees you and wants to take a walk on the wild side. Yeah, I've been there. And no, it doesn't fucking work out for guys like us."

"Oh, Q. Did a girl break your heart?" The totally sincere question comes from Bump. "I had no idea, buddy. That's so mean."

Q rolls his eyes at the kid and keeps talking. "Just watch yourself. You've kept every woman at arm's length for a fucking long time for a reason, Gabe. I just want to make sure you're not setting yourself up for a fall."

"He's already falling. They text all the time. He gets this look on his face every time his phone buzzes."

This time, I glare at Bump and the dopey expression he's making. The kid doesn't know when to keep his fucking mouth shut.

Q's expression takes on a new level of concern at Bump's admission. "If you want to bang her, fucking bang her. Get it out of your system. But whatever you do, don't let her in. You keep your circle small on purpose, Gabe. Remember why."

With a nod at me, Q ducks out of the doorway, and I frown at Bump.

"Did you really have to tell him that?"

"Q's family. He just wants what's best for us."

Leaving the office, I walk up toward the VIP section,

under the guise of wanting to make sure everything is ready to go. Down on the floor, Q and Zoe are meeting with the staff and security.

I slip my hand into the pocket of my black slacks and pull out my phone.

LEGEND: *I'm ready for you, ladybug. See you soon.*

SCARLETT

T he lop-eared bunnies are tap-dancing in my stomach as we approach the club. Harlow, Monroe, and Kelsey went all out, posting where we'd be tonight and making sure everyone who's anyone will be at Legend.

Gabriel's club is going to be safe. At least, as safe as I can make it.

I just wish I could say the same for my heart. Because it's in serious jeopardy.

"I can't believe you told Flynn she couldn't come. She's almost twenty-one, and her fake ID is damn good."

I glance at Monroe sitting in the row behind me and Kelsey. "He asked me to help save the club, not bring in known minors to give the cops a reason to close the club down or fine him."

"Like they'd ever find out."

"Leave it alone, Monroe. We've got more important things to worry about tonight," Harlow says, shutting Monroe up.

"Yes! Because Scarlett's getting *laid tonight!*" Kelsey yells, and the cheers and screams in the SUV nearly deafen me.

"You guys! Stop. You'll make me lose my nerve."

"Not a chance. We all saw how you danced with him, and I know you, Scar. You don't let anything stop you from getting what you want. Legend is going to find out exactly what that's like tonight."

More cheering fills the cabin of the Escalade as we turn the corner to pull up to the building that houses Legend, which looks like a Roman temple.

I turn to look at Monroe, who is checking her lipstick in a compact in the back seat. "Is Nate really coming with some of the team tonight?"

"He's definitely coming, but I don't know about the other players. They had that charity thing, so there's a good chance they'll want to get loaded and have fun after. We'll see. If they're not here by midnight, they're probably not coming."

I make a mental note to look around at midnight to see if they made it . . . and then a dreamy smile stretches my lips. *What if I'm gone by midnight?*

It's ten thirty right now. I have absolutely no idea how long it takes to seduce a man, but I'm giving it my best shot.

The Escalade rolls to a stop at the curb, and it's a completely different scene from last week. The line behind the velvet rope goes down the street and wraps around the corner. A red carpet is rolled out to the curb, and paparazzi stand near the street, anxious to get a shot of whichever VIPs arrive next.

Kelsey reaches over to squeeze my hand. "Are you ready to do this?"

My hair and makeup are perfect. Kelsey made sure of that. I glance down at my white dress, knowing the fabric is going to shimmer under the lights and make me look better than I may have ever looked in my entire life.

"As ready as I'll ever be. Let's do it."

Ten minutes later, we're in the VIP section of the club with champagne flutes in hand, and the girls are chattering with friends who arrived before us. The DJ is killing it, and the dance floor is packed.

A warm feeling washes over me, because I helped make this happen. Gabriel's club is a hot spot again, and that's a reason to celebrate.

I take a step toward Kelsey and the railing that looks down over the dance floor, but the hair on the back of my neck stands on end, and I pause.

He's here.

Slowly, like I'm afraid I'll spook a wild animal, I turn in the opposite direction.

The dim lighting leaves him mostly in shadows, but he's never looked more devastating. Black slacks, black shirt open at the throat, a silver watch glinting at his wrist, and his dark blond hair slicked back against his head.

Oh. My. God.

My mouth actually waters at the sight of him.

From his posture, he looks like an arrogant god, come down from Mount Olympus to survey the humans out of pure boredom. At least, until I get to his eyes. The piercing blue rakes over my body, and his nostrils flare as his chest rises and falls. Each breath seems more labored than the last.

It's the breathing that gives me confidence. I walk toward him, my hips swaying, closing the distance one measured step at a time. In the dim light of the club, I can barely make out the pulse at the base of his neck, but I'm pretty damn sure it ticks faster the closer I get.

Thank God. Because I couldn't handle it if I were the only one falling apart inside right now.

He holds up a hand like he wants me to stop, and I freeze

where I stand. His eyes rake up and down my body, as if he's memorizing exactly how I look. I wait one beat, two, then three . . . until he finally moves.

His hand slides into mine and he pulls me close, until I can feel the heat radiating off his body.

"Fuck. Me. You look incredible." His voice is normal volume, but competing with the din of the club, it sounds like a whisper.

My nipples peak, and even the lining of the dress and the built-in bra cups won't be able to prevent him from seeing how much he affects me.

"You look pretty amazing yourself," I tell him, squeezing his fingers.

"I can't see you like this. Not with people around us. I can't be held responsible for what I'll do to you if you turn around and I see the back of that dress."

I don't know if the devil's riding on my shoulder, or if I'm just hedging my bets, but I pull away from him and slowly turn around in a move that would make Bad Scarlett proud. "You mean like this?"

"*Fuck.*" The word comes out raw and guttural, but I don't have a moment to appreciate it.

Suddenly, his hand is back in mine and I'm being pulled away from the VIP section to an alcove in the corner, where he pins me against the wall with his front to my back and his lips at my ear.

"I have never faced temptation this strong and been able to walk away." His breath tickles my skin, raising goose bumps all over my neck.

"Maybe that's exactly what I was planning," I tell him, turning my head so our lips are only an inch apart.

His palm wraps around my thigh, a few inches above the knee, and glides upward until it's under the hem of my dress.

"I sure as hell hope so. Because if you want me to let you go, you're going to have to say so right now."

His fingers move so close to the burning heat of my center that I can barely form a conscious thought.

"Please . . ." I whisper the word against his lips, and his fingertips ghost over the tiny scrap of lace I wore for modesty's sake. But there's absolutely nothing modest about what I'm feeling right now.

"Oh, fuck. Me. Jesus Christ, you're so hot," he growls in my ear. "You want me to touch you? Right here? Where anyone can see us?"

I totally forgot where we were. If someone came over to this alcove, there'd be no question that something private was happening. Old Scarlett, the Scarlett who existed before Gabriel Legend, would have freaked out, but with his hand hovering over my pussy while my body is going up in flames . . . I don't care at all.

"Please. Touch me." I arch my back, pushing my ass against him, and the hard shaft of his cock presses against me.

"How the hell could I say no to you?"

The pad of one of his fingers makes contact with my panties, sliding up and down my slit, until a moan breaks free from my throat as my head drops back against his shoulder.

"Oh God." My hips buck against him, my body trapped between his hand and his cock, and the need that's been climbing all day flares into an inferno. One more brush over my clit and I'm poised to come, just like that.

How is this even possible?

"Fuck, ladybug. You are a goddamned miracle." The rough timbre of his voice in my ear, combined with the sizzle of his breath over my skin and the added pressure on my clit, snaps my control.

My entire body shakes as the orgasm washes over me. Gabriel wraps an arm around my waist and pulls me flush against his body, holding me tight as I ride it out. As soon as I stop shaking, he spins me in his arms and crushes his lips against mine.

The kiss is feral, totally out of control, and completely not fit for an audience.

I couldn't care less.

I didn't even notice Q standing behind Gabriel until he clears his throat and Gabriel's mouth releases mine.

"Take this off the floor before you get attention you don't want."

Gabriel growls something at him, and then we're on the move again—but this time, through a door I didn't even know was there. Moments later, I'm almost running to keep up as he rushes down a corridor made up of two-way mirrors on one side through which you can see the entire VIP section. I remember the day I met with Zoe and thought I felt someone watching us.

He was here. Behind this glass. I don't need an admission to know it's the truth. I felt it. That's how attuned to him I am. And the fact that I don't ask him where we're going shows exactly how much I trust him.

Two minutes later, he pulls me into that wood-paneled office from the very first day and shuts the door behind him.

We've come full circle. This is where it all started.

Except the man in front of me no longer elicits fear. No, I feel something completely different now.

Because he's mine. And tonight, I'm claiming him.

Gabriel stalks toward me, and I back up until my ass connects with the desk. With one hand planted on either side, I lean back.

My words are bold, and I own them. "This is happening. You and me. Right now."

CHAPTER FIFTY-FOUR

LEGEND

"Fuck yes, it's happening right now. Jesus fucking Christ, Scarlett. You walk into my club looking like you just stepped off a cloud from the heavens, and any chance I had of keeping my head is fucking gone. You're a goddamned angel, and I don't even deserve to touch you, but I don't care. This is happening. You and me."

As soon as I say the words, one of her heels slides to the side, and it's all I need. I've never moved so fast in my entire life, not even in the ring, when I was fighting to save my own ass.

"I'm glad you like the dress," she whispers as my lips touch hers.

I reply against her mouth. "It's not the dress. It's you. Everything about you. Fuck, the way you came out there? There aren't words." A nervous laugh leaves her lips, and I nip at the bottom one. "You're laughing?"

"I've never done that before. Not so fast. Not like that. Especially not with someone else touching me."

My hand curves around her hip and lifts her off the desk so I can cup her ass.

"Oh yeah? I fucking love that." My palm slides down until it's skin on skin, and then I reverse directions, pushing up the hem of the dress as I go. "You're so fucking soft."

Her hips lift and push against me, and it's all the invitation I need to go for it. I slide my fingers beneath the flimsy little strap of her thong and follow it between her legs until all I feel is hot, wet heaven in the form of the sweetest pussy I've ever had the pleasure to touch.

"Oh God." She bucks against me, rocking back and forth across my fingers, and my dick threatens to bust through the zipper of my slacks. "More, please. Harder. Oh God. I'm so close."

The whimpers and moans send all the blood in my body roaring south. All that's left is a chant in my head. *Make her come, make her come. Take her, take her.*

When I plunge my middle finger into her tight cunt and grind my cock against her clit, she screams.

"Oh my God, oh my God. Oh my *God*!"

Her fingernails dig into my shoulders, threatening to tear my shirt, and I couldn't fucking care less. The only thing that matters right now is getting inside her and feeling her grip my cock while she screams.

CHAPTER FIFTY-FIVE

SCARLETT

I can't stop coming. The friction from his cock, combined with his fingers and everything else happening in this moment, overwhelms my senses until all I can think is *more*.

"I need you. All of you. Please. More. Now."

Voicing my request unleashes the beast inside Gabriel, and he locks his lips onto mine and fucks my mouth with his tongue as he pulls his hand from between my legs.

I try to argue, to tell him to put it back, but there's no chance to speak. He picks me up and slides my ass farther back on the desk.

My panties disappear with a snap of elastic and my dress is shoved up to my hips.

With his hands on my thighs, my pussy bared before him, he pauses.

"Sweet fucking Christ. I don't know how else to say this, but you've got two seconds before I'm buried inside you. You want to change your mind, now's your chance."

I don't know what he's expecting me to say, but I only have one word for him.

"Condom?"

"Fuck yes."

One hand leaves my thigh and goes to his back pocket—so I know he was hoping for the same outcome tonight as me. I reach out, my fingers tangling with his as I undo the buckle and he pops the button on his slacks. The zipper slides down and . . . *oh my God.*

His thick cock springs free, slapping my hand. I wrap my fingers around it, squeezing and stroking for a second before he peels them away.

"You do that, and I'll blow my load all over your hand, ladybug. I'm not coming anywhere but inside you tonight."

As soon as I lose my grip on him, he tears open the condom and rolls it on.

Burning blue eyes lock onto mine. "Last chance."

"I want all of you, Gabriel. Right. Now."

With a look on his face that is equal parts saint and sinner, he steps between my legs and cups my cheek with his left hand. A moment later, the head of his cock presses against my entrance, and I suck in a breath.

One hand cups my ass, and the other strokes my cheek as he drives forward, inch by inch.

My hands scrabble for purchase, one gripping his bicep and the other grasping the edge of the desk as he buries himself to the hilt.

"Holy fuck." He whispers the words like a benediction as my inner muscles clamp down on his cock in a stranglehold.

We both still for a beat.

"Hold on, because this isn't going to be sweet or easy."

I dig my nails into his shirt, signaling that I want exactly what he's about to give me, and Gabriel explodes into the most beautiful display of raw need that I never knew could exist.

Stroke after stroke, he pounds into me, pulling me close

with each thrust until our bodies collide. Somehow, he manages to thumb my clit, and I'm a goner. My neck can't support the weight of my head, and it drops back, lolling from side to side as I whisper and scream and thank God that I finally know what it's like to be fucked by a real man.

My orgasm hits like a rogue wave, sweeping me away until I'm nothing but need and feeling and whimpers.

"*Scarlett.* Fuck yes!" Gabriel groans as he keeps going, taking me higher.

I can't stop coming. I'm going to freaking shatter into a million tiny little pieces at any moment.

Moments later, Gabriel roars out his climax so loudly that the entire building seems to shake.

LEGEND

The earth stands still. Stops turning. Every other human on the planet ceases to exist.

As my heart hammers and sweat drips down my brow, I try to catch my breath as I stare at the beautiful face of the woman in front of me. In that moment, I know she has the power to break me.

Q had the reason for his concern wrong. She's not just out of my league. She's the kind of woman I'll never recover from.

Everything I ever thought I knew before was bullshit. Scarlett Priest is it. The kind of woman I'd kill to keep—and would kill me to lose.

I lean forward, touching my forehead to hers, inhaling the scent of sex and sweat and sweetness that's all her.

She will break me. It's a fact.

"Thank you," she whispers, her breath cool against my overheated skin. "You have no idea how badly I needed to know this was possible. To know that I can feel like *this*."

I don't know exactly what she means, but my dick is in

danger of sliding out of her, so I press a kiss to the tip of her nose.

"Thank *you*," I say, pulling out.

She scrambles off the desk, and I walk around it to grab a box of tissues from a drawer. I hold it out to her, and she takes a handful.

"Let me take care of this, and you can clean up in the bathroom."

I walk through the attached doorway and dispose of the condom, wash my hands, and do up my pants before letting her have the restroom. She closes the door with a smile on her face that strikes fear so deep inside me, it threatens to take me to my knees.

I keep my expression fixed until I lose sight of her, and then I spin around and jam my fingers into my hair.

What the fuck did I just do? What the fuck am I going to do now? I can't do this. Not with her. If something happened to her . . . I won't survive it. I don't know how I know this fact, but I do.

My stomach churns. How the fuck do I face her?

Q's warning from earlier hits me like a sucker punch. *"Whatever you do, don't let her in. You keep your circle small on purpose, Gabe. Remember why."*

I remember why. Because when my circle's not small, people die.

I'll never forget the sight of Bump's bleeding body crawling toward me as tears streamed down his face. *"Jorie's dead."* Then he passed out, and I thought I'd lost them both. Regret ripped through, shredding the fabric of my fucking soul.

I can't go through that again.

Moses will find me. With my name and picture in the papers after the shooting, I've known it's only a matter of time before he tracks me down to finish the job he fucked up when they shot Bump and Jorie.

I refuse to put Scarlett at risk.

The sound of the flushing toilet tells me I have only a couple of minutes to decide what to say, and I keep coming up blank.

The moment I see her face, I'll want to give in. Tell myself it could work. That I can protect her.

But that's a lie.

The pain of the realization threatens to level me, and I know what I have to do.

CHAPTER FIFTY-SEVEN

SCARLETT

When I step out of the bathroom, I try to shake off the lingering awkwardness I feel. What do you say after having the hottest sex of your life with a guy you've only known two weeks, but you're pretty sure you're falling for?

I silently rehearsed it in the mirror, and I can only hope it doesn't sound as stupid as it did in the bathroom.

Gabriel's back is turned toward me. *I can do this.*

I take the plunge. "I want to make this real. I want us to give this a shot. You and me. Together." My voice sounds steadier than I expected, but the last few words still waver.

His entire body seems to freeze, and my heart hammers.

"I've never put myself out there like this before, Gabriel. I need you to know that. But . . . there's something about you, and we need to see where this goes."

After what feels like the longest ten seconds in the history of the planet, he turns to face me, and the only way to describe the expression on his face is one of complete devastation. And when he speaks, his voice is raw and ruined.

"Before you, I would've said there'd never be anything I

wanted more than the life I thought I was supposed to have." He lifts his tortured blue gaze to meet mine. "I know now that I was wrong. It's you, Scarlett. You'll always be what I want most. But I can't have you."

He drops his chin, breaking eye contact, and his words echo in my brain.

"You'll always be what I want most. But I can't have you."

My breath catches as I comprehend what he's saying. *No. No. That's not possible.*

"What?" I ask, hoping I heard him wrong.

"You should go. And don't come back, Scarlett. This isn't happening."

Pain radiates through my body like someone just ripped out my heart. And not just any someone. The man who turns and strides to the door . . . and walks out. Leaving me alone, wondering what the hell just happened.

Gabriel and Scarlett's story continues in *House of Scarlett,* and concludes in *The Fight for Forever* the third book of The Legend Trilogy.

ALSO BY MEGHAN MARCH

Magnolia Duet
Creole Kingpin
(March 2020)
Madam Temptress
(April 2020)

Legend Trilogy
The Fall of Legend
House of Scarlett
(December 2019)
The Fight for Forever
(January 2020)

Dirty Mafia Duet:
Black Sheep
White Knight

Forge Trilogy:
Deal with the Devil
Luck of the Devil
Heart of the Devil

Sin Trilogy:
Richer Than Sin
Guilty as Sin
Reveling in Sin

MOUNT TRILOGY:

Ruthless King

Defiant Queen

Sinful Empire

SAVAGE TRILOGY:

Savage Prince

Iron Princess

Rogue Royalty

BENEATH SERIES:

Beneath This Mask

Beneath This Ink

Beneath These Chains

Beneath These Scars

Beneath These Lies

Beneath These Shadows

Beneath The Truth

DIRTY BILLIONAIRE TRILOGY:

Dirty Billionaire

Dirty Pleasures

Dirty Together

DIRTY GIRL DUET:

Dirty Girl

Dirty Love

REAL DUET:

Real Good Man

Real Good Love

ABOUT THE AUTHOR

Making the jump from corporate lawyer to romance author was a leap of faith that *New York Times*, #1 *Wall Street Journal*, and *USA Today* bestselling author Meghan March will never regret. With over thirty titles published, she has sold millions of books in nearly a dozen languages to fellow romance-lovers around the world. A nomad at heart, she can currently be found in the woods of the Pacific Northwest, living her happily ever after with her real-life alpha hero.

She would love to hear from you.
Connect with her at:
Website: meghanmarch.com
Facebook: @MeghanMarchAuthor
Twitter: @meghan_march
Instagram: @meghanmarch